Emily's Hope

RUGGED CROSS RANCH
BOOK TWO

JILL DEWHURST

JILL
DEWHURST

FAITH FILLED FICTION

ISBN 978-0-9995228-3-7 Paperback

ISBN 978-0-9995228-4-4 Ebook

Dedication

A mountain of gratitude belongs to my husband Bob, who has been not only my faithful encourager in the writing of this book, but also my faithful friend during difficult seasons of waiting for God's timing in our lives. God truly blessed me beyond measure when He chose Bob to be mine.

May the God of hope fill you with all joy and peace in believing, so that by the power of the Holy Spirit you may abound in hope.

~ Romans 15:13 ~

Contents

CHAPTER 1
Matthew

The sun shone brightly as Julie sat in the rocking chair on her front porch listening to the gentle wind rustling the leaves and smelling the sweet fragrance of fresh cut hay from the nearby field. With misty eyes she gazed into the face of her newborn son. Matthew looked so much like a little version of Buck. God had taken Julie's first husband home not long after their first anniversary, but He had given her this precious gift, a living remembrance of Buck to remind her of the wonderful love they had shared.

In God's perfect plan, He had also given her another amazing gift. Luke loved her just as much as Buck ever had. From the moment Buck died, she had known Luke's unconditional love. He was now her husband, and he was so proud to be a dad. That Matthew was not his blood never mattered. Their son was his.

Buck and Luke had been brothers on this ranch, born in different families, and brought here as orphans with their four other brothers. Luke had admired his half Kiowa brother from the first day Buck had come to live at the ranch, for Buck was a man of unwavering faith and integrity who was strong, yet gentle, quiet, yet confident. He stood for what was right. His actions were thoughtful and deliberate, and he never quit anything he set his mind to do.

Julie smiled as she thought of the many ways Buck and Luke were alike in character and personality, though their appearance was vastly different, from Buck's Kiowa bronze skin, black hair, and brown eyes to Luke's fair skin, blond hair, and bright blue eyes. Her adoptive Kiowa father, Runs Like the Wind, had been right. Many maidens had never known a husband that truly loved them, but she had been blessed with two.

She and Buck had lived in a tepee Buck had built on land along the northern perimeter of the ranch, just south of the river. When Julie and Luke married, Luke and his brothers had begun construction of a small house in the clearing near the tepee. They had hoped to finish the house before the baby was born, but the busyness of spring on the ranch kept them from reaching their goal. Julie didn't mind. Somehow, spending Matthew's first weeks in the tepee just seemed fitting.

Now their new home was complete, and Emma's gift to her was the rocking chair in which she was sitting. To Julie, Emma seemed more like a big sister than the aunt she was, but more importantly, she was a close friend.

Luke would be home from morning chores soon, so Julie really needed to get breakfast ready, but she just couldn't pull her eyes from the boy in her arms. She was indeed blessed, blessed with a loving husband, blessed with this precious little life.

Finally, the call of work to be done pulled her from the rocker. Julie stood with her baby and stretched her petite frame. She wore a green calico dress and a white apron, with her long, wavy brown hair neatly tied at the nape of her neck with a green ribbon. When she had entered their home to prepare breakfast, Julie gently laid Matthew in the cradle that had been crafted for him by Josiah, the youngest of Luke's brothers here on the ranch. Just as she finished cooking, she heard familiar humming as Luke neared the house. She plated his breakfast as he entered the door.

Instead of reaching for his plate, he strolled over to the cradle and reached for his son. This simple action warmed Julie's heart. Once Matthew was securely tucked in his father's arm, Luke returned for his plate. "I don't know how you get anything done with this bundle of cuteness lying around."

Julie replied, "You nearly didn't get breakfast because I didn't want to stop rocking him."

Luke stepped close to his wife and kissed her. "I love you."

"I love you, too. Sit before your food gets cold."

He turned and sat at their kitchen table, and Julie served her plate and sat with him. They held hands, and Luke began to pray. "Our loving Father, my heart is overwhelmed with your blessings and goodness toward us. Thank you for this gorgeous summer day, for my beautiful wife, and for the son you have entrusted to our care, and thank you that Julie loves me enough to make me breakfast. In our Savior's name, Amen."

Julie glanced up to see the teasing twinkle in her husband's eyes and couldn't help the laughter that escaped her lips.

After breakfast, Julie took Matthew from Luke's arms and nursed him while Luke played with his son's little hands and feet. Julie playfully swatted his hands away, "Leave him alone and let him eat."

"That's no fun," Luke teased.

When Matthew had a full tummy and a clean diaper, Julie handed him back to his dad, who held him in his left arm and extended his free hand to his wife. After Julie hefted their laundry basket to her hip, Luke and Julie walked hand in hand to the barn. There Julie took her son once again and wrapped him snugly against her with a long fabric scarf that secured him and freed her hands. Luke went to the tack room to retrieve his horse Dakota's saddle to prepare for today's ride.

Julie crossed the corridor to the first stall, and Cinnamon saw her coming and met her at the stall door. She reached up to stroke the soft muzzle. Of the three horses in this barn that connected with her heart, this chestnut mare had known her the longest. When Julie had been cared for by a band of Kiowa after her family had been killed, her adoptive parents had given her Nutmeg, her first horse. Known as Desert Rose in the village, Julie had trained Nutmeg and found freedom on their daily rides. During Julie's years with the Kiowa, Nutmeg had become one of her closest friends. Cinnamon was Nutmeg's filly. An unfortunate accident caused the chief to order Nutmeg to be put down. Before Cinnamon was old enough to train, she was sold by the chief to another Kiowa village, and Julie would not know for many years what had become of her.

Not until Buck brought Cinnamon to the ranch did she learn that she had been sold to the village where Running Buck, her Buck, lived. He was the one who had raised her and trained her. Before he had even met Julie, he had bred Cinnamon with his own horse, Wind Dancing. Their filly, Spice, was waiting for Julie in the next stall. Remembering how God's sovereign hand had tied them all together warmed Julie's heart with a renewed sense of awe and trust in His faithfulness.

Julie led Cinnamon out to the pasture to graze and returned for Spice. She, too, met Julie at her door. "Good morning, beautiful." She reached into her apron pocket for a carrot and let Spice munch while she spoke to her in soft tones. "Do you remember how well you did yesterday letting me lead you to the pasture and back? We're going to do the same thing again today." Julie gently slid the halter over her nose, and Spice stayed relatively still while she buckled it in place and rubbed her neck. "Good girl." Julie lifted the lead rope from the hook on the wall and fastened it to the halter. Spice eyed her, but didn't recoil. "Now I'm going to open the door and walk with you to your mama."

Luke had Dakota saddled and was fastening his chaps when Julie led Spice from her stall. His instinctive desire to protect her caused him to watch her every move until she had released Spice in the pasture. He marveled at her gentle way with the horses. She had earned their trust, and they obeyed her. He had admired this same talent in his brother Buck. It was a talent he would love to learn from Julie.

When Julie reentered the barn to make her third and final stop, Luke was still standing there looking at her. "You'd better get going, or Josiah is going to wonder where you are," she teased.

"It's your fault. You're too beautiful, My Love." He waited in front of Wind Dancing's stall for her to reach him. When she drew near, he wrapped his arms around her, careful to give Matthew enough room between them, bent his head, and kissed her gently on the lips. A moment later he released her, saying, "I really should get going. Josiah is going to wonder where I am." He smiled with that familiar twinkle in his eyes before turning to meet his horse, and Julie swatted at him with the tail of the scarf securing their son.

Wind Dancing nodded his head as if to show his approval. Julie stepped toward the stately Indian paint horse. His very appearance symbolized her first beloved, for the color splotches were half dark brown and half white. Even his mane and tail bore both colors. Likewise, Buck had been half Kiowa and half white, though his features were decidedly Indian. When he had come of age, he had chosen to live here on this ranch, just as his horse still did. Julie and Wind Dancing shared this common bond, their love for a man whose soul was now in Heaven with his Savior. Rather than extending his nose toward Julie, he gently nudged the neatly wrapped newborn on her chest. Somehow, he seemed to know this little one carried the blood of his dear friend. Julie rubbed his muzzle, "I know, Wind Dancing. I still miss him, too. One day, our son will ride with you, and you can care for him as you did his father." As with the others, she led him to the pasture before strolling over to the ranch house to help Emma with the laundry.

Julie always enjoyed spending the day with Emma, even if it was laundry day. As they settled into their work, they chatted and shared their hearts.

"Do you feel like you are getting settled in your house?" Emma asked.

"Yes. We really didn't have much to move. Between you and me, I was afraid the house wouldn't feel as much like home as the tepee, but I have to admit that my heart does feel at home. Didn't Luke and his brothers do a fine job on the construction?" There was pride in Julie's voice.

"I know they were disappointed they didn't finish before Matthew was born. They wanted everything to be perfect for your baby."

Julie smiled, "I don't know if there has ever been a baby as loved as Matthew. Honestly, though, I am thankful Buck's son was able to spend the beginning of his life in the tepee. Now he will have a connection to his heritage that he wouldn't have known otherwise." The rhythm of Julie's hands against the washboard had lulled Matthew back to sleep.

Early Friday morning, as Luke finished mucking Cinnamon's stall, his oldest brother James ambled by with an armload of straw. "James, Julie and I would like to invite you and Emily over for dinner tomorrow night as our first official guests."

James nodded, "Thank you, Luke. I'll ask Emily this

afternoon and let you know." James always looked forward to his Friday afternoon walks with Emily. He would pick her up in the buckboard and drive to one of their favorite scenic places. There he would enjoy an hour of uninterrupted conversation with the one he loved.

The afternoon finally arrived. After James knocked on the door of the simple wood-framed parsonage, he smiled at the cacophony of noises emanating from the house. That one house could contain such sound was a testament to the number of siblings living there. Though Emily was the eldest of the six, she was the most demure of the bunch. She nearly always wore a smile, and she showed amazing patience when mothering and teaching her siblings. Laura, the next oldest, was struggling to transform her outspoken, often fun-loving, but sometimes bossy self into a young lady of seventeen.

Robert was the only boy. At fourteen, he was still all boy, having not yet learned to temper his energy and strength into gentleness when necessary. He had a good heart, but he still needed to learn self-control. James remembered being much like Robert before his parents died. Then he had to grow up nearly overnight. He was so thankful that Emma's husband Daniel had found him soon after he was forced to live on his own. The way Daniel lived his faith was what had impressed James' heart and brought him to the Savior. Daniel then mentored him in his walk with the Lord and became the Dad his teenage heart so desperately needed. If Daniel had not been there, James' life could have easily turned out much differently.

Susan was nearly as rambunctious as Robert. Though twelve, she had definitely not outgrown her tomboy ways. Sarah, at ten years old, was bubbly and talkative. She had enough energy to keep up with Robert and Susan, but she desperately wanted to be just like Emily, who had just that morning discovered Sarah wearing her clothes and shoes in front of the long mirror in the bedroom. Beth was a soft-spoken six-year-old who shared more words with her "dollies" than anyone else. She seldom smiled, though she was not an unhappy child. Her expression was more pensive. Beth's big brown eyes noticed everything. Something about her especially endeared her to James. If he could pick a favorite among Emily's siblings, she would be the one.

James' thoughts were interrupted when the door opened, revealing a lovely young lady wearing a blue cotton dress with a lace collar, standing just under five and half feet tall, with long, wavy blond hair, blue eyes, and the sweetest smile in the world. How he loved his Emily! Well, she wasn't really his yet, but he couldn't wait until she was. James offered his arm to Emily and asked, "Shall we?"

Emily reached up for his arm, and they strolled over to the buckboard. She took a slow, deep breath and sighed a happy sigh.

"What was that for?" James asked.

"This is the first chance I've had to slow down enough to enjoy the pretty day. Thank you for coming."

James chuckled, "I come every Friday."

"Yes, but I never want to take you for granted."

James wanted to draw her into his arms, but instead he extended his hand to help her up and slowly made his way around the back of the buckboard. Emily trusted him, and he needed to be worthy of her trust. He climbed up the opposite side and clucked the horse into motion.

"Where are we headed today?" Emily inquired.

"How about Johnson Lake? It's been awhile since we've walked there."

"That's a great idea. The flowers in the surrounding meadow are probably in full bloom."

As they crested the rise that sloped down to the lake, James saw that Emily was right. The meadow that encompassed the side of the hill was covered in yellow daffodils.

Emily remarked, "I was just teaching my siblings the poem 'The Daffodils' by William Wordsworth this morning. Now I understand why he was moved to write his poem. This is beautiful."

"The flowers are pretty, but not nearly as pretty as you." James' compliment was sincere, and Emily blushed.

After James had parked the buckboard and helped Emily down, they strolled side by side along the circumference of the lake. She asked him about his day, and he in turn peppered her with questions about hers. Emily seemed so content where the Lord had placed her for this time, taking care of her siblings. He could learn from her example. The Lord knew he had been struggling with patience lately. Maybe he should spend some more time alone with God.

Before they reached the buckboard again, Emily gladly accepted James' invitation to Luke and Julie's home on the morrow. He would tell Luke when they met during evening chores.

After breakfast the next morning, Emma brought two cups of coffee and moved to a chair next to James, who was seated at the foot of the kitchen table in the ranch house. This weekly meeting between mother and son began as ranch owner and foreman. He opened the stack of ledgers and began reviewing everything with Emma from hay yields and planting schedules to cattle head counts and supply inventory. Emma opened her financial ledger and began the list of needed supplies for their next trip to town.

God had indeed blessed this ranch Emma and Daniel had started. Even after Daniel's passing, the herd was continuing to grow, and the market prices had been favorable. None of this progress would have been possible without the hard work of Emma's boys, rather, her men. She was so proud of them.

Their meeting ended and the ledgers were closed. James leaned back in his chair and lifted his cup for a sip of coffee. Emma, always Mom first, leaned forward and rested her arms on the table. "All right, James, what is it that is bothering you? You haven't been entirely yourself for the last couple of weeks."

James looked at Emma and gave her half a smile. "Sometimes you are too perceptive."

"It's called mother's intuition. I'm listening."

James took a slow, deep breath and began, "I'm happy for Luke and Julie, really I am."

"But . . ." Emma encouraged.

"When I stood in the garden with Emily listening to Julie and Luke say their vows last fall, I wanted that to be us. Now when I see the two of them with Matthew, I am constantly reminded of my desire to marry Emily and begin my own family. Two of my younger brothers have now married the one they loved, and I'm ready for it to be my turn."

"What is stopping you?" Emma asked.

"You know how much Emily's dad depends on her since her mom died. She efficiently runs the household and has become mom to her brother and sisters. He would be lost without her, and I don't want to put Emily in the position to choose between her father and me."

"You are thoughtful to think of him, but he can't keep Emily forever. What does she say?" Emma inquired.

"To be honest, I haven't really asked. How do I know when the time is right to discuss it?"

Emma reached over and rested her hand on his arm, "Follow your heart. Pray for wisdom. You will know."

That evening, Luke and Julie welcomed James and Emily into their home. Though Julie and Emily did not have the opportunity to meet often, they were good friends, and they really enjoyed this time of conversation and laughter. James and Luke were also friends as well as brothers. Together, they had wonderful fellowship at the dinner table. Once the dishes were cleared and washed, Julie excused herself to nurse Matthew and give him a clean diaper before getting settled on the sofa.

"Emily, would you like to hold Matthew?"

Emily's eyes lit up as she smiled, "Oh, yes." Julie carefully laid him in her arms. As Emily gazed into the newborn's face, she was overcome with unexpected emotions. She suddenly realized that holding a baby felt, well, so right. She had held each of her siblings, of course, but that was so many years ago, under her mother's watchful eye. Until this moment, she had not thought of her arms as empty. Matthew stretched and cooed. Emily was mesmerized. Within minutes, he nodded off, but she just couldn't take her eyes from his face.

Julie looked on in wonder. She glanced up at Luke standing across the room and caught his gaze. He nodded, for he had seen it, too.

Luke and James were leaned back against the kitchen counter with their coffee cups in hand and their ankles crossed in front of them. Luke looked over at his brother and commented quietly, "James, you need to marry that girl."

"What makes you say that?" James wanted to know.

Luke gestured toward Julie and Emily with his coffee cup. "Just look at the expression on Emily's face. She is ready to hold a baby of her own."

James gazed intently at the woman he loved. Luke was right. He had been wrestling with his own impatience so much that he had failed to see that Emily might feel the same way. Just then, Emily lifted her misty eyes to meet his. What he saw there was a jumble of emotions: wonder, love, and tenderness, certainly, along with -- Was that sorrow he saw hiding there masked behind her shaky smile? Holding a baby looked so natural, so picture-perfect. Suddenly he felt the twinge of sorrow he had seen in Emily's eyes. Maybe sorrow was not quite the right emotion. More of a painful longing, knowing their arms would still be empty for some time.

After James set down his empty cup, he moved away from the counter and ambled toward the sofa. He sat next to Emily, careful not to disrupt the now-sleeping baby and reached up to gently caress the black hair on Matthew's head. He leaned close to Emily's ear and whispered, "I'm looking forward to the day you will hold our baby." Emily just nodded, for she could not trust her voice to speak. "You will be an amazing mother." As he continued to study her face, a single tear dripped from her lashes onto her cheek. James glanced up at Luke, who was still leaning against the counter. Luke gave him half a smile that silently said, "Told you."

Many minutes passed before Emily finally found her voice, "Julie, he's beautiful."

James offered his hand to help Emily into the buggy and rounded the buggy to climb in the other side. Instead of wearing her usual smile, Emily wore the expression of one deep in thought. James signaled to the horse to set him in motion and turned the buggy to head out beyond the south pasture. He was taking the scenic route to the parsonage. By the time James slowed the buggy to a stop at the crest of a hill with an unobstructed view of the clear night sky, neither of them had yet spoken a word. James was the first one to break the silence. "Emily, watching you hold Matthew tonight was -- well, it was beautiful." Emily looked up and met his gaze. "My heart has been yearning to make you my wife for a couple of years now. I have struggled with and prayed for patience, for I understood how much your family needed you. The last thing I wanted was to put you in a position where you had to choose between your dad and me. Over the last few weeks my desire for us to have a home and someday a baby of our own has become so strong it almost hurts. Tonight was the first time I felt a glimmer of hope that maybe you are feeling the same way. You have always seemed so perfectly content."

Emily quietly responded, "I strive to be content because that is God's command for me, not because I do not desire for the next chapter of my life to begin. Spending this evening with Julie and Luke in their home just reminded me of everything I'm still waiting for." She wanted James to understand, "Honestly, though, I'm not envious of them. I just want us to be able to share the same joy they have."

A slow smile spread across James' face. "Do you think your family would be all right without you?"

Emily nodded thoughtfully. "Yes, I think so. After all, Laura is now seventeen and fully capable of taking my place. The others are older, too, and able to help her with household responsibilities."

James could not have stopped smiling if he tried. "Does that mean it would be all right with you if I spoke with your dad?"

A matching smile appeared on Emily's face. "Yes."

Later that night, as Julie leaned against Luke's shoulder while they were cuddled close on the sofa before the empty fireplace, she commented, "Wouldn't it be wonderful if the Lord used our little Matthew to be the nudge that finally gets James to propose?"

"James isn't the one who needs a nudge. He's been wanting to propose for a long while. I think he's just been waiting on a cue from Emily that she's ready. That is where Matthew performed beautifully tonight."

As if responding to his name, Matthew scrunched up his face and began to cry. Julie's soft voice replied, "Yes, it is time for your bedtime feeding, then we'll tuck you in your cradle."

"James has so much to look forward to," Luke said as he moved the cradle from the main room to the bedroom next to Julie's side of the bed. There they both tucked him in and prayed over him before crawling into bed themselves.

The next morning, Julie woke with a startled fear to sunlight streaming in the window. With one movement, she jumped out of bed and covered the short distance to Matthew's cradle. Her heart was racing in her chest as she looked down at her baby. He was sleeping peacefully, without a care in the world. She had enjoyed her first full night's sleep in weeks. Matthew had finally slept through the night.

CHAPTER 2
The Meeting

Sundays at the ranch began especially early, for the boys needed to finish their chores in enough time to clean up and change for church. Every Sunday since Matthew was born, Luke would hitch up the buggy after he finished in the barn and drive home for breakfast. He enjoyed driving his family to church. The other brothers still took turns taking Emma in the buckboard. Today was James' turn to drive Emma, and she immediately noticed the change in him.

Once Tim, Jacob, and Josiah left for church on horseback, Emma ventured, "The conversation with Emily must have gone well."

"How do you know that?" James asked in surprise.

"Mother's intuition, remember? Your smile finally made it back to your eyes. I love seeing you genuinely happy."

James chuckled, "You've got this Mother thing down. Good thing, too. You may be getting a daughter-in-law soon. I'm going to ask Pastor if we can meet this week."

Emma's face glowed. "James, I am so happy for you both. I'll be praying your meeting goes well."

"Thank you, Emma."

When they arrived at the church, James offered a hand to help Emma down, then he followed her up the steps and into the building. Emma slipped into the pew beside Julie and Luke, and James met Emily in the aisle for a short greeting before she made her way to the piano. James sat down with the Pastor's family across the aisle from Emma. Though part of him missed having Emily sitting next to him during the first part of the service, James loved listening to her play the piano. He could get lost in her music. She began to play "When I Survey the Wondrous Cross," and the room filled with the beautiful melody that sounded smooth and effortless. Suddenly, he was struck with an idea. If he and his brothers received their usual bonus after the next cattle drive, he would buy Emily a piano for their home. The thought made him smile. Their home. He couldn't wait.

When the hymns finished, Emily came down from the piano. She smiled up at James as he quietly rose to his feet and stepped into the aisle to let her slip into the pew beside her sister Laura. James couldn't help but return her smile. He resumed his seat next to Emily and thought of his upcoming conversation with her dad, but he reminded himself to focus. This was a time of worship when he could learn more of the truths from God's Word. Pastor's sermon was a continuation in a series on the life of Jacob, a man transformed by God from a deceptive little brother to a patriarch of Israel.

Today's message was about God teaching Jacob to learn patience. Pastor read from Genesis 29. When Esau sought to kill Jacob, Jacob fled to his uncle's home. There he fell in love with Rachel, but his Uncle Laban made him work for seven years before he would let him marry Rachel. After Laban deceived him and gave him Rachel's sister Leah, he finally relented and gave him Rachel also, with Jacob's promise that he would work another seven years.

Pastor Kendrick continued, "From this passage, we can

plainly see the evidence of the truth in Galatians 6:7 'Do not be deceived: God is not mocked, for whatever one sows, that will he also reap.' Jacob had sowed seeds of deceit and trickery in his life, and that is exactly what he received from Laban. What I want us to dwell on today, however, is that God is always teaching us to be more like Him. One of the fruits of the Spirit listed in Galatians 5 is patience."

"God had an amazing plan for Jacob's life, but Jacob was going to need to learn to be patient and wait happily for God's blessings. God had promised that the lineage from Abraham to the Messiah would pass through Jacob, not Esau, but when Jacob and his mother became impatient and took things into their own hands, sin was the result. Just as Rachel was worth waiting for, so God's future blessings would be worth the wait."

"The same is true in our lives. We must learn to trust God enough to wait for His perfect timing in our lives. Then we will know His blessings to their fullest."

James and Emily understood this all too well. They truly wanted God's plan for their lives. The Lord had helped them be patient, and now their wait was almost over. James glanced down at Emily, and she met his gaze just long enough to let him know she was thinking the same thing. She was his Rachel, and she was definitely worth waiting for.

When the service concluded, James chatted with Emily for a few minutes to allow the church building to empty a bit. He wanted Pastor's full attention when they arranged their meeting. James finally rose from the pew and walked slowly down the aisle with Emily at his side. When they reached the back door where Pastor Kendrick was standing, Emily quietly excused herself to finish Sunday dinner.

Pastor smiled and extended his hand to James, who returned his firm handshake. "Good morning, Pastor. Your message this morning spoke to me. I've always been quick to be hard on Jacob, but sometimes waiting on God's timing is hard. Thanks for the reminder to be patient."

Pastor clapped James' shoulder, "I'm glad God is working in you, son." James smiled at his calling him "son" and was encouraged to continue.

"Pastor, I was wondering if I could meet with you sometime this week."

Pastor Kendrick's smile faded a bit as he donned a look of concern. "Is everything all right?"

"Yes, sir."

When Pastor's face relaxed, he pondered, "Why don't you come over for dinner on Tuesday, and we can meet afterwards."

"That would be great. Thank you."

What followed were the two longest days of James' life. At least, that is the way it seemed to him as he awaited Tuesday evening. After James arrived at the parsonage, he dismounted and took a deep steadying breath as he wrapped the reins around the hitching post. James didn't think he had ever been so excited . . . or so nervous. He walked up to the front door and knocked.

Pastor Kendrick opened the door and welcomed James into their home. The table was already set for dinner, and Emily was finishing the last-minute preparations for the meal. The smells coming from the kitchen made James' mouth water. Pastor directed James to the sofa in the living room to chat, and Beth was suddenly there to crawl up in James' lap. He pulled her up, and she laid her head against his chest. She listened carefully, then pulled away to comment, "Your heart is beating harder than usual. Are you going to ask Emily to marry you?"

James glanced up at Pastor, who was busy admonishing Robert for running in the house. His gaze returned to Beth, and he whispered, "I hope so."

With a serious expression that made her seem much older than her six years, Beth replied, "Everything will be okay. You'll see."

"Thank you, Beth." That sweet girl definitely had him wrapped around her little finger.

Emily had made shepherd's pie for dinner, for she knew it was James' favorite. In truth, she could have made liver and onions, and he still would have loved every bite tonight. How he enjoyed looking across the table at Emily's smile!

As soon the meal was finished, and Pastor rose. "James, join me in my study, and we'll talk." James quietly cleared his place at the table and laid his plate on the counter. He looked at Emily, who had cleared her place and was standing beside him.

"You look anxious. Are you sure you want to talk with Dad?"

"I've never been more sure of anything. I'd do anything for you, Emily." She blushed and could not help the smile that emerged. James followed Pastor into his study and closed the door.

Emily wished she could be the proverbial "fly on the wall" in her dad's study. All she could hear was the low hum of the men's voices as they conversed. Soon, the rest of the kids finished their dinner and made a clatter clearing their plates.

The noise they created obscured the hum she was working so hard to hear.

She had to remind herself that the discussion going on in the next room was between James and her dad alone. She must be patient. To divert her attention, she cleaned the kitchen and promised a bedtime story. Her siblings clamored upstairs to get ready for bed before coming back down to surround Emily on the sofa.

James opened the study door and stepped out.

When Emily looked up at him from where she was sitting, reading the promised bedtime story aloud, her smile and the light in her eyes were extinguished like a candle being snuffed out. Another onlooker would have seen James' clenched teeth and stern expression and assumed he was angry. Emily knew better, for she had seen the pain in his eyes. In a strained whisper, he managed, "I must go." Then he turned and made his way to the door. The soft click as he exited portrayed an odd feeling of finality to Emily.

Her heart dropped as she realized James' conversation had not ended the way they had hoped. Sarah broke her musings, "Emily, please finish the chapter. I want to know what happens." Emily wondered how her own chapter was going to end, but she finished their story and ensured they were all tucked in bed before she hesitantly made her way to her dad's study.

He was still sitting behind his desk, with his hand holding the weight of his forehead. Emily asked softly, "Is everything all right?"

"James asked for permission to marry you." He paused, and Emily waited quietly. "I told him no."

Emily was overcome with the urge to beg *"Why?"*, but

instead she opened her mouth to defend James, to remind her dad what a fine man he was.

Before she could utter another word, however, her dad cut her off. "I do not wish to discuss it."

The pain in her heart was real and was mirrored on her face. Her dad did not notice, for he never looked up. She knew she had been dismissed, so she slowly turned and left the study. For her dad to speak so abruptly was out of character for him. Now she had no one to talk with, no one but One. Emily quietly made her way to her bedroom and readied for bed, careful not to disturb her sleeping sisters. She picked up her Bible and sat at the writing table by the window where the light of the full moon was bright enough for her to read the words on the pages without a lamp. Her tears, however, obscured her view. She spoke silently to the One who had promised never to leave her or forsake her. *"Lord, my heart hurts so much that I don't even know what to pray. I know James is the man You have chosen for me. I love James and want nothing more than to marry him and make a home for him, but I love Dad, too, and would never marry without his blessing. Please give me the patience to wait on You."*

A few miles away, James was sitting on the bench on the Hill. This tall mound behind the ranch house had been Daniel's favorite place to meet with God. This is where James had opened his heart to the Lord and had accepted His gift of salvation and forgiveness. Daniel had taught James to come here when he needed to be alone with God. Now Daniel, Buck, and Buck and Julie's baby girl were buried here. Something about this place continued to draw James' soul. He finally let the tears that he had been fighting fall as he poured out his heart to the One who is always ready to listen. He prayed for wisdom, for patience, and for the one he loved. He knew she would need comfort, and he wanted to be the one to give it, but now he could not.

The following morning at the Kendrick breakfast table was a difficult time for Emily. For the sake of her siblings, she wanted to conceal the emotions that overflowed her soul. Her dad was subdued, quietly eating his meal before excusing himself to his study.

Emily desperately wanted to know what had happened the night before, what had influenced her father's decision. In her mind, his decision did not make any sense. What possible objection could he have? She knew he thought highly of James. He had been immediately approving when James had asked to court her four years before. James was a hard worker and a perfect gentleman who lived out his continually growing faith in his Lord. She was now twenty-one. Her mom had already been married for two years by her age. In fact, Emily had been born when her mom was twenty-one. Surely her age was not the issue.

Emily was still pondering these thoughts behind a forced smile as she cleaned the dishes and prepared to teach her siblings their lessons. Beth came up next to her big sister, "Why are your eyes sad?"

Emily laid a gentle hand on her shoulder. "You, sweet girl, never miss anything, do you?" Beth shook her head. Emily paused, wanting to be careful with her words, "Something has happened, and it seems I must wait longer than I expected for my dreams to come true."

"James loves you."

"Yes, I know, sweetheart."

Beth seemed to plead with her brown eyes, "Don't forget."

"I promise not to forget." Emily assured her.

Beth seemed satisfied and found her place at the table.

Their day of lessons began with a Bible study, then they pulled out their slates and chalk to begin their various levels of arithmetic. Emily breathed a deep sigh. The day had begun without anyone but Beth noticing anything was wrong. The busyness of the rest of the day allowed her to hide behind her many tasks.

In the afternoon, Emily found a pocket of time to head to the church before starting dinner. Her soul needed the soothing sounds of music. While she played, she prayed for wisdom and patience. In the end, she decided not to ask her dad about his conversation with James again. When he wanted her to know what had happened, he should be the one to initiate the discussion.

Beth's urging to remember that James loved her haunted her with a sense of foreboding. What did Beth notice that she was not revealing to her?

As she played her final song before heading back to the parsonage to prepare dinner, Emily let the strains of "Trust and Obey" speak to her soul. She must trust the One who loved her more than either James or her dad.

When Friday arrived, Emily wondered if James would be by for their usual afternoon walk. She wore one of his favorite dresses, just in case. The time of his pending arrival came and passed. Emily's heart sank. Though she was in a house full of people, she suddenly felt rather lonely.

At the ranch, Luke looked up as James saddled his horse for an afternoon check on the cattle. Surprised, he asked, "Shouldn't you be heading over to Emily's?"

James didn't look up as he responded, "Not today." He

tightened his horse's girth strap with a bit more force than usual and led his horse from the barn. Luke had been wondering why his brother's demeanor had been off the last couple of days. Now he was concerned for him. While Luke continued his chores in the barn, he prayed for his big brother. After all, that is what brothers were for.

The Saturday morning ranch meeting between James and Emma began as usual. Once the business had been discussed, James was not the least bit surprised when Emma gently asked, "What happened? I've been wanting to speak to you since Wednesday morning, but I haven't been able to find you alone."

"I know. I've been avoiding you." James confessed.

"Yes, I had gathered as much." Emma quietly waited for James to speak.

James took a sip of his coffee. When he finally met Emma's gaze, she saw tears in his eyes. "Well," he began, "our wait isn't over yet."

"James, what happened?" Emma asked again.

"To be honest, I'm not exactly sure. Pastor and I were talking about Emily, sharing stories, laughing together, and agreeing how wonderful she is. When I asked his permission to marry her, his visage immediately changed. Emma, he not only said 'no,' but he asked me not to court her or even speak to her at all for now."

"Oh, James, I'm so sorry. Did he give his reasons?"

"No." James looked down at his coffee cup. "If I hadn't asked to marry her, at least I would still be able to spend time with her."

"You mustn't second guess your decision to ask him. It was the right choice."

"It sure doesn't feel like the right choice right now."

"I know. Don't lose hope. God is faithful. Keep trusting Him," Emma admonished.

James nodded. "Emma, would you do something for me? Would you speak to Emily tomorrow and tell her . . . Tell her that I love her? Give her this message from me: 'I Corinthians 13:7.' I don't want her to think I've changed my mind."

Seeing the pain in James' eyes nearly broke Emma's heart. "Of course, I will deliver your message." With that, James nodded again, gathered his ledgers, and exited the kitchen door. James might be a man, but he was still her son, and she ached for him. Before she resumed her morning chores, she, too, prayed for him and Emily.

For the first time that he could remember, James dreaded the coming of Sunday morning. He wanted to see Emily and hear her play the piano more than anything, but he needed to honor and respect her father's wishes with a good attitude. He had to consciously fight the urge to be upset with the man he still hoped would one day be his father-in-law, and he was afraid his inner battle would show on his face and be read as something other than what it was. As he rode on horseback to the church, he prayed for grace.

The man who had caused his turmoil was still his Pastor, and James prayed that the message God had for him would still reach his heart and not be deterred by the one giving that message today. James climbed the steps to the church. He entered the building, but kept his gaze downward until he reached the pew where he normally sat with Emily's family. He forced himself to look toward the right side of the aisle instead, and asked Julie, "May I sit with you?"

"Of course," Julie replied as she and Luke slid down a bit to give him room to sit. Julie looked up at Luke with a quizzical expression, and he simply shrugged in response.

James leaned forward with his elbows on his knees and kept his gaze toward the floor. He heard the swish of a skirt in the aisle and glanced up to watch Emily walk toward the piano. Then he swallowed hard and returned his gaze downward. The service began, but he couldn't sing. Instead, he just listened to the piano. Was it his imagination, or was the melody not as cheerful as usual? When Emily made her way down to her seat, James looked up and their eyes met for a brief moment. The pain he saw in her eyes made his heart ache.

The sermon began, and James sat straight, careful not to turn his eyes to the beautiful woman across the aisle from him. He tried to give his attention to the message, but he just could not concentrate. When the service ended, he smoothly exited the building before Pastor could reach the back door. He just wouldn't be able to face him yet.

Emily still did not know the details of the conversation last Tuesday night, but she made sure to wear James' favorite dress again on Sunday, with the hopes that she would be able to talk with him. She could not hide her disappointment when James sat across the aisle. It was as if he were purposely avoiding her. All she could think of was Beth's reminder that James still loved her. When she came down from the piano, James' eyes reflected the pain in her own. Laura asked her a question when the service ended. Once she had answered, she looked across the aisle, and James was already gone.

Julie filed out of the pew across the way and hugged Emily. Julie whispered in her ear, "I'm not sure what happened, but I'm praying for you. If there's anything I can do, let me know."

"Thank you, Julie." Emily watched as Luke exited the pew and walked down the aisle with Julie and Matthew. She wasn't able to hold back a quiet sigh.

Emma stepped beside Emily, "Walk with me." Emily nodded, and they exited the church together. Once out in the sunshine, Emma spoke again, "James is heartbroken over his talk with your dad. You need to know that he still loves you very much. He is merely trying to honor your dad's instructions. I'll tell you what I told him: Keep trusting the Lord, Emily. Don't lose hope. James asked me to give you a message: I Corinthians 13:7." Emma hugged Emily and turned toward where Jacob was waiting at the buckboard.

Emily walked slowly home. Beth was right. James still loved her. She pondered his message. Emily knew I Corinthians 13 was the chapter on love, but she could not think of what verse seven was. Getting dinner finished and on the table was her first priority right now. She would find some time alone this afternoon to look up the exact verse.

Once the kitchen was clean after dinner, Emily took her Bible and walked behind the parsonage where a swing hung from a large oak tree. She sat and closed her eyes to picture James' smiling face. Then she opened her Bible to I Corinthians 13:7. "Love bears all things, believes all things, hopes all things, endures all things." This was God's message to her first and now James' message to her.

Emily thought of the love she and James shared. That love had borne her through the passing of her mother and him through the passing of Daniel and then Buck. That love had believed in each other and in their Lord. That love had hoped and must continue to hope that her dad would give his blessing to their marriage. Now their love must endure this test. If their love was true, and Emily believed it was, it would endure.

Though Emily was not yet privy to her dad's instructions to James, she would trust James and trust that his love for her was also true. She, too, needed to focus on honoring her dad's wishes. With the Lord's help, she would be content and patient while she was bearing, believing, hoping, and enduring. She would cling to the promise of I Corinthians 13:7.

CHAPTER 3
The Blacksmith

S eth Carter guided his team carefully down the wagon trail away from his beloved ranch. His life's dream had been to own a cattle ranch, and under his knowledgeable hand, their ranch had prospered. Now he was leaving his dream behind, for his wife was ill. She needed medical care that was unavailable in their remote part of southern Kansas territory. Besides, ranching did not provide the steady income required to pay the doctor she needed. When his uncle wrote and invited him to come to Prairie Hills and help him in the blacksmith shop, Seth recoiled at the very idea. He had worked too hard just to give up his ranch.

Then, when Susanna became weaker, his uncle's offer seemed to haunt him. One morning, as Seth was reading his Bible by lamplight before morning chores, his eyes became glued to one verse in Psalm 37. "The steps of a man are established by the Lord, when he delights in His way."

Seth's heart was stirred. He had been stubborn and selfish. Yes, the Lord had blessed this ranch, but the ranch belonged to God. He was merely His steward. If the Lord was directing him to leave for Susanna's sake, he needed to let go of his pride and obey. "Lord, you have given me this ranch, and I love it here, but I love Susanna more, and You most of all. I feel as if I have been wandering aimlessly these last few weeks. Please help me to delight in Your will, so you can establish my steps. Whatever Your will is, show me, and I will follow."

Later that morning, as Seth finished his chores in the barnyard and saddled his horse to ride out and check the herd, a stranger approached on horseback. Seth called, "Hello. May I help you?"

The man dismounted and addressed Seth, "I do hope so." He extended his hand for a handshake. "I am Jeremy McClintock. My wife and I were headed West to homestead and begin a ranch of our own, when the Lord seemed to impress upon our hearts that we had traveled far enough. I know that must sound strange."

"Actually, no, it doesn't," replied Seth.

Jeremy continued, "We were riding past your ranch yesterday and simply fell in love with it. I am here to make an offer to purchase your ranch." The offer he presented was not extravagant, but it was generous.

Seth was overcome with the perfection of God's timing. "Sir, the same Lord who has impressed you to stay is the One who has been working in our hearts to move on. Of course, I will need to discuss your offer with my wife before I give you our decision. Where might I find you?"

"We are camped near the main road just on the north side of town."

"I will ride out just after dinner to give you our answer. Thank you for coming by." Seth left his horse tethered and strode to the house to see Susanna.

When he sat on the edge of their bed holding her hand and told her about his time with the Lord that morning and the arrival of the strange visitor, Susanna lightly squeezed his hand, and a solitary tear trickled down her cheek. "Seth, this is the answer we've been praying for. I will miss this place, this home that God has allowed us to build together, but I have peace that our time here is complete. Best of all, the Lord is going to use our ranch to be a blessing to another family."

Seth nodded. "Then I will ride out and accept Mr. McClintock's offer. On my way back, I'll stop by the telegraph office and let my Uncle Caleb know we'll be coming to Prairie Hills."

Susanna extended her arms, and Seth bent down into her embrace. "You've worked so hard to start this ranch. Are you all right with all of this?"

"Honestly, before this morning, the answer would have been 'definitely not,' but after the Lord used his Word to change my heart, I am certain that this is the right decision."

She whispered, "I am so sorry that my illness has caused the necessity for all of this."

"Shh. You are far more important to me than this ranch. If the doctor in Prairie Hills can give you the care you need so you can heal, every heartache will be well worth it. I love you, Sweetheart." He released his arms from around her and kissed her, then asked, "Is there anything you need before I check on the herd?"

"Where are the children?" she asked.

"They are working together in the garden."

"My illness has made them grow up too quickly. I fear I have stolen their childhood." Tears began to well up in her eyes.

"Nonsense. If anything, your illness has given them a heart to help others. Louisa most of all. Now get some rest." Seth stood and exited the bedroom, focused on finishing the tasks of the day before dinner so he could ride out to deliver their answer to the family camped just north of town.

Jeremy McClintock's visit had been two weeks ago. Seth now gingerly guided the covered wagon toward Prairie Hills, and twelve-year-old Louisa stepped up behind where he was driving, "Mama's sleeping."

"Good. Though it's a wonder she can sleep with all this jostling. The recent rains have really pitted the roads. Thank you for taking care of her back there."

Six-year-old Anna was sitting next to her dad. "Louisa, would you braid my hair again. It keeps blowing in my face."

Louisa smiled, "Sure. I'll get your brush." Once she had retrieved Anna's brush, she worked out the tangles and began to braid her long blond hair. "If you wore your bonnet, the wind wouldn't blow your hair so much."

"You sound like Mama," Anna retorted.

"That was a nice compliment," Louisa replied. Anna just rolled her eyes.

Jonathan, a constantly growing boy of ten, remarked, "I'm glad I'm not a girl. My hair is too short to tangle or get in my face. Right, Dad?" Seth chuckled and nodded. Leave it to Jonathan to make a comment like that. He was always looking for ways to claim a spot as a man in the family.

When they entered Prairie Hills a few days later, Seth found the blacksmith forge at the far end of town next to the livery and pulled to a stop. He dismounted the wagon, and his uncle exited to meet him, wiping his hands on a thick towel before extending his hand to his nephew. "Seth, you finally made it. I was starting to get concerned that something had happened on your trip."

Seth explained as he shook the offered hand, "The heavy rains have deeply rutted the roads, so I needed to drive slowly for Susanna's sake."

"Did she tolerate the travel well?" Uncle Caleb asked with concern. When he glanced up at the wagon, he spotted two of Seth's children looking at him.

"She never complains, but she looks exhausted."

"I had thought about giving you the apartment over the shop, so you could be closer to your family during the day, but the noise from the forge is pretty deafening. Instead, I'll give you directions to the house I purchased recently so you can get her settled. It's just on the edge of town, so it will be convenient for you but still give Susanna some rest and privacy. It may need some repairs, but we can take care of that later." He stepped toward the wagon seat and addressed the children, "You must be Jonathan and Anna. I'm your dad's Uncle Caleb. I'm glad to finally meet you."

Anna replied with a shy "Hello," but Jonathan extended his hand for a handshake and proclaimed confidently, "I'm Jonathan, Dad's right-hand man."

Uncle Caleb chuckled, "I'm sure you're a big help." He turned to Seth. "Follow this main road and take a right just before the general store. The fourth house on the left is yours. There is a wooden picket fence out front. I'll come by later, and we'll discuss work hours."

"Thank you, Uncle Caleb." Seth climbed back into the wagon seat and clucked the team into motion once again. Anna turned to wave at her dad's uncle as they drove away. After he turned right at the general store, Jonathan started counting houses, "One, two, three, four . . ." At first, Seth thought they must have miscounted, but he glanced back up the lane and counted again. His heart fell. This must be the right house, for it had the picket fence, but it needed more than "a few repairs." The front steps were broken, the door appeared to be warped, and part of the roof was sagging. He turned to his kids, "Wait here a minute." He dismounted and entered the picket gate as one of the hinges gave way. The weed-covered ground inside the fence was probably once the garden. He carefully pushed open the creaking door to reveal a house covered in dust and cobwebs. How could he bring Susanna here?

Though he was tempted to ask God if he had misunderstood His leading, Seth swallowed hard and reminded himself to look beyond the needed cleaning. The floor was sound, with only a few loose boards. The cookstove appeared to be in good working order, and the fireplace was along the central wall of the house, good for heating in the winter. The building had three bedrooms, a living area, kitchen, and a spare room off the kitchen that could be used as a private bathroom. Exiting the backdoor revealed a small treed yard with the outhouse. This was the home he had been given, and he would be grateful.

Knowing his attitude would set the mood for the entire family, he forced a smile and returned to the wagon. "Well, kids, we will need to clean up a bit before we move in. Who is ready to help me?"

Louisa, Anna, and Jonathan all jumped down, eager to help. The four of them pulled down cobwebs and dusted as well as they were able in a short time, for they wanted to move their mama into the house as soon as possible. Seth looked around. The house was far from "Mama clean," but it would have to do for now. "Jonathan, come help me move the bed pieces inside. Louisa, would you bring in my toolbox?" Jonathan and Louisa immediately followed behind their dad, and in a few minutes, the bed was assembled. Louisa and Anna fluffed the mattress and made the bed, finishing just as Seth walked into the bedroom carrying Susanna.

He laid her in the bed, and she immediately relaxed a bit. "Oh, this feels heavenly. You are all so sweet to bring our bed in first."

As Seth bent down and kissed his wife on the forehead, he spoke, "We are going to let you rest while we unload the rest of the wagon."

Anna piped up, "We love you, Mama." Susanna extended her arms, and Anna returned her mama's hug.

"I love you, too."

"Come on, kids, let's try to get the wagon unloaded before dusk." Seth reached out and guided the children from the bedroom, then turned and whispered, "I love you, Sweetheart." He softly closed the door behind him as he exited.

The four worked as a team, reserving the lightest items for Anna to carry, while the "men" shouldered the heavier crates. Louisa alternated carrying in crates of food staples and staying inside to set up the kitchen. She knew she needed to have the kitchen somewhat organized to begin dinner soon. Their dad had a knack for making even work fun, so they were able to accomplish their task before the sun dipped below the horizon.

Once the lamps were lit, Seth and Jonathan assembled the two remaining beds. Anna put on the linens while Louisa cooked dinner. Louisa placed a taller crate on its end in the middle of the living area, and moved four smaller crates in a circle around it. This makeshift dining set would be their eating place for the foreseeable future. When they were all seated, Anna remarked, "This is fun. I feel like we're camping."

Seth reached over to rest his hand on Anna's hair, "We may all feel like we're camping until we get settled. I'm proud of you for finding the fun."

Just as they finished dinner, a knock sounded on the door.

Seth opened the warped door with a strong jerk to reveal his uncle. The elder spoke, "This house needs a few more repairs than I realized. I nearly fell on the broken steps."

"We're thankful that you provided our lodging for us. Come on in."

The two sat on the crates and discussed the work shifts at the blacksmith shop. Seth would start early in the morning and take a break midday to meet with the doctor in town.

After chores the next morning, James announced to Luke, "Trigger threw a shoe. I'm going to take him into town to be reshod. I'll be home in a couple of hours. Would you go with Tim to check the herd in the north pasture?"

"Sure. I'll saddle up and be ready to ride in a few minutes," Luke approached Trigger, speaking smoothly and laying a hand on the horse's rump. "Hey, big guy, let me have a look at that hoof." He gently lifted the left hind leg and carefully examined the hoof. To James he reported, "The hoof looks healthy. You should be able to ride him home."

"Thank you, Luke."

Luke raised his hand in a wave of acknowledgement, already on his way to the tack room for his saddle.

James pondered as he led Trigger from the barn. Though part of his life seemed upside down right now, he was thankful that he could always count on his brothers. As he walked beside his horse on the way to town, he spent some time talking with his Lord. He knew he still needed an attitude adjustment toward Emily's father, and the Lord was the only One who could change his heart.

Some time later, James arrived at the blacksmith shop. He

called, "Hello, Caleb," but the man who exited garbed in the thick brown leather apron was not Caleb. This stranger was considerably younger and taller than the blacksmith he knew, with thick brown hair, blue eyes, and a friendly smile.

The newcomer extended his hand to James, "I'm Seth Carter, Caleb's nephew. What can I do for you?"

Returning the handshake, James replied, "I'm James McAllister. Pleasure to meet you. My horse has thrown the shoe on his left hind hoof and needs to be reshod. Are you a farrier?"

"Yes, I am a farrier, among other things," Seth answered. He expertly raised the offending hoof and began his measurements. When the measuring was complete, Seth went to the forge to begin molding the needed shoe.

Something about this newcomer seemed familiar, and James was drawn to him. James watched him work and immediately noticed his confidence and skill. When Seth finished shaping the iron, he quenched the shoe in water to harden the metal. While they waited for the shoe to cool, James inquired, "What brought you to Prairie Hills?"

"My wife is ill and needs more medical care than we had available in southern Kansas territory. God used my Uncle Caleb's offer of work to bring us here."

"Where are you staying?" James wondered.

"Our family moved into the fourth house behind the general store."

"The one with the picket fence?" James asked in surprise. When Seth nodded, James continued, "That was Sam Adler's place. Before his wife died, his house was the prettiest house in town. When he aged, he became unable to keep up the place, but he refused any offers of help. I can only imagine the shape it's in now."

Seth gave a half-smile and a small sigh as he ran his fingers through his thick hair, "Yes, it is definitely in need of some repairs." He was quick to add, "But we're thankful for lodging nonetheless."

James asked, "Would your wife be up for a visitor? My mama makes the best apple pie in the county and never misses an opportunity to greet those new to our community."

After pondering the offer for a moment, Seth responded, "Susanna is too weak to get out of bed on her own right now, but if your mama doesn't mind not being entertained, I know Susanna would really appreciate making a friend."

"Good, I will let her know."

When the new horseshoe had sufficiently cooled, Seth nailed it to Trigger's hoof and instructed James, "Walk your horse around in a circle and let me be sure his gait is even." James untied Trigger's reins from the hitching post and led him around in a large arc. "He looks good."

"Thank you, Seth." James paid him and extended his hand, and Seth returned the firm handshake.

"Anytime," he waved as James mounted and started the return trip home. When James arrived at the ranch, his first stop was the main house. He spotted Emma planting annuals in the flower garden next to the house.

As he approached her, she stood and stretched. "I didn't mean to interrupt you."

She waved off his comment. "I needed a break anyway. My feet were falling asleep. What's on your mind?"

James told her of his conversation with Seth. "I offered your friendship and your apple pie. I hope you don't mind."

"Mind?" She reached up to rest her hand on her son's shoulder. "I would have only minded if you hadn't offered."

James smiled, "Yeah, that's what I thought."

"Would you bring up a basket of apples from the cellar?" Emma asked. "I'll finish here and bake that pie before lunch."

"Sure thing," James replied as he smiled and turned to walk around the house to the cellar.

When Uncle Caleb arrived just before eleven o'clock, Seth walked down the street to the doctor's office and knocked on the door. "Come in, the door's open," called Dr. Mason.

Seth entered to find the doctor with a young patient and his mother. The doctor gave instructions to the boy's mother while speaking directly to his patient, "I've put some medicine on your cut to prevent infection. Keep this bandage on until tomorrow, then take it off and let the cut stay open to air. If it starts draining or turning puffy or red, come see me again."

The mother nodded her understanding, and the boy looked up with teary eyes, "Thank you, Doc."

Dr. Mason reached out and tousled the boy's hair, "You're welcome."

Seth glanced at the wall and took notice of a framed diploma from Harvard University Medical School. A combination of surprise and reassurance grew within him, for he had researched enough to know there were only three formal medical schools in the country, and most doctors received the majority of their training on the job. To have an academically trained physician in this small town was indeed a blessing.

When the patient and his mother exited the office, Dr. Mason washed his hands, then turned toward Seth. "Good Morning, I'm Dr. Mason. Most folks around here just call me Doc. How may I help you?"

Seth replied, "I am Seth Carter. I'm hoping you'll be able to help my wife."

"You must be Caleb's nephew."

"Yes, sir."

"I understand your wife has been in declining health the

last few months. I don't have any appointments here for the next couple of hours. Would you like me to examine her now?"

"Susanna is too weak to walk right now, but if you don't mind making a house call, I'd appreciate your seeing her."

Dr. Mason crossed the room to procure his medical bag and returned to where Seth was standing. He extended his hand toward the door. "Lead the way."

Something about Dr. Mason's demeanor immediately put Seth at ease. Every spare minute of his morning, Seth had prayed about this meeting, that God would give the doctor the wisdom to apply his diagnostic and treatment expertise to heal Susanna. He normally did not worry about much of anything, but when something so seriously affected his beloved wife, he struggled to push aside his worried thoughts and trust the One who loved them both.

The doctor flipped the sign on the door window that said he would be back soon, and the two men exited the office and began the short walk to the Carters' new home.

While they walked, Doc inquired, "When did your wife's illness begin?"

"I'm ashamed to say that I'm not exactly sure. Her weakness seemed to come on gradually, but she never complained. After the hectic days of spring were finished, I noticed that she seemed weary after just a short time in the garden, but I thought she was just run down and needed rest. The kids then told me she had been getting easily tired for a while, and they had been trying to help her more."

"In early May, Susanna fainted while she was cooking dinner. Jonathan ran to the barn to get me, and she was still unconscious when I arrived. She came to a minute later, but in that long minute I was sure I had lost her. Her strength has steadily declined since."

Doc commented, "A gradual onset of illness can mean many things. We should have more answers shortly."

When they entered the Carter home, Louisa and Anna were making sandwiches for lunch. Seth introduced his daughters to Dr. Mason just as Jonathan burst through the back door with a bucket of fresh water, sloshing a bit onto the floor as he went.

Louisa fussed at him, "Please be careful with that bucket. I just cleaned the floor."

"It's just water. It will dry." Jonathan retorted.

Doc had to stifle a chuckle.

"And this is my son Jonathan," Seth continued. "Susanna is here in the bedroom." Doc followed Seth into the referenced room. "Susanna, this is Dr. Mason."

Susanna smiled politely and reached out a thin, pale hand to the doctor, who shook it gently.

"You are blessed to have a husband who loves you so much."

Glancing over to where Seth stood at the foot of the bed, she agreed, "Yes, I am."

Doc instructed, "Please tell me the details of your illness. Do not omit any symptoms, even if you think they are insignificant."

Susanna began, and Seth was surprised to learn that her decreased energy began back in February.

Doc noticed the look on Seth's face and asked, "Why did you not tell your husband at that time?"

A faint pink color tinged Susanna's cheeks. "To be honest, I thought I might be in the family way. I was incredibly tired during the first few months carrying all three babies. Spring is always so busy. By the time I realized I wasn't expecting again, I just figured I wasn't as young as I used to be."

"The evening I fainted, I had been having sharp stomach pains for most of the day. Once again, I dismissed the pain, assuming I had eaten something that didn't agree with me. After I fainted, my first memory was looking into Seth's ashen, tear-stained face. At that moment, I finally admitted that something might be seriously wrong."

"After I slept nearly a day, I pushed myself to resume life as usual, but even the easiest task was exhausting. The children continued to assume more of my daily duties, much to my chagrin. Finally, God showed me that my pride, not my illness, was causing my frustration. He had instilled in my children the desire to help, and I should not steal that blessing from them. Until our move, I had still been able to do small tasks, with breaks between, but the travel seemed to deplete whatever energy I had left."

"Are you still having the stomach pains?"

"Yes, though the intensity of the discomfort varies. At its worst, the pain is sharp and nearly unbearable. Right now, it is only a dull ache."

"May I examine you?"

Susanna nodded.

Doc lifted his medical bag onto the side of the bed and pulled out a handful of instruments. After a thorough physical examination, he shared his assessment. "Your heartbeat is strong, your lungs are clear, and though you are weak, your muscles and nerves seem to be working properly. There are two things that concern me. First, your skin is very pale, even for someone who hasn't been exposed to much sunlight recently. You are probably anemic, meaning your blood count is low for some reason. Secondly, you have a hard swelling in your abdomen that shouldn't be there."

"What can we do, Doc?" Seth asked.

"The most likely cause of the anemia is internal bleeding. Until we find and treat the cause of the bleeding, we must seek to correct her blood count in other ways. Most importantly, she needs to eat more iron. The best source of iron is beef, especially liver."

Susanna scrunched her face, and Doc understood. "I know.

I don't care for liver either, but enduring the flavor will be worthwhile if it will give you more strength." He looked to Seth and continued, "The best beef in Prairie Hills can be found at the Rugged Cross Ranch. Emma Taylor and her boys run the ranch and would give you a good price on meat. Fresh air and a bit of sunshine might restore some of your energy, too."

"I'll ride out there this afternoon. What about the swelling?" Seth wanted to know.

Doc looked soberly at Susanna, then over to Seth. "The swelling could be any of several things. Only one of the possibilities would be good news, but as you correctly surmised, you are not in the family way. My best guess at this point is that it is some kind of growing tumor. Your skin is not yellow, so I don't believe your liver is involved. I need to determine if the anemia and the swelling are related or are two separate issues."

"Can the growth be removed?" Susanna asked.

"If indeed the hard swelling is a tumor, surgery can be done, but only as a last resort. Surgery alone can be fatal. If you were to survive the surgery, the risk of a life-threatening infection is high. For now, let's treat what we know we can, and I'll examine your abdomen regularly to see if the swelling changes. If we restore your iron level and your blood count, perhaps the swelling will decrease."

"If you do not mind, I will send my findings to a former colleague in Boston and confer with him about your treatment."

"I don't mind. 'In an abundance of counselors there is safety.'"

Dr. Mason reached out to place his hand on Susanna's shoulder. "Proverbs 11:14 is a verse I live by. If you need anything at all, just ask. Before I leave, may we pray together?"

"Please," Susanna responded.

Seth came around the other side of the bed to sit and hold

his wife's hand. With his hand still on her shoulder, Doc began to pray. "Our Loving Lord, You alone are the Great Physician. Our bodies are wonderfully made, but they are imperfect. We come before You now asking for wisdom. Help me to find the answers we need to treat Susanna's illness. Above all, we want You to be glorified. Guide us as we depend on You. In Jesus' name, Amen."

When the two men left the bedroom, Louisa had lunch waiting for them. Though Seth's heart was heavy, he took the time to praise his daughter. "Thank you, Louisa. You are a wonderful hostess."

As the men joined Anna and Jonathan at the makeshift table, Louisa took a plate into the bedroom, but her mama was already asleep.

CHAPTER 4
Making Friends

About an hour after lunch, Emma filled her basket with dinner fixings and her fresh-baked apple pie and exited the ranch house to find Jacob tethering the hitched buggy to the front post. He extended his hand to help her up, then asked, "Are you sure you don't want me to drive you?"

"You are sweet to offer, but I'm not sure how long the visit will be. If I make a friend, we may be chatting for a while."

Jacob raised his hand in mock resignation. "Okay, you have a good point." He stepped aside as Emma clucked the horse into motion.

As the buggy traveled down the lane that bordered the south side of the north pasture, Emma could see Tim and Luke working together, checking the herd. She was reminded again just how blessed she was to be Mama to these hard-working men. The horse exited the ranch and conveyed Emma toward town, giving her time to pray for the new blacksmith's wife. Though she didn't even know her name, Emma desired to be a help and blessing, and she asked the Lord to show her the opportunities to do just that.

Several minutes later, Emma reached the edge of town and traversed the only main road, turning at the general store and pulling up to the hitching post in front of the Adler's former home. She remembered this house in its prior glory and couldn't help but think that Miriam Adler would be saddened to see the condition her home was in now. This wasn't the time to dwell on the past, for Emma was on a mission to make a new friend. She still had a few butterflies, though, not knowing exactly what to expect. Nevertheless, Emma alighted from the buggy, lifted her basket, and hummed a soft tune while she picked her way carefully to the front door.

The soft knock was answered by Louisa. The girl of five feet stood with waist-length dark brown hair and a blue calico dress. She had an expressive face with a pleasant smile and spoke a soft greeting, "May I help you?"

Returning a smile, Emma replied, "Yes, I'm Emma Taylor. My son met the new blacksmith this morning and offered some of my apple pie. I just baked one fresh and thought I'd bring it over while it was still warm."

The face of a boy not much younger than Louisa popped around his sister's shoulder, "Let her in, Louisa, I could smell that pie from across the room. Can I have a piece?"

With a grown-up air, Louisa retorted in a whisper, "Jonathan, it is 'May I have a piece?' not 'Can I have a piece?' and you're being rude."

Emma laughed, "My boys still appear out of nowhere to try to get a piece of apple pie before it cools, and they're old enough to know better. As long as your mama approves, I'll cut you a piece right now."

That was the only invitation the young boy needed before he disappeared to ask his mama for permission to have pie. Louisa looked back to her visitor with a sheepish expression, "Please come in. I'm sorry about Jonathan. He's usually much more polite."

"Don't give it a second thought. I have six boys," she paused and corrected herself, "Well, only five here now. They are all sons to be proud of, but even they have a lapse in manners every now and again," Emma reassured her. She stepped into the home and discretely observed the structure around her. Tiny bits of light filtered through cracks in the siding, enough that she could feel a slight draft, though the breeze outside was light. A few of the floorboards were noticeably loose, the table and chairs were nonexistent, and the ceiling had a sag that extended from just beyond the front door toward where the main bedroom was located. This entire scan took but a few seconds before she returned her attention to the young lady before her.

"I'm Louisa, and Jonathan is my brother. Our little sister Anna is taking a nap. The last several days have been pretty tiring," she explained. "Dad told us at lunch that a visitor might be coming by. Mama is eager to meet you." Louisa lowered her voice, "She's really weak after the move, but she can sit up in bed, if you don't mind sitting in the bedroom."

Emma set down the basket on the tallest of the crates. "I wouldn't mind at all. Do you think she'd like a piece of apple pie?"

Louisa's hesitation vanished, "Oh, yes. Mama loves apple pie."

As Emma unpacked her basket, she handed the dinner items to Louisa, then pulled out the pie, followed by plates, forks, and napkins. "I wasn't sure how much you had been able to unpack yet, so I brought extras. There should be enough pie for now and for dessert tonight, and I'll fix dinner for you before I head home."

Louisa's expression brightened more, "Thank you. I'll tell Mama you're here." She turned toward the bedroom door and lifted her hand to knock just as Jonathan opened the door and burst through.

"Mama said it's okay to have pie," he announced enthusiastically.

Louisa rolled her eyes at her brother, and her mama softly asked, "Yes, dear?"

"Mrs. Taylor is here to see you. Do you want me to bring her in?" Louisa inquired.

"Why, yes. That would be fine."

When Emma had finished slicing the pie, Louisa led her into her mom's bedroom. Once there, Louisa realized there wasn't a chair, so she offered, "I'll go grab one of the crates and be right back."

"Thank you, Louisa." Emma wasn't exactly sure what she expected to see facing an invalid, but the woman in the bed surprised her. She was quite thin and her skin was rather pale, but her smile and the light in her eyes seemed to overshadow the effects of her illness.

Louisa's mother extended her frail hand toward Emma, "Hi, I'm Susanna. Thank you so much for coming by. I haven't seen Jonathan so excited about anything in some time." Her laugh was soft and almost melodic, and whatever of Emma's butterflies still remained instantly flew away.

The two women told stories about their children and discovered a shared faith in the Lord. They smiled and laughed until they cried. Emma never thought to mention what ages her boys were now, and Susanna looked at this new friend about her age and assumed they were the age of her own children. An hour later, Emma noticed that Susanna's energy seemed to be fading. Emma excused herself under the guise of getting dinner on the stove so she could get home in time to do the same. Before she left, however, she politely asked if she could bring her boys by the next day to help Susanna's husband with some of the repairs. Though Susanna wondered how much work the boys would indeed accomplish, she gladly accepted Emma's kind offer.

When Seth finished the last order of the day at the forge, he asked his uncle directions to the Rugged Cross Ranch and explained the reason for his errand. Seth saddled his horse and rode toward his destination, praying that the beef would indeed give Susanna the strength she needed to recover. As he passed beneath the sign at the entrance of the ranch, Seth felt a twinge of nostalgia, for he was reminded again of the ranch he had left behind and the ready supply of beef he had had there. His gaze focused on the long lines of wooden fence that lined both sides of the lane and framed the large pastures.

James was completing his afternoon perimeter ride when he spotted a rider entering the ranch. He neared the center lane and recognized the new blacksmith. Waving at the newcomer, he called, "Hello, Seth."

Seth returned the wave and pulled his horse to a stop while James dismounted, led his horse through the pasture gate, and relatched it before coming to meet him.

"Welcome to the Rugged Cross Ranch. What can I do for you?"

"Dr. Mason examined my wife today and recommended that she eat your beef to get her strength back. I came to see if I could purchase some from you."

"Sure. Follow me to the smokehouse." James smoothly swung himself back into the saddle and led the way past the ranch house and the bunkhouse, dismounting just in front of the smokehouse. "What cuts are you wanting today?"

"Our cold storage isn't that large. Could I get one-eighth beef and a couple of beef livers? That would give us roast, steak, and extra meat to grind for beef patties."

"Of course. Do you have a place to butcher your beef, or

would you prefer to have us do the butchering for you and bring the meat to you tomorrow?" James asked.

Seth rubbed his chin in thought. "That's a good point. How much extra do you charge for the butchering?"

James quoted a fair price.

"All right, why don't you do the butchering, then. Do you have any liver I could take with me today?"

James assured him, "You can have all the beef liver you want. I'll even include it at no extra charge."

Seth nodded in understanding, "We don't care for liver, either, but Dr. Mason said Susanna needed the iron."

"Emily Kendrick can make liver almost not taste like liver. I'll see if Mama can get Emily's recipe to you."

"Thank you."

"Come on in the smokehouse and choose your cut. We'll deliver the meat in the morning."

Seth chose what he wanted. James weighed the beef, and Seth paid him. James wrapped up two beef livers and assured the blacksmith, "When you need more, just ask."

They exited to wash their hands at the water pump then shook hands before Seth departed.

Not long after Emma had begun her trip back to the ranch, Seth arrived home, met by the mouth-watering smell of beef stew. "Mmm. Louisa, that smells delicious."

"Mrs. Taylor made dinner before she left, but we wanted to wait until you got home to eat."

"That was very thoughtful. Let me just see your mama for a few minutes, and we'll eat." Seth opened the bedroom door that was already ajar and saw that his wife was sleeping. He placed a kiss on her forehead and quietly exited the way he had come.

Jonathan came bounding into the living area and gave him a bear hug, "Dad, you're home!"

Seth hugged him but quietly admonished, "Not quite so loud, young man. Your mama is sleeping."

Nodding, he changed his voice to a whisper that was still nearly as loud. "Mrs. Taylor makes the best apple pie! We saved you some."

"Dinner and dessert. That was very kind of her to come by." Having met James, Seth pictured his mother as an older woman with graying hair. He hadn't noticed the differing last names.

Louisa filled the bowls, and Anna carried one to her daddy and one to Jonathan before taking hers to her crate-chair. Once Louisa was settled with her bowl, Seth prayed, thanking God for their food and many blessings and asking for healing for his wife.

Seth asked, "Louisa, there is enough stew for your mama when she wakes up, right?"

"Oh, yes. We probably have enough for dinner tomorrow night, too. Mrs. Taylor said she has boys. They must eat a lot."

Looking over at Jonathan, who had nearly emptied his bowl already, Seth agreed, "Yes, boys tend to do that."

Emma invited Luke and Julie to join the rest of the family at the ranch house for dinner that evening. Just as everyone was finishing their meal, Emma announced, "After you clear your dishes, I'm calling a family meeting."

Tim blurted, "We must not be in too much trouble. I smell apple pie."

"You have the nose of a bloodhound when it comes to Mama's pies," James commented.

"I can't help it if she makes the best pies around."

Emma laughed. "All right, you may have some pie."

Once everyone was gathered in the living room, Emma told them of her visit to the blacksmith's family and of the many repairs that were needed on their new home. Everyone was eager to help. James formulated a plan. "Jacob, why don't you help me finish the butchering so we can pack their beef. Tim, split a few cedar shakes for the roof. Tomorrow, Jacob and Tim can do the roof repairs. Josiah, plan to tame what used to be the garden. I'll fix the steps, porch, and front door. Luke, you tackle the loose floorboards and the holes in the chinking. All of you collect whatever tools and supplies you will need in the wagon bed tonight."

Emma added, "Julie, could you fix up some kind of reclining chair for Susanna to rest outside while we clean indoors? The sagging roof extends into the bedroom, and I wouldn't want the falling debris or the noise to bother her."

"Yes, I know just the thing. I'll clean the cot in the barn and cover it with a soft tick mattress and quilts. I'll bring some cushions so she can be propped up to a comfortable angle." Another thought occurred to her. "Do you think Susanna might enjoy some curtains? I still have some extra fabric here at the house from our curtains. If you don't mind my using your treadle sewing machine, I could sew them tonight."

Emma reached over to rest a hand on Julie's arm, "That's a wonderful idea. I know she would love them. I'll prepare a lunch basket for all of us and gather the cleaning supplies. Is there anything we've forgotten?" Emma asked.

When no one had any other ideas, James interjected, "Let's

get to work, then." The family rose, carried their empty pie plates to the kitchen, and got busy with their tasks to be ready for the morrow.

CHAPTER 5

Helping Neighbors

The next morning Seth woke early, hoping to use his first day off to get as many repairs done as possible. He started to make a list, then stopped when he began feeling discouraged at the length of it. Instead, he decided to eat breakfast and start repairing the front steps. He was just nailing a freshly-cut board in place on the bottom step when he heard the lumbering rattle of a wagon and looked up.

When the wagon came to a stop, James jumped down and approached the blacksmith. "Good morning, Seth. My family is here to lend a hand with some repairs and cleaning." While he was speaking, the rest of the family filed out of the wagon one by one. Seth was dumbfounded at the crew gathering before him. James continued, "Before Tim and Jacob get started on the roof, Julie is going to make a comfortable place for your wife under the tree in the backyard, where she will be safe from anything falling from the ceiling."

Jacob was already securing the ladder against the side of the house. Tim set a stack of split roof shakes on the ground and walked up to Seth, greeting him with a firm handshake,

"Hi, I'm Tim." He pointed to the roofline. "Does the sagging beam extend the length of the house or just to the center?"

"Just to the center."

"Good. Then we shouldn't mess up the load bearing of the roof to replace that section. We'll get to work as soon as the room beneath is unoccupied." He turned back to the wagon to set up the sawhorses and pull the tools to the edge of the tailgate.

Luke had helped Julie from the wagon and carried what she needed around to the backyard. Now he approached Seth with a bucket of chinking in one hand. He, too, shook Seth's hand as he introduced himself, "Mornin'. I'm Luke. If it's all right, I'll repair any loose floorboards inside and replace any worn chinking."

"Your house will be sealed as tight as a drum when he gets through," James remarked. He gestured toward his remaining brother. "Josiah is going to help Emma first, then he'll work on the garden. I'll help you with the front porch and steps. It will take two of us to rehang the door. Oh, and we brought your crate of beef, too."

Seth looked around at these grown men, organized and ready to work. "I'm a bit speechless, and I'll admit that doesn't happen often. Let me tell my kids what is going on, and I'll move Susanna."

Seth pushed open the front door with a little force from his shoulder. "Jonathan, we're going to have some assistance with repairs today. Why don't you head outside and see where you can help out?" Looking around, he asked, "Where are Louisa and Anna?"

"They are with the pretty girl in the backyard making an outside bed for Mama."

When Seth opened the bedroom door, Susanna was awake. "I forgot to tell you. Did Emma's boys come to lend a hand?"

"Yes, they did."

"Are they big enough to be of some real help?"

Surprised at her question, Seth replied, "Yes, they are. I'm going to move you to a bed the girls have set up for you in the backyard so the roof can be repaired."

"Some fresh air sounds lovely."

Seth helped her don her robe and gently lifted her in his arms to carry her outside. There they found a bed covered with colorful quilts and cushions. Beside it was a small table with a pitcher of fresh-squeezed lemonade and a couple of glasses.

Julie's back was to them as she fluffed the pillow once more. When she turned around, both Seth and Susanna were surprised to see a young lady with a sleeping infant secured to her chest. "Perfect timing. Your daughters helped me fix up this bed for you. They were such good helpers. I hope you will be comfortable."

"Are you part of Emma's family, too?"

"Yes, I'm Julie, Luke's wife." She patted the back of her baby boy. "This is our son Matthew."

Seth gently laid Susanna on the bed. "This is comfortable. The temperature is perfect here in the shade, especially with the gentle breezes blowing." When he bent close to tuck the lightweight quilt around her, Susanna asked, "Is Luke one of Emma's sons?" Seth nodded. "I wouldn't have thought any of her sons would be old enough to marry."

Still not understanding their difference of perspective, Seth crinkled his brow. "The sons I met are grown men or nearly so."

Susanna was puzzled. She sat deep in thought and tried to think. The Emma she met couldn't have children that old. What was she missing?

Tim knocked and entered the Carters' home. Jonathan just stared up at him, then spoke in awe. "You're really tall."

With laughter in his eyes, Tim replied, "Yep, that's what they tell me."

"How did you get that tall?"

"One inch at a time." Tim eyed the youngster. "Do you want to help me measure this wall?"

"Boy, would I!" For now, Tim had a sidekick.

Tim started his measurements from inside the house while Julie and Emma covered the bed with a tarpaulin. Emma inquired, "Will you be able to shore up this beam?"

Tim rubbed his chin. "No, it's badly warped and needs to be replaced. If we brace these two weight-bearing posts, we should be able to remove the beam without having to rip up the entire roof on this half of the house. Putting the new beam in place will take all of us, though."

Emma nodded, tying a kerchief on her head that covered most of her hair, and exited the front door to find Josiah. "Take the chimney brush up to the roof. As soon as I cover the hearth opening, brush the soot down from above. When you finish the chimney, use the smaller brush on the stovepipe."

"Yes, Ma'am." Josiah replied. He went to grab the tools while Emma reentered the house to seal the hearth from the downpour of soot that was to come. She finished her task just as she heard footsteps on the roof and walked over to begin cleaning out the stove. When she knelt before the open oven door, cleaning out the wood pieces and ash, Emma realized too late that Josiah's steps above her had moved to the stovepipe. Before she could close the door, a cloud of soot billowed out and covered her entire upper body, including her face and exposed hair. Not only was she a mess, but the floor around her would now need a thorough scrubbing.

Emma's first reaction was frustration, but she looked up to see Anna hiding her giggles behind her hand. Instead of allowing herself to become angry, she chose to see the humor and laughed with the little girl.

Just then, Seth entered the back door and looked over to where Emma was kneeling before the cook stove. The first reaction to appear on his face was shock. The shock soon softened into a merry laugh.

Emma was suddenly flustered. She was glad her reddening cheeks were hidden behind the soot. "I am so sorry to have made such a mess. Josiah finished sweeping the chimney faster than I had expected, and he swept the stovepipe before I was ready. This stove will be squeaky clean before I leave. Don't you worry."

"I'm not worried in the least. I presume you are Emma?" When she nodded, he continued, "Anyone who has sons who work this hard for a stranger would certainly have no problem wiping up a little soot. I am grateful you and your family have come, though I don't envy your next laundry day." Still chuckling, he exited the front door to meet James and tend to repairs there.

Tim set to work measuring and cutting the replacement beam, while Josiah descended from the roof and fetched the hoe, ready to tackle the tangle of weeds within the picket fence.

Jonathan approached Josiah, "What are you doing?"

"First, I'm going to remove the overgrowth from the gate to the front steps, so we can level the stone path. After that, I want to clear some of this brush away to prepare for a garden."

"The garden was always my job. May I help you?"

"Sure. There's another hoe in the wagon. Grab it, and we'll get to work."

Jonathan went over to the wagon to get the hoe. Tim was close by sawing the new beam and looked over at the young man. Jonathan hesitated, "Um. I offered to help in the garden. Is that okay with you?"

"Of course. I'm getting ready to climb on the roof anyway.

I'm sure your mama would rather your feet stay firmly planted on the ground."

Jonathan quickly returned to Josiah, and they started clearing the walkway.

Inside, Luke had swept the ceilings and the walls so dust wouldn't get onto the wet chinking. After he sealed the leaks in the house and secured the loose floorboards, he went outside to repair the picket fence and the gate.

Julie swept the floors and cleaned the windows while Emma finished cleaning the hearth and the cook stove. Anna sat in a chair outside until her mama fell asleep, and Louisa dusted the furniture. Soon all four were on their hands and knees scrubbing the floors. When they finished, Emma stood and stretched her back, saying, "Now that that's done, Louisa, would you help me serve lunch?"

Emma retrieved the large picnic basket and a small crate of additional foodstuffs, and Louisa helped her unpack. Julie called to James, "Please tell the boys it's lunchtime."

James' resounding voice proclaimed, "Lunch break, everyone."

Julie blocked the doorway. "Don't even think about coming inside; we just finished scrubbing the floors."

The whole crew washed their hands and sat around on the front porch while Emma and Louisa served lunch. Julie went to check on Susanna and bring her some lunch, too.

Susanna was awake and welcomed the food and the company. "Please sit down and chat for a bit."

Julie ate with her before nursing Matthew.

"There is something I can't figure out, but I'm not sure how to ask without sounding rude," Susanna declared.

"Ask anything you want."

"Well, the Emma Taylor I met yesterday was about my age. Seth and I had children right away, and my oldest is twelve. How can Emma have sons who are old enough to marry?"

"Did you not meet Emma's boys?"

"No, not yet."

"You would be even more confused if you met them. None of them look alike, well, except for Jacob and Josiah, but they were born brothers."

Seeing Susanna's puzzled expression, Julie explained, "Let me start at the beginning. Emma and Daniel moved here to homestead their ranch. God didn't give them babies of their own, but He gave them the opportunity to open their home and hearts to six teenage orphan boys: James McAllister, Buck Matthews, Tim O'Brien, Luke Hamilton, and Jacob and Josiah Collins. Emma is only about twelve years older than James, but she is Mama on the ranch."

"I think I'm beginning to understand now. Do all of her boys still work on the ranch?"

Julie felt a lump in her throat. "All but one. Buck, my first husband, died of influenza last fall. Our son Matthew looks just like him."

Reaching out to rest her hand on Julie's, Susanna replied, "Oh, my dear, I am so sorry. You are so young to have endured such sorrow."

"Thank you. This past year has not been easy. Some nights I went to bed physically and emotionally exhausted wondering how I would make it through another day without Buck, but God always had just the right amount of strength and comfort waiting for me when I awoke. Every day He proved Himself faithful in my life. He delivered His comfort through His Word and through two amazing gifts: my husband Luke and my son Matthew."

"When I am reminded of a vivid memory of Buck, I am finally to the point that I can smile for a moment before the tears come. Luke is so understanding. Buck was his closest brother on the ranch, so he feels Buck's death deeply, too. While I do not have a photograph of Buck, I see his likeness every time I look at the face of our son. The Lord is always good, even during the tough times."

Julie suddenly realized, "You asked about Emma, and I have rambled on. Please forgive me."

"Don't apologize. God just used you to speak to my heart. Sometimes I forget to look for the blessings in the midst of the trials of life. God is faithful, and I need to trust Him. My illness has been frustrating and humbling, to say the least. When I am tempted to be discouraged, I need to remember to move my focus from myself to others. Some days I feel rather useless. I've been praying that God would show me some kind of ministry I can do at home. The Lord has blessed me with a godly man and three precious children, but I don't even know what I could do for them right now."

"Never underestimate the power of words," Julie reminded Susanna. "Many of the conversations I had with my mama still come to mind from time to time, and she died just before my ninth birthday. You can have a tremendous impact on your children by sharing how they can live out the truths in God's Word. That impact is what discipleship is all about."

Susanna's eyes brightened. "What a wonderful reminder! My time with my children is precious. I need to pray for more opportunities to share God's grace with them."

Realizing Susanna needed more rest, Julie secured Matthew snugly to her chest once more and rose to gather the dishes. "Is there anything you need before I head back inside?"

"No, you have been most kind."

When Julie reentered through the kitchen door, Emma and Louisa were nearly done washing the lunch dishes. Emma looked at the young lady beside her. "Since you know what food staples you generally use, why don't you sort through your inventory of dry goods? Once you have a list of what you need, you and Julie can head to the general store for supplies."

Louisa nodded and found a piece of paper and a pencil to start jotting notes.

Just then, all of the men came in to replace the roof beam. They made quite a ruckus, despite the fact that they had left their dirty boots in disarray on the front porch, but working together, they got the beam up and secured. Seth remarked, "The bedroom looks bigger now that the ceiling doesn't sag."

"Now you won't have to worry about the roof falling on you while you're sleeping," Tim added.

When they finally exited, Julie and Anna swept and tidied the bedroom once more. Julie noticed that the little girl's eyes were drooping. "I know it's too noisy to sleep in the house with the men still nailing shingles to the roof. Would you like me to get a quilt and pillow so you can lie on the grass near your mama for a bit?"

"Yes, please," was Anna's sweet reply.

Julie gathered a quilt and pillow, and Anna followed her to the back yard. Susanna was resting quietly. As soon as Julie laid the folded quilt on the ground, Anna curled up on top of it. By the time Julie lifted Anna's head to slip the pillow beneath it, the little girl was already asleep. *What a little sweetheart,* she thought.

Louisa had just finished her shopping list when Julie returned to the house. Emma stood from where she had been cleaning the lower kitchen shelves and stretched her back. "Julie, why don't you lay Matthew down on a quilt here in the kitchen and walk with Louisa to the general store." When Louisa was almost to the front door, Emma leaned in toward Julie and whispered, "Put their supplies on the ranch's account."

Julie smiled and nodded. She placed the small quilt on the newly-cleaned floor and laid down her sleeping boy. To Emma, she commented, "After carrying him around all morning, I feel twenty pounds lighter."

With the shopping list in hand, Louisa and Julie exited the open doorway and descended the front steps. Josiah had nearly finished the footpath, and Luke was repairing the hinges on the front picket gate. The latter stood and held the gate open for the ladies to walk through. When Julie passed him, he noticed she wasn't carrying her usual bundle and inquired, "Where's my boy?"

"He's sound asleep. Emma is keeping an eye on him for me."

Luke lowered his voice. "I love you."

"I love you, too."

Luke tipped up her chin with his finger and gave her a quick kiss.

"Hey, you two," James teased as he passed to get more nails from the wagon.

"Sorry, I can't resist." Luke's gaze followed his wife as she turned to walk with Louisa. Then he knelt down to finish his repair.

Once again, James was reminded of Emily and their seemingly endless wait, but he pushed the thought quickly from his mind. He had work to do.

The bell on the door jingled as Julie and Louisa entered the general store and made their way toward the dry goods. A short time later, the bell sounded again, and Julie looked up to see her best friend. "Emily!" They met each other halfway and hugged. "I'm so glad to see you. You've been on my heart a lot lately, and every time I think of you, I pray for you and James."

"Thank you, Julie. Please continue praying." Emily blinked

away the encroaching tears and asked, "Why are you in town today?"

"Our family has invaded the new blacksmith's house to help with repairs and cleaning."

"And restocking, I see."

"Yes, quite so. I'd like to introduce you to Louisa Carter, the blacksmith's oldest daughter. Louisa, this is Emily Kendrick, the pastor's oldest daughter."

Louisa's soft voice politely replied, "It is very nice to meet you."

"And I you. Welcome to Prairie Hills. Julie, did your entire family come?"

"Yes, James is helping Louisa's dad repair the porch and front door."

A bit of pink colored Emily's cheeks, for Julie had known what she was asking. Emily nodded, and they both excused themselves to finish their shopping. The store clerk neatly packed Julie and Louisa's purchases in two boxes. They turned to leave, and Julie whispered to Emily, "The Carters have moved into the Adler's house."

When Emily had paid for her items, she descended the front steps and started to cross the street. She wrestled with what to do, but she just had to stop and look. Julie had just made it up to the front of the house and was speaking with James. He stopped what he was doing and looked down the street. When their eyes met, the distance between them did not matter. Any doubt that James still loved her vanished in that moment. They were not allowed to speak, but his eyes mirrored the feelings of his heart. Emily forced a shaky smile, and James touched the brim of his invisible hat in a gentlemanly gesture. James stayed rooted where he was, and though Emily wanted this moment to last, she knew she could not stand there all day. She turned slowly and made her way toward the parsonage, and James' gaze followed her until he could see her no longer.

Seth's voice interrupted his thoughts, "James, will you help me rehang the door now?"

"Yes, I'm coming."

"Is that your girl?"

"Yes." Then he realized his error and amended his answer, "Well, no, I guess not. It's complicated."

Realizing there was an important part of the story he was missing, but not wanting to intrude, Seth simply replied, "I see."

By the time the front door was repaired, Julie and Emma had hung the curtains, and the brothers were all finishing up their tasks. James' authoritative voice sounded, "Good work, everyone. Gather your tools and clean up. We need to get home for evening chores."

Seth stepped back to the picket fence. He was amazed at what he saw. The house did not look anything like the one they had moved into. This one had a sturdy picket fence with a stone pathway, even steps, a door that opened easily, and a straight roofline. The ground to the right of the footpath was cleared and ready for a garden. The grass to the left of the footpath had been clipped short. When the boys passed by him with their tools and supplies, Seth thanked each one individually.

Soon, Julie and Matthew came, followed closely by Emma, whose face was still mostly obscured by smeared soot. Emma addressed Seth, "There was still plenty of beef stew from yesterday, so I have it warming on the stove. The clean stove, I might add. The inside is ready for Susanna."

"Let me get her before you leave." Seth walked through the house to collect his wife.

When he carried her into their home, Susanna gasped, "Seth, is this the same house? Look, they even hung curtains!"

"I had the same thought about the house. Just wait until you see the front." He exited the front door to find everyone still loading the wagon.

Susanna was glad Julie had explained her family or she would have surely embarrassed herself gaping at this group of men. "Thank you to all of you. Our home looks brand new, and the curtains are beautiful." Just then, she spotted Emma. "Emma, what happened?"

"Just a little run-in with the cook-stove. It dealt the first blow, but I won the fight."

Laughing, Susanna replied, "I'm glad to hear it. Jonathan, I see you have made some new friends, but you have to stay here with us."

"I know, Mama."

Josiah added, "You are welcome to come to the ranch and visit anytime."

"Thanks, Josiah," Jonathan beamed.

"I'm guessing we'll see them at church tomorrow, too," Seth remarked.

James replied, "We'll be there. Your family will love our church." He stopped short of saying "and our Pastor," then mentally chided himself for the omission. He needed to go up to the Hill tonight after dinner and spend more time with his God.

The family piled into the wagon and waved as they pulled away.

CHAPTER 6
Winds of Change

J osiah helped Emma from the buckboard in front of the church Sunday morning just as Seth Carter and his kids were arriving. "Hi, Josiah," Jonathan called.

"Hello, there," Josiah replied. He looked up at the new blacksmith, "Welcome to our church. I'll introduce you to Pastor Kendrick." Jonathan was all but glued to Josiah's side as they ascended the front steps. "Pastor, this is Seth Carter, the new blacksmith, and his children Louisa, Jonathan, and Anna."

Pastor extended his hand toward Seth for a handshake, but Jonathan reached his hand first, "We're pleased to meet you."

Seth placed his right hand on Jonathan's head before returning Pastor's handshake also. "What he said."

To Jonathan, Pastor said, "I love your enthusiasm, young man." To the entire Carter family, he added, "I'm delighted you are joining us this morning."

The group filed through the doorway, and Jonathan whispered to Josiah, "Can I, I mean, may I sit with you?"

"Sure, as long as it's all right with your dad."

Jonathan looked up and received an approving nod from

his dad. He followed Josiah into the third pew with Tim and Jacob, and Seth and his daughters filed into the pew behind them. Waiting for the service to begin, Seth glanced around the congregation. Two rows in front of him, he spotted James, Julie, Luke, and another young woman. He briefly wondered if she were the wife of one of the other men at the ranch, then dismissed the idea when she was sitting next to Luke, whom he knew was married to Julie. Missing the obvious connection, he had another passing thought, *"Where was James' mother?"*

Seth was distracted from his musing when he noticed the silent exchange between James and the pretty girl from the street. Louisa gently tugged on her dad's sleeve, "That's Emily, the Pastor's oldest daughter. We met in the general store yesterday. She seems really nice."

He put the name together. Emily Kendrick. James had recommended her recipe for beef liver, so he must have eaten her cooking at some point. Maybe more than once, if he had had to endure liver. This was another evidence that there was more to the story. Noticing relationships was Susanna's expertise. Maybe she was rubbing off on him a bit.

James had again chosen the seat closest to the center aisle. He did not know if he were just torturing himself, but he needed Emily to know he was still there for her as much as he could be. Thankfully, he felt a bit more relaxed than the Sunday before. When Emily was ready to leave her seat for the piano, she glanced over at James and found his deep brown eyes gazing at her. She responded with her best attempt at a shaky smile. How he wished he were allowed to speak to her!

Emily knew seeing James would be bitter-sweet, but she, too, chose the spot on the aisle. She was reminded once again of her promise to Beth. James loved her; she would not forget.

Pastor stepped behind the pulpit and opened the service by leading the congregation in "Trust and Obey." Emily marveled, knowing this very hymn had been the one to encourage her heart these last couple of weeks. Once again, she let the message of the words speak to her soul.

Sitting in the congregation, James was exhorted by the words he sang. The title alone should be his goal. When the song ended, he prayed silently, *"Lord, help me to trust You and obey."*

The sermon this morning was on discipleship. Pastor emphasized, "Discipleship is not just for pastors and church leaders. God has called every one of his children to teach others about Him. Discipleship does not have to be formal instruction. It takes many forms. Those of you with young children have the opportunity to disciple them in God's truths every day. Sometimes, discipleship looks more like Titus 2, where the older men are told to teach the younger men; likewise, the older women to teach the younger. If God lays someone on your heart, follow His leading. You may never know the impact you might have in someone's life."

Seth sat soaking in the service, but when Pastor spoke about mentoring others, the face that appeared in his mind was not that of his children, but of James. Perhaps he should set up an informal meeting with him sometime soon.

When the service concluded, Seth waited a few moments

while Jonathan conversed with Josiah and Tim. He was glad his son already felt so accepted among this group of fine young men. James walked up and shook Seth's hand.

"Thank you again, James, for the work you did on the house."

"You're welcome. We're always happy when the Lord can use us to be a blessing."

"You certainly were that. I was wondering, is there is a cafe here in town?"

"Yes, there is one next to the telegraph office," James replied.

"Would you be able to come into town one day this week for lunch? My treat."

"Name the day, and I'll be there."

"How about tomorrow at eleven o'clock?" Seth asked.

"Great. I'll look forward to it."

Soon Luke and Julie walked past, followed by the unknown young woman, who stopped to ask, "How is Susanna today? I hope we didn't tire her out too much yesterday."

"When we left for church, she was resting comfortably, reading her Bible." Seth was certain that Julie was the only younger woman at the house yesterday, so he was compelled to ask, "I'm sorry. Have we met?"

Though surprised by his question, Emma responded casually, "I'm Emma Taylor."

Still fully expecting James' mother to be a middle-aged lady, he asked incredulously, "You're Emma?" When she nodded, he transformed what he knew must be a look of shock to one of amusement. "I guess I didn't recognize you without the soot."

Still a bit flustered over the cookstove incident, Emma responded, "Oh, I must have looked a sight."

Realizing he had embarrassed her, Seth quickly responded, "I'm glad there were no long-lasting ill effects."

"Is there anything I can do for Susanna?"

"You have already done more than you know. She is so thankful for your friendship."

"Would it be all right if I stopped by one afternoon this week?"

"I know she would love your visit."

"Wonderful, I'll plan on it then."

When Emily was gathering her Bible, Mrs. Lucinda Horne approached her. "Emily, you play the piano so beautifully. Would you consider teaching piano lessons to Millie and Opal? We could pay you fifty cents a week."

"To be honest, I would really enjoy teaching them. When would you like the lessons to begin?"

"I know it's only June, but could you start this week?"

"Oh, I don't mind. I teach my siblings school through the summer to help them better retain the material." Still wanting to keep Friday afternoons free for when James could come again, Emily suggested, "How about three o'clock Tuesday afternoon?"

"I'll have them here. Thank you, Emily."

"You're welcome. See you Tuesday."

Emily had just exited the church when Mrs. Amanda Cooper stopped her. "Emily, I just heard that you're teaching piano lessons. Would you teach Maddie, too?"

With her mind whirling a bit, Emily responded, "I have lessons scheduled until four on Tuesday. Would Maddie be able to come then?"

Amanda smiled, "Yes, that would be perfect. Thank you."

Emily walked to the parsonage and marveled at how

quickly life can change. She had gone from simply playing piano to becoming a piano teacher to three students in about ten minutes. The thought of teaching music made her heart sing. The only downside was that she was unable to share the news first with James.

CHAPTER 7
Teaching

After Sunday dinner, Emily retreated to her room. She knelt before her wooden chest and carefully pulled out items that were dear to her. Near the bottom, Emily found what she was looking for: the beginner piano books she had used as a new student. She laid them gently on her bed and neatly returned the rest of the contents to her chest before closing the lid.

With a swish of her skirt, Emily turned and moved the books to the small writing desk before the window, where she sat, lifting and carefully turning page after page of her piano books, trying to remember back to her first lessons. She was surprised to find one thing conspicuously missing: a simple music staff with the notes and their names.

Emily slid the desk drawer open and removed a single sheet of paper, a wooden ruler, and a pen. With practiced hand, she dipped her pen in the ink and drew the treble clef staff with quarter notes neatly labeled. This is where she would begin. One more time, she withdrew another sheet of paper and outlined her lesson plans for the first month. She knew she could always tweak her lessons as she went, but a teacher with a plan is the one who reaches a goal.

At five minutes before eleven o'clock on Monday morning, James tethered Trigger to the hitching post in front of the cafe. Seth was walking down the boardwalk from the forge, and they met at the front door. "Morning, Seth."

Seth extended his right hand to shake James' and clapped him on the shoulder with his left hand. "Good morning, James. Shall we head in and order? I'm starving."

"Sure thing."

The men were seated and presented menus. Once they had both ordered the day's special, Seth spoke up. "My family really enjoyed the church service yesterday."

"Yes, we are thankful to have such a church in our small town. The sermons are true to God's Word, and those in the congregation truly care for one another. Did you have a good church before you moved?" James inquired.

"Our home in Kansas was a significant distance from the nearest town, much less a good church. We would meet as a family on Sunday mornings for a time of worship and Bible study, but that just wasn't the same as meeting with fellow believers." Seth added, "The sermon yesterday on discipleship spoke to me. I don't know why the Lord laid you on my heart, for I'm practically a stranger and certainly no theologian, but if you ever need a listening ear, I'm here."

The pronouncement could have been awkward, but it came as a comforting embrace to James' soul. Until this moment, he would have been unable to put his finger on what was missing in his life, other than Emily; but the Lord had known exactly what he needed. "Thank you, Seth. I think God knows I need extra guidance, for He has always provided a mentor at just the right times."

"Susanna told me a bit about your family at the ranch. How long have you lived there?"

"Since I was fourteen. My family was killed by an Indian raid while I was traveling to a neighboring farm on an errand, and I was suddenly alone. The clerk at the mercantile knew I was looking for work and introduced me to Daniel, Emma's husband. Though my dad was a farmer, he had a small herd as well, and I had developed a love for cattle ranching. When I learned that Daniel was a rancher, I hoped he'd give me a chance, but I was just a kid and didn't think he'd really offer me a job. But he did give me a job -- and so much more. Daniel invested his life in me and became my father during a time when I needed one desperately. Emma gave me her motherly love and care. She still does."

Seth nodded. "If I'm not mistaken, there is another young lady who would like to give you love and care."

James swallowed hard and pinched his brow in a pained expression. "Yes, there is."

"Would I be overstepping if I asked you what happened?" Seth asked with hesitation.

"Emily and I have been courting for just over four years. When I asked her dad for permission to marry her, he refused and has forbidden me to even speak to her. She may not have my presence right now, but she still has my heart. Everything in me wants her to be my wife."

Seth could see what it cost James to share those words and silently prayed for wisdom. "You have made the right decision to honor her father's wishes."

"Knowing it is the right decision doesn't make it any easier."

"No, being withheld from the one you love is anything but

easy. Susanna grew up in an affluent family. Her mother had expectations for the social circles Susanna would join, whom she would be close to, whom she would marry, what her future would hold. Needless to say, the common boy who wanted to head West was not in her plans. I first met Susanna when I was standing on the street corner selling newspapers. She purchased one from me and wouldn't let me give her the change, insisting that I keep it. Her attitude was generous, not arrogant. She was so beautiful! Not long after, I got a job at the dock and soon discovered that it was her father's shipping business. When I was up at the main office to collect my first paycheck, I saw the beautiful girl again and learned her name. Though in time I was promoted enough for her father to notice and approve of my work, Susanna's mother would not relent her aversion to my courting Susanna. Her father encouraged me to blend into the aristocratic circles, but the debutante life was not for me, even if I had been born to privilege."

"Like you, I was forced to wait. Finally, Susanna's mother realized what a wonderful man I am." Both of them laughed. "Seriously, though, she finally consented to our courtship, and you know the rest of the story. Not only am I married to the girl of my dreams, but with the blessing of her family. That blessing is worth the wait."

"Thanks, Seth. It's good to hear that from someone who's been there." James paused, then added, "Though I must admit that I feel restless, like I should be doing something."

"I obviously don't know you well, but from what I've observed, my guess is that you'd rather be a man of action than one to sit and idly wait."

James sighed, "Yep, that's me, all right. Always learning patience."

"Action and patience don't have to be mutually exclusive," Seth stated matter-of-factly.

"What do you mean?"

"Take Noah for example. He was waiting for the animals and the rain that would follow, but he did not sit idle. He built an ark. Likewise, Elijah prayed for rain after several years of drought. He sent his servant to check the sky seven times. When a cloud only the size of a man's hand was spotted, Elijah sent word to the king to prepare for the abundance of rain."

James crinkled his brow. "I don't follow the correlation."

"Are you convinced that Emily is the girl God had chosen for you to marry?"

"Without a doubt."

"Then prepare for rain. Pray about what you should be actively doing while you wait, then obey in faith."

For the first time in weeks, James felt as if a weight had been lifted from his shoulders.

Later that night at the Hill, James sat on the bench underneath the wide branches of a wizened oak. He was reading the stories of Noah and Elijah from Genesis 6-8 and I Kings 18. Though his soul yearned for action, he deeply wanted God's will more than his own. "Lord, you know I am often tempted to run ahead of your plan rather than be patient, but Seth's words were so freeing. I know Emily is the woman you created to complete me. Would it be all right with You if I prepared for rain? Please give me peace about what to do. If Your answer is to be still and wait, please give me the patience to obey."

No words echoed from Heaven. James gazed into the deepening sky as the first pinpoints of light began to appear. For some reason, his thoughts returned to Noah, and he reopened his Bible to Genesis and read again the detailed instructions God gave Noah regarding the Ark's construction.

Suddenly an unexpected thought came to his mind. *"That's it! I could build our home. I've already saved up for the cost of the lumber. The construction will keep me busy, and I won't be violating Pastor's instructions. Perfect."*

When Tuesday afternoon approached, Emily wrapped up the lessons with her siblings a few minutes early, gathered the piano books she had procured from the chest in the bedroom, and made her way the short distance to the church. She sat on the piano bench, propping the note chart and the opened first level book on the music stand, and mentally rehearsed what she wanted to teach today.

Millie and Opal Horne arrived a few minutes before three o'clock. Their mother walked with them down the center aisle to the front. The bouncing brunette ringlets Millie wore pulled away from her face with a blue bow matched her exuberant personality. Opal's neatly combed straight light brown hair was demure like her manner. Millie was bubbling with excitement, but Opal looked terrified. Emily stepped down from the platform. She smiled at both girls, but her words were meant for Opal. "Hello, girls. Today you will begin learning one of my favorite things. Do you know how I learned to play the piano?" When Opal shook her head, Emily continued, "One note at a time." Opal gave a shaky smile. "Millie, why don't we start with your lesson first. Opal, you may sit here on the front pew with your mother and listen so you will know what to expect."

Emily began by showing Millie how to find Middle C on the keyboard and how to recognize the corresponding note on the staff. She emphasized the fundamentals of how to sit properly on the bench, keeping the back straight and shoulders relaxed, and how to curve the fingers and hands while keeping the wrists lifted away from the piano ledge. By the end of the lesson, they had covered C, D, and E and had begun learning the first couple measures of "Mary Had a Little Lamb."

Millie bounded from the platform. "Did you hear me play notes, Mama?"

"Yes, I did. They were lovely." Lucinda Horne patted her daughter's knee as she plopped down beside her.

Emily knelt in front of Opal. "Are you ready for your first lesson?" The little girl still looked unsure. "Come with me." Emily stood and reached out her hand. Opal placed her hand in Emily's, and they walked up to the piano together. Though Emily covered the same material she had with Millie, she added more words of encouragement and praise for Opal.

By the end of the lesson, the little girl nearly had a smile as she added, 'Thank you, Miss Kendrick."

"You are welcome, my dear." When the pair reached Opal's mom and sister, Emily instructed, "I know that you do not have a piano at home. For this week, I would like the girls to practice their hand position at the edge of the dining table. Remind them to keep their wrists off the table as they gently tap the surface with their fingers, one at a time."

"Thank you, Emily. I will be sure they practice." Lucinda Horne paid Emily for the lessons. The girls waved at their teacher, and the trio turned to leave.

Amanda Cooper and her daughter Maddie entered the church as the Hornes reached the back pew. Millie bounced up to Maddie and whispered loudly, "Playing the piano is so much fun. You will love it."

Half an hour later, Emily strolled back to the parsonage feeling a wistful satisfaction. Laura was filling the bucket at the water pump out front, and looked up when she heard Emily approaching. She pushed the sweat-curled tendrils from her forehead and asked, "How'd it go?"

"Quite well, I think. Millie and Maddie were eager to learn, but shy little Opal was a bit overwhelmed. In the end, they each had a good first lesson."

Laura lifted the filled bucket, and they both walked into the house. "Better you than me. I don't think I'd ever have the patience to teach anyone anything."

"That's not true. You just taught Susan how to make soap last week," Emily reminded her.

"Making soap is fun. That's hardly the same as teaching."

"To me, making soap is work, but playing piano is fun. It's all a matter of perspective."

"You have a gift, Emily. You know how to explain even the most difficult concept so anyone could understand, and you enjoy doing it. I'm living proof. You taught me geometry."

Emily looked sideways at her sister, "I wasn't sure we were both going to survive geometry."

"Yeah, I gave you a hard time. Sorry about that, but we did survive, and I passed my high school diploma examination. I'd have never been able to do that without you."

"To have a student fully grasp the concept you are teaching is very fulfilling."

"Well, having taught all of us and now three piano students, I'd say you must be very fulfilled. I think you've found your calling."

When Laura moved past her older sister to carry the water bucket into the kitchen, Emily paused at the bottom of the staircase and pondered her words. *"My calling. I do enjoy teaching. Is it terrible that this isn't the calling I want? My heart's only desire is to be James' wife and someday a mother. Maybe God allowed Dad to make his decision to force me to pursue another direction. I do want God's will for my life, but I love James so much."* A troubled sigh escaped

Emily's lips as she ascended the stairs to put away her piano books.

About an hour after lunchtime on Thursday, Emma knocked on the Carters' front door. Jonathan swung open the newly hung door with a bit too much gusto. Seeing Emma, he blurted, "Hi, Mrs. Taylor, did you bring more apple pie?"

"Jonathan!" came Louisa's reprimand from the kitchen.

Emma chuckled, "You sound like Tim. No, I don't have apple pie; but I did bring two loaves of pumpkin bread."

Jonathan's eyes lit up. "Yum. That sounds good, too."

With flushed cheeks, Louisa appeared beside him. "Please come in, Mrs. Taylor."

"Thank you, Louisa." Emma stepped into the house and spotted Anna playing with her dolls in the corner. "Hi, Anna."

"Hi, Mrs. Taylor. My dolls and I are going to have a tea party. Would you like to come, too?"

Emma walked over to the little girl and knelt down close to the circle of handmade dolls. "That is a lovely offer, my dear." She rested her hand on Anna's blond curls. "Would you mind if I visited with your mama for a little bit first?"

Anna nodded. "That's fine. Take your time. We'll save you some tea."

A couple of minutes later, Emma was seated at her new friend's bedside. Susanna was sitting upright, with pillows propped behind her back. Her pale face held a bit more color in her cheeks. "Are you feeling a bit better today?"

"Yes, I have been getting gradually stronger. Last night, I was able to sit with the family at the dinner table. That might not sound like much of a triumph, but I hadn't been able to join them for a while. Thank you for Emily's liver recipe. Even still, I have to discipline myself not to pinch my nose when I eat liver in front of the children." She gave a small shiver of disgust, and Emma laughed.

"The recipe was her mother's. When I asked Emily about it, she told me that when she was a little girl, their church members were mostly start-up ranchers who frequently 'blessed' their pastor with beef livers. None of her family cared for liver, but her mother got creative in the kitchen to make it more palatable, and this recipe was the result."

"Well, I appreciate the suffering they endured for my benefit." After a pause, she continued, "The kids' education has been on my mind a lot lately. Is there a school here in Prairie Hills, or did you teach the boys?"

"We don't have a school here, though the way the town is starting to grow, I wouldn't be surprised if that changes in the next few years. My situation was a bit different, since the boys all came to our family half grown. Most of their education was already completed. They were all good readers. Even Buck was reading English fairly well when he first arrived. I would have them read literature during the winter months and would help them with grammar and composition skills. Daniel evaluated and completed their training in arithmetic and taught them the practical skills of the ranch."

"I have always enjoyed teaching my three, but since February, most of our learning time has taken place right here, with them sitting on the bed with their books. They are starting to fall behind in their studies, and I've come to the humbling conclusion that I may need to ask someone else to teach them until I'm back on my feet again."

"What about asking Emily? She has been teaching her siblings since her mother became ill, giving her experience at all grade levels. Laura finished last year, leaving more room at the table. Besides, Robert has always had to learn with his sisters; I know he would love to have another boy around."

"Do you think she'd mind? She sounds like she has her hands full already."

"I tend to think she'd welcome the challenge, but you won't know until you ask."

On Friday afternoon, Seth walked from the forge to the parsonage and knocked. As Emily opened the door, Seth observed her four youngest siblings seated quietly around the table, bent over their paper, writing.

"May I help you?"

"Hello, Emily, I'm Seth Carter." He glanced over at the table again. "I was wondering if you might have enough room around that table for three more students. Until my wife's health improves, she is simply unable to teach them, and I haven't enough time after my shift at the forge." When Emily didn't respond right away, he added, "I'd pay you, of course."

When Emily recovered from the surprise of his question, she replied, "Oh, pay wouldn't be necessary, and I'm sure we could fit three more here. I met your children on Sunday, and they seem very sweet. What are their ages?"

"Louisa is twelve; Jonathan is ten; and Anna is six."

"They will fit right in. I would like to begin by evaluating their levels, but they should be able to study right along with Susan, Sarah, and Beth. We usually begin our learning time around eight o'clock, right after chores and breakfast. Would that be all right?"

"The timing would actually be perfect. I can walk here

with them on my way to the forge. When would you like them to start?"

"Monday morning would be fine."

The lines in Seth's brow relaxed a bit, and he replied, "Great. Monday morning it is." Just to clarify, he added, "And I'm still planning to pay you."

Seth excused himself, and Emily quietly closed the door and murmured, "Changes are happening faster than the winds in a tornado. Lord, I really miss James, but I'll be content talking with You."

She had barely turned around when Sarah exclaimed, "Emily, Susan poked me with a pencil!"

"Just because I am pulled from the head of the table for a moment does not give you permission to pester each other. Be kind and finish your paragraph." Susan and Sarah glared at each other before returning to their assignment.

Robert leaned forward inquisitively and asked, "What did Mr. Carter want?"

"Finish your paragraph first, then I will tell you."

He poised his pencil to continue writing. "Hmph. I hate writing."

"Yes, that is a common sentiment, especially among boys, but you must learn to write well, and the only way to accomplish that is to practice."

"Practice is boring."

"Practice will teach you diligence, perseverance, and the value of hard work."

"I don't want to be diligent."

Emily placed her hand on Robert's shoulder and chuckled, "I trust you for that. Nevertheless, diligence is a character quality that should be developed in every godly man. Now, finish your paragraph."

Realizing he was losing this dispute, Robert exhaled loudly

and once again started writing his cursive words across the paper.

Emily's hand was still on his shoulder, and she bent down to his ear, "I want you to grow to be the man God wants you to be because I love you."

Robert whispered back while continuing to write, "I know. I love you, too."

A few minutes later, Robert laid down his pencil and handed his paper to Emily. "Finished. Now, tell us about Mr. Carter."

Four pairs of eyes were fixed on Emily. "Well, we will have three more students around our table beginning Monday."

The buzz of excitement started immediately. Even Beth's eyes lit up. "Can Jonathan sit by me?" Robert pleaded.

Emily corrected, "May Jonathan sit by me, not can; and we'll see."

Ignoring Emily, Robert enthusiastically assured his sisters, "School will be much more fun now!"

"What, it isn't fun already?" Emily asked in a mock offended tone.

Robert just rolled his eyes in response.

Emily lifted a hand to gain everyone's attention. When they were all quiet, she continued, "Remember, Mrs. Carter has been sick for some time, and the Carter kids have just moved from the only home they have ever known. If they are behind on their studies, we can all help them catch up. Most importantly, you can all be good friends to them so they feel welcome in our community and in our home." After making sure all her siblings understood, Emily transitioned, "All right, let's do arithmetic."

On Sunday afternoon, Emily again sat at the writing desk in the girls' bedroom, composing a list of topics that should be evaluated in her new pupils. She didn't want her evaluation to feel like a test on their first day, so she developed creative ways to assess their progress and include her siblings in the process. Emily had always taken her teaching responsibilities seriously, but somehow her duties seemed even more important, even somewhat daunting, when entrusted with the education of students who were not related.

She paused her planning and bowed her head, *"Lord, I filled Mama's teaching shoes out of necessity and discovered a love of teaching. Now on the eve of teaching three new students, I feel inadequate and overwhelmed. I need You. Please give me wisdom and help me to be the best teacher I can be. Help me to be attuned to the needs of all of the students under my tutelage, both academically and otherwise. Enable me to be a blessing. In my Savior's name, Amen."*

CHAPTER 8
School Days

O n Monday morning, Seth gathered his children together after breakfast. "Today will mark a milestone in your education. For the first time you will have a teacher other than your mama. I expect you to listen to Miss Kendrick, learn from her, and be respectful to her."

In unison, the three replied, "Yes, Daddy."

"All right, then give Mama a hug and kiss, and we'll be on our way." They obediently entered their parents' bedroom to do just that.

Louisa was the last to hug her mama. As she released her embrace, she looked at her mama with concerned eyes. "Are you going to be all right while we're gone?"

Susanna reached up and stroked Louisa's hair. "Yes, sweetheart, I will be just fine. Now go and learn new things so you can tell me all about it when you get home."

Louisa seemed reassured and turned to follow her brother and sister out of the bedroom and out the door. Seth reminded Susanna, "I'll come check on you at lunchtime. Love you."

"Love you, too."

A few minutes before eight o'clock, Seth and his trio of children arrived at the parsonage. When he knocked, Emily opened the door. She spoke to her new students, "I am so glad you are joining us. Jonathan, you may sit next to Robert. Louisa, please sit next to Susan. Anna, sit between Sarah and Beth." As the new arrivals went to their places, Emily turned back to Seth.

"Would you like me to have Robert walk them home when we finish?" Emily asked.

Seth paused, then replied, "I may take you up on that one day soon, but today I'd like to walk with them. I'll swing by as soon as my shift ends."

From where she was sitting, Anna called, "Have a good day, Daddy."

"I will, Sweetheart. All of you, learn well." With that, he turned with purposeful stride toward the forge, and Emily closed the door and took a deep, steadying breath before facing her class.

Emily walked confidently to the head of the table, though inside she was quivering like a leaf in the breeze. One by one, she calmly met the gaze of all seven pairs of eyes looking her way before she spoke. "'Learning is not attained by chance; it must be sought for with ardor and attended to with diligence.' Those words were penned by Abigail Adams, the wife of our country's second President. She received her education at home, under the teaching of her mother, and became a very well-read and respected influence during the Revolutionary Era. Her husband entrusted her with all the decisions during his many diplomatic trips abroad."

"Though educated primarily by tutors, her son John

Quincy Adams also received much instruction from his parents, who took personal responsibility for his education as well. By the time he was eighteen, he knew several languages and had traveled to Europe with his father to assist in diplomatic meetings. Later that year he was admitted to Harvard College and subsequently graduated second in his class. As you know, he also became our sixth President."

Emily paused before continuing, "Learning is tremendously important. Though it is not always easy, learning is always worth the effort. Whether you are taught by your mother or someone else appointed to that post, learn with diligence."

The features on Emily's face softened into a gentle smile. "Now, let's begin our day with prayer." When everyone had bowed their heads, Emily prayed, "Dear Lord, we are grateful for a new day and for this time You have provided to enrich the minds you have given us. Thank you for the students you have entrusted to my care, and make me the teacher I need to be. Give each one of us the opportunity to be a blessing to someone today. In Jesus' name, Amen."

"Now, before we begin our academic work, let's start with our Bible study. Please turn in your Bibles to Daniel, chapter 1. We have been studying the book of Proverbs, specifically the verses about wisdom. Robert, what is wisdom?"

"Applying God's Word to our lives," Robert responded without hesitation.

"Right, knowing what God's Word says is important, but until we let it change how we live, it is merely knowledge. We should strive to grow in wisdom. Making the choice to do right is easier when your parents are watching. Making the choice to do right when no one will ever know is godly character. Daniel's life is a perfect example of this. Robert, begin reading in verse one, and we'll go around the table, each one reading a verse, until we finish the chapter."

Other than needing to lend a pronunciation with the

Babylonian names, each of the children, other than Anna, read appropriately for their age. Emily made a mental note to spend a bit of time with her one-on-one at some point during the day.

"Nicely done. Now I want you to put yourself in Daniel's shoes for a minute. He was taken from the only home he had ever known, a home in a rural agricultural area, and transported hundreds of miles to the most advanced city of his day. There, he was taken to the king's palace. Can you imagine how beautiful and grand it was? The Hanging Gardens is still considered one of the wonders of the ancient world. Daniel was living in the home of the most powerful ruler in the world. No parents. No rabbi."

"Remember, he didn't have the entire Bible we have today. He didn't know how the story was going to end or even that his own life's story would be included in Scripture. He could have chosen to blend in, to do what everyone else was doing, but he didn't. Why? Look at verse 8. Daniel had resolved, had purposed in his heart, to do what was right, no matter what."

"Think about this: Daniel did not wait until he was faced with temptation to make a decision of right or wrong. He had already determined that he would do right. When the temptation came, his decision had already been made. In the same way, if we wait until we are tempted to do wrong, we will fail every time. Make the choice today to do what is right, whether or not someone is watching. For, of course, God is always watching, hoping, as do our fathers, that we will choose to do right."

"As we read the rest of Daniel's life in the upcoming days, we'll see that he became a leader, first to his Hebrew friends, then among the counselors to three different kings. Always he was faithful. Be a Daniel."

"Sarah, please close our Bible study with prayer." After Sarah's sweet and simple prayer, Emily said, "All right, everyone stand and jump up and down twenty times. Good. Stretch up to the ceiling as high as you can then reach down and touch your toes. Now have a seat. Pull out your slates, and we will begin arithmetic."

Robert and Jonathan both groaned simultaneously. "Boys, be a Daniel with your attitudes, too." When all the slates were out, Emily explained, "Today, we are going to play a game. We'll have a bit of fun and review your combinations at the same time."

Jonathan leaned over to Robert and whispered, "That doesn't sound too bad." Soon they were all enjoying the math challenge game. Then from one subject to the next, the morning progressed smoothly. At half past eleven, Emily dismissed her class for lunch. The Kendrick siblings included the Carters as they prepared sandwiches in the kitchen and wandered into the backyard to sit on the grass and soak up some fresh air and sunshine. Just before noon, the Kendricks led the others back into the kitchen, where they washed dishes and cleaned up.

"What's next?" Louisa asked Susan.

"Reading hour. Do you have a book already?"

"No, not one I haven't read."

"Then come over here and pick one from our library. Have you ever read *Pride and Prejudice* by Jane Austen?" Louisa shook her head. Susan pulled the volume from the shelf and handed it to Louisa. "You'll love this story."

Louisa carefully accepted the book and followed Susan over to the hearth rug to sit and read.

Emily pulled an early primer from the bottom shelf. "Anna, come sit with me on the sofa, and we'll read together." The look of worry on Anna's face after she listened to Louisa and Susan's exchange nearly vanished, but not quite. Anna settled on the cushion next to her new teacher. Despite the warm breeze that was flowing through the open windows, Anna gave a little shiver.

Emily's heart melted for this little girl. What Anna did not know was that Emily had taught all of her siblings to read, even when her mama was still alive. Some of Emily's siblings had caught on right away, others . . . well, not so much. They were all fine readers now. Emily guessed that Anna, at only six, had probably not had much opportunity to learn since her mama had been so ill, and she was right.

To the others seated around the room, Emily instructed, "Read carefully, for after our reading hour, you will write two sentences summarizing what you have read." Her siblings were used to this procedure, but Jonathan and Louisa looked up, nodded, and returned to their reading.

Gently opening the primer in her hand so Anna could see, Emily pointed to the alphabet, showing upper case and lower case, each with a corresponding picture. "Anna, have you had a chance to learn your alphabet?"

Anna nodded, "I know most of them." She looked to the ground and whispered, "I usually get stuck somewhere after 'n'."

"Whenever something is hard for me to remember, I make it into a song." Emily began to softly sing a little tune with the entire alphabet, and Anna's eyes grew wide. "Listen to it one more time and follow the letters in the book with your finger while I sing." Anna obeyed. "I'll tell you a secret. I don't really like singing by myself. Would you sing the alphabet song with me?" Anna nodded, and they sang it together several times until Anna knew her letters in order.

"That's wonderful! Now that you know the names of the letters, you can learn their sounds. Five of the letters have special jobs; they are called vowels." Emily taught Anna the vowels and spent the rest of the reading hour on a "scavenger hunt," helped by Anna, turning the pages of the primer to find the words with "a" and practice its sounds.

When the time came for reading hour to end, Louisa approached Emily rather bashfully. "Miss Kendrick, I did not realize my sister didn't know her alphabet." She was quick to defend her mama. "Mama has been so weak, but she always reads to all of us before bedtime. It's Anna's favorite time of the day."

Placing out her hand on Louisa's shoulder, Emily assured her, "Your mama has already given Anna a love for reading. She will be reading on her own before you know it."

"Thank you, Miss Kendrick."

"You're welcome." Emily stood by the sofa while her pupils returned to the table while all but Anna took out a piece of paper and wrote a brief reading summary. When Anna was instructed to draw a picture instead, she drew a bright red apple with a black letter "A" beside it. When the science lesson had ended, Emily filled the remaining time before Mr. Carter's arrival by sending everyone out for leaves to be the feathers on their bird drawings while she mixed the flour and water to make glue.

When Seth arrived, they were all busy designing their art projects. Emily interjected, "All right, everyone, be sure your name is on your drawing before you lay it on the hearth to dry." When they had stowed their artwork and collected their books, they each chorused, "Thank you, Miss Kendrick" and joined their dad through the doorway.

Emily waved, "See you tomorrow." As she latched the door, she sighed a happy sigh and thought, "The first day went well. I wonder what tomorrow will bring."

CHAPTER 9
Ranch Business

Emma turned the calendar page to July. The calving season had concluded a few months ago. Typically, all of the cows were bred sixty to ninety days after calving in the spring, but guided by a series of articles in *The Cattleman* magazine, Emma and the boys had decided to breed only half of the cows in their usual timeframe with the intention of breeding the other half of the herd during the winter for an autumn calving. Early research showed that autumn-born calves tended to be healthier and grow faster than spring-born calves. Splitting the herd had two benefits: dividing the risk by having two incomes each year rather than one and keeping the cattle drives smaller and more manageable for the brothers.

The time had come to plan ahead for the winter breeding. The Rugged Cross Ranch had seventeen bulls and nearly five hundred cows. A successful breeding season was essential to the prosperity and longevity of the ranch. Having healthy bulls was paramount. Being naturally very territorial, the bulls had to be separated throughout the ranch, each with their own collection of cows.

After breeding, several more cows than usual were barren.

Now it was up to Luke to determine why. James stepped out of his office in the barn just as Luke walked by with a wheelbarrow of hay. "Luke, when will you do the breeding soundness exams on the bulls?"

"I just spoke to Tim about them this morning. He's going to help me after morning chores."

"Good. Let me know what you find."

"Will do."

Tim, six and a half feet tall and still lanky, entered the barn, thankful that he didn't have to duck into this doorway. His long loping gait took him to the place where Luke was mucking his last stall. He folded his arms and leaned them on the top of the stall wall. "Are you ready to go, little brother?"

Luke was just over six feet tall, but he was still shorter and younger than Tim, making him "little brother" on two accounts. "Just about. I still need to spread some fresh straw here and saddle Dakota."

"You get the straw; I'll get your horse saddled." He stood to his full height and turned toward the tack room.

"Thanks, Tim." Luke finished his task and met Tim at the hitching post in front of the barn. Luke fastened his chaps around his legs, and they both mounted their horses, the leather squeaking as they settled in their saddles.

Tim squinted in the bright sunlight. "Where do you want to start, little brother?"

"Let's start with the closest pastures and work our way out. The older bulls are on the outskirts of the ranch. A couple of them were borderline on their examinations last year; they might not pass this year. Besides, the older ones are a little more cantankerous. We'll save them for last."

They started off toward the nearest pasture. Luke looked over at Tim as they rode. "Just out of curiosity, why do you call me 'little brother'? I don't think I've ever heard you call Jacob or Josiah 'little brother'."

Tim opened his mouth to speak, then closed it to think a moment. "I don't know. Maybe because you and I joined the family about the same time, and for awhile, you were my only little brother. I was happy not to be the youngest anymore. When Jacob and Josiah came, they seemed to have each other, already being brothers. Though I think of them as my brothers, too, you were the first, so I guess it stuck."

After a moment, Tim asked Luke, "Why did you ask me to ride with you?"

"You're the best roper of all of us, and the bulls know and respect you as their boss. I need them under control while I perform their physical exams, and I know I can trust you to protect me if they get out of line. Right, big brother?"

One by one, each bull was closely examined. By the end of the second day, they had finished their rounds. Luke found James in the foreman's office and discussed his findings with him.

"Let's meet with Emma. If we need to make changes to the herd, we need to start the process soon." James and Luke walked together to the ranch house where Emma greeted them. They sat at the kitchen table, and she poured each of them a cup of coffee.

"Okay, Luke, how were the breeding soundness exams?" Emma inquired.

"Twelve of the bulls passed, but five of our older bulls are now subfertile."

Emma responded. "That certainly explains our barren cows. I knew this would have to happen sometime soon. We haven't supplemented the bull herd since just before Daniel died."

James pondered for a moment, then stated, "We really have only two options. We can either cull the underperforming bulls and redistribute the cows for the bulls we have left, or leave the ratios the same and take the opportunity to introduce new genetic characteristics to our herd."

Emma appreciated the way James could analyze any situation logically. Daniel had been very much the same way and had taught James well. She mulled over the options. "Using the twelve remaining bulls leaves us with bulls we know perform well, but adding so many cows to each one could lead to an even larger number of barren cows. We certainly have the savings to purchase a few new bulls, but I don't know of a herd around here I would want to mix with our herd. What do you think, Luke?"

"The fertile bulls are getting older, too. We will not be able to rely on them forever. Tim recently read that there is a breed of longhorn cattle in Texas that grows bigger and leaner, adding weight, yet also improving the quality of the meat."

"That's a good thought. James, what do you think about sending a telegram inquiry for more information about this Texan breed?"

"Sending for more information is never a bad idea," James replied. "I'll be in town tomorrow; I'll send the telegram then."

"Why are you going into town?" Emma asked.

"Just to run a couple of errands," James answered evasively as he stood and carried his coffee cup to the sink.

After dinner, James lit a lantern and strode over to his foreman's office in the barn. Once seated at his desk, he slid open the right-hand drawer and pulled out his drawings of the house he wanted to build for him and Emily. To call them blueprints would be an exaggeration, but he hoped they would be detailed enough for the mill owner to determine how much lumber he would need. He studied the drawings carefully and made a few revisions based on what he had learned helping with the construction of Luke and Julie's home. Though he and Emily had never had a formal discussion about the house she wanted, he had listened to her mention one detail or another and would apply them to his sketches. His original intention had been to present the house plans to Emily after he proposed so they could dream together and discuss any changes. Now he was choosing to trust that he knew her enough to know what she would want. Yes, he was taking a risk, but he felt confident this was the right decision.

Finally, the last alteration was made. James shuffled the papers to find the sketch of the front of the house. As he held it in his hand, he leaned back in his chair and allowed himself a moment to daydream about showing Emily their finished home. He closed his eyes and whispered, "Emily, I love you. I will never stop loving you. One day, we will live in this house together, and I will be the happiest man in the world."

His chair creaked as he sat forward and reached to the very back of the drawer. He pulled out a short rectangular metal box. Lifting the lid revealed his entire life savings. He carefully placed the drawings and the box's contents into his saddlebag. He had been planning on this expenditure for some time. Now he was ready to make this purchase—and one other.

The next morning, James saddled Trigger right after morning chores and returned to his office for his saddlebag. As Tim prepared his horse to leave for his morning check on the herd, he spoke to Luke in low tones. "Something's up with James, but I can't figure out what. He was actually whistling in the bunkhouse this morning, and I caught him smiling during chores. I haven't seen that in awhile."

Just then, James walked from his office with his saddlebag slung over his shoulder and started to whistle again.

Tim gestured toward the whistler as one who had just obtained evidence for his claim, "See what I mean?"

James tossed the saddlebag across Trigger's back and tied its leather straps securely to his saddle, oblivious to his brothers standing nearby.

Luke prodded Tim, "Just ask him."

James finally looked over at them. "Ask me what?"

"Why are you suddenly so happy today?" Tim blurted.

Raising his eyebrows slightly in surprise, James responded, "Just a man on a mission."

"What kind of mission?" Tim asked.

James swung himself up in the saddle and grabbed the reins before he replied, "Preparing for rain."

Tim looked at Luke quizzically and mouthed, "Preparing for rain?" Luke simply shrugged in response as Trigger and James exited the barn.

Looking through the barn doorway at the cloudless sky, Tim shook his head, "James must have spent too long in the sun yesterday."

James arrived in town just as the stores were starting to open. After tethering Trigger, he slung his saddlebag over his shoulder again. Knowing his thoughts were preoccupied, he stopped by the telegraph office first. The attendant was seated at the telegraph and greeted him with a "Good Morning" as he entered.

"Morning. I'd like to send a message to the Texas Cattlemen's Association."

"Certainly, sir." The attendant stood and walked over with a pad of paper and pencil. "What would you like to say?"

"To Whom It May Concern: Stop. The Rugged Cross Ranch would like to request information on the Texas longhorn breed to determine if they would be the right bulls to supplement our herd. Stop. Sincerely, James McAllister, Foreman. Stop."

"Is that all?" When James nodded, the attendant counted the number of characters and quoted the price.

Once the telegram had been paid for, James exited the telegraph office and fixed his eyes on the sign for the lumber mill office across the street. He could feel his heart rate quicken. He took a deep breath and tried to suppress his smile as he ambled to the other side. Just as he stepped onto the opposite boardwalk, Seth walked toward him on his way to the forge.

"Good morning, James," Seth greeted.

"Good morning, Seth."

"I just dropped off the kids at the parsonage. Emily has agreed to teach them along with her siblings until Susanna is up to the task again. All three are enjoying 'Miss Kendrick,' but Anna is especially taken with her."

Ignoring the small twinge of disappointment that he was hearing this news secondhand, James replied, "I hadn't heard she was teaching your children, but they are indeed blessed. Emily is a wonderful teacher." James' tone was full of admiration.

"Wait, is that actually a smile I see?" Seth asked.

"I'm taking your advice. I'm going to prepare for rain."

Raising his eyebrows, Seth asked, "Oh, how so?"

James patted his saddlebag. "I have the plans for the home

we will share someday and am getting ready to place the order for the lumber so I can start construction soon."

Seth smiled and clapped James on the shoulder, "James, I'm proud of you." Something about that gesture made James' heart swell with confidence. "Resume your task. I need to get to work."

As Seth strode down the boardwalk toward the forge, James reached for the handle of the lumber mill's office door and stepped in. "Mornin,' Fred."

The mill's owner, a middle-aged businessman of average height with salt-and-pepper hair, turned from the papers strewn on his desk to face James and extended his hand for a handshake, "Good morning, James. What can I do for you?"

"I'd like to place an order for a load of lumber."

"Is Emma building another barn?"

James spoke as he pulled the drawings from his saddlebag and handed them to Fred. "No, this order isn't for the ranch. It's for me."

Glancing at the sketches, Fred asked, "Are you leaving the ranch?"

"No, but I'd like to move out of the bunkhouse and have my own place."

Fred walked to a raised table in the middle of the office and spread the pages to study them. "Three bedrooms? No second floor? Isn't this a lot of house for a bachelor?"

James nervously cleared his throat. "I'm not planning to be a bachelor forever, and—" He started to say Emily's name and caught himself just in time. "—Some women prefer not to carry laundry up and down the stairs."

Fred was a member of their church, and he had seen the recent separation of James and Emily as they sat conspicuously across the aisle from one another. He had assumed they had had a tiff, but now he wasn't so sure. Thankfully for James, he had enough propriety not to ask. "You are sure this is what you want?"

"Yes, sir," James replied confidently.

Nodding, Fred instructed, "Have a seat and give me a few minutes to calculate the amount of lumber you will need."

Settling into a nearby chair, James draped the saddlebag over his left knee and waited. If he were being honest, he had expected to have some doubts at this juncture, but he had none, just eagerness to get the project started.

Several minutes later, Fred looked up from his ledger. "All right, James, here are the figures for you." James stood and walked over to him as Fred turned the ledger toward him and pointed with the tip of his pencil. "Here is the amount of lumber required and my quote for the price. If you pay in full today, I will give you a 15% discount."

"If you make your discount 20%, I will pay you in cash right now."

Having conducted ranch business with James before, the mill owner expected nothing less than a bit of negotiation. "Done, 20% it is." Fred smiled and reached for his order book, writing the invoice for the agreed amount. After carefully removing the invoice, he stood and handed it to James, who reviewed it and counted out the correct sum of money. The money exchanged hands, and Fred again extended his hand for a handshake, "Pleasure doing business with you, James." The owner gathered James' building plans together and handed them back to him. "This order should be ready in a few weeks. Would you like us to deliver it for you, free of charge?"

James tucked the pages carefully back into his saddlebag. "Yes, please." He waved as he departed the lumber office. "Thank you, Fred."

The lumberman watched James close the door behind him and mused aloud, "I wonder if Emily knows what he's up to. Don't worry, James, your secret is safe with me."

James mentally crossed lumber off his errand list and followed the boardwalk toward the general store. One more purchase. He stopped for a moment to look in the shop window and smiled when he spotted what he was looking for. It was perfect, and he had just enough money left. He opened the door, and the bell's tinkle announced his arrival.

The shopkeeper looked up while boxing a customer's purchase. "Hi, James, do you have a list from Emma?"

"Not today." He paused. There were several customers milling about, and he thought, *"Perhaps I should come back another day. On second thought, there will probably always be customers. I need a plan."* To the shopkeeper, he said, "I'm just going to look around and place my order in a few minutes." He must have been satisfied with James' comment, for he merely nodded and returned to his work.

For several minutes, James milled about aimlessly looking at everything and nothing. As soon as a customer or two would exit, another would arrive. *"What was I thinking? I can't buy it with anyone around. Word would certainly get back to Emily or her dad in this small town."*

James made his way to the exit, and the clerk asked, "Didn't you have an order, James?"

"No, I see you're busy. It's no rush; we'll just get it the next time we're in town." The tiny bell sounded again as he once again stepped onto the boardwalk. He couldn't deny that he wasn't disappointed, but it was his own fault. He hadn't thought his plan through. When James made his way down the boardwalk toward the place where Trigger was patiently waiting, he looked toward the end of the street and saw the sign for the forge. He walked right past Trigger, seemingly drawn to the forge.

Seth was working at the anvil, hammering a red-hot billet of Damascus steel that would become a beautiful knife. He looked up and saw James standing in the doorway. "I'll be with you in just a minute." When the steel was finally the right thickness and shape, Seth quenched the blade in oil. Fire and smoke spewed from the quench tank for just a few seconds. When he withdrew the blade and checked the hardness of the steel with a file, he nodded that he was pleased, set the blade on his workbench, and walked over to James.

"Did you accomplish what you set out to do?" Seth asked.

"Mostly. I ordered my lumber, and Fred gave me a price that was more than fair. The order should be delivered in a few weeks."

"That's fantastic news! So tell me, why aren't you smiling?"

"I had planned one more purchase, but apparently I didn't think it through quite enough."

"How can I help?"

James shared the details.

"Do you have the money to buy it?" When James nodded, Seth added, "Just to clarify, there is only one in the window? I would hate to buy the wrong one."

"There is only one," James assured him, but he described it in detail, just in case.

"Give me the money, and I'll stop by the general store on my way to pick up the kids this afternoon. I'll bring it by the ranch tomorrow and pick up a couple more beef livers."

James handed him the cash. "Thank you, Seth."

"You're welcome. See you tomorrow afternoon." Seth folded the money, tucked it in his pocket, and returned to the blade on his workbench.

James walked over to Trigger to tie his saddlebag back on before briefly popping into the telegraph office in case there was a reply.

"Yes, the reply came just a few minutes ago," the telegraph operator said as he handed the paper to James.

"Thank you."

The telegraph read, "To James McAllister, Foreman,

Rugged Cross Ranch: Stop. A packet of information on the Texas longhorn has been mailed to you in today's post. Stop. If you decide to make a purchase, send another wire to arrange delivery. Stop. Sincerely, Texas Cattlemen's Association. Stop."

James addressed the operator once again, "Have a good day." A minute later, he tucked the telegram in his saddlebag with his house drawings and mounted Trigger for the ride home.

The following afternoon, Seth rode up the lane at the ranch and found James chopping wood near the barn. "Preparing for an early winter?"

Wiping the sweat from his brow in the summer heat, James replied, "Nope. Chopping wood clears my head." With the hint of half a smile, he added, "How many beef livers can I wrap for you?"

"Another two will hold us for a while."

James walked over to the water pump and washed his face and hands before heading over to the smokehouse with Seth. The latter dismounted and stealthily pulled a box from his saddlebag. Once inside, Seth handed it to James.

Carefully lifting the lid, James whispered, "It's perfect. Thanks for your help, Seth." Closing the box, he set it carefully on a clean shelf before wrapping two beef livers in butcher paper. "They're still free."

"For the record, you have nice taste. I think Emily will love it." He took his meat parcel and left for home.

CHAPTER 10
Mrs. Margaret Lange

O n Saturday afternoon, the thundering of hoofbeats and the creaking of the large wheels of the stagecoach came to a stop in front of the general store. The owner of the store, who doubled as the town postman, handed the mail bag up to the man riding shotgun and received one in return.

Nathan Lange and his family were waiting under the shade of the awning for a passenger to disembark. Not just any passenger. Nathan's newly-widowed mother. From Boston. The coach door opened, and the feather plume of her hat exited before her rather plump, well-dressed figure. The lines of her face were pinched in a scowl as she stepped onto the street and ordered the coachman to bring her trunk and valise.

Nathan moved forward to greet his mother, "Welcome to Prairie Hills."

Ignoring his greeting, she put her handkerchief to her nose and commanded, "Get my things so we can leave. This town smells, and there is dust everywhere. I'm just covered in it."

Looking up at his wife, who was trying to keep her smile in place, and his children, who had eyes like saucers, Nathan spoke pointedly in low tones, "Mother, this isn't Boston. Please stop complaining. You are scaring your grandchildren."

She stood aghast and pointed to the two children clinging to their mother. "Those waifs are my grandchildren? This is going to be worse than I thought."

Nathan quickly pursed his lips tightly to prevent words he would later regret and collected her valise. *"Dear Lord, calm my anger, and let me show Your love."* To the older woman before him, he said calmly, "Mother, this is my wife Molly and our two children, Thad and Amy. Let me guide you to our buggy, and I'll come back for your trunk."

"I don't know why I ever agreed to come here. This is such a disgrace."

Placing a hand on her elbow to guide her, Nathan took a steady breath and instructed, "Right this way, Mother." After she was settled on the buggy seat, he returned for his family and his mother's trunk. Before he hefted the cargo, he approached his wife and gently reached for her hand. "I'm so sorry for Mother's behavior. Thank you for being the sweetest wife ever." He could see the tears brimming on her lower lid and knew she was trying to be brave for the kids. "Thank goodness we were able to find a house within her budget here in town."

He loaded the trunk in the back of their buggy, and his wife and children climbed into the back seat. When Nathan found his place next to his mother, he signaled the team into motion and began another conversation with her. "Mother, you know I love you. I know you have been uprooted from everything you know and deposited in a very different world. In case you did not receive my latest letter before your departure, I was able to purchase a lovely little home on the edge of town with the money you wired. It will not be the extravagant surroundings you are accustomed to, but it will be both private and convenient. We are now on the way to our farm for dinner, and I trust you to please keep any unwelcome comments to yourself. Molly has been working all day in the kitchen, and you will find her roast is scrumptious, outdone only by her cherry pie. After dinner, you may decide whether to spend your first night in Prairie Hills with us and have me drive you to your new home tomorrow morning or whether you would prefer to be in your own home tonight. Molly has cleaned your home for your arrival, and you will find your bedroom furniture already in place. Your other shipping crates are opened, but not unpacked."

The atmosphere at dinner was strained, at best. Molly felt as if she were under constant scrutiny. Nothing she did was "the way it was done in Boston." *"Of course not,"* Molly thought. Nathan's mother had moved from a large house with wait staff, a maid, and a butler. The tension climaxed when Thad summoned the courage to tell his Grandmother about the frog he had caught that morning. The elder stopped him in his second sentence to declare that, "Children are to be seen and not heard."

Molly could keep her peace no longer. "May I call you Mother?"

"Mrs. Lange will do," she answered coldly.

"Mrs. Lange, as you have well surmised, this is not Boston. Here, we encourage our children to engage in conversation to foster family relationships and social interaction and convey our love for them." Turning to her son, she gently spoke, "Thad, tell us about your frog. We want to hear all about him."

He glanced at the stranger with big eyes, then at his mama, who seemed very eager to hear this tidbit of news. "Well," he began slowly, picking up speed as he went, "I was down at the pond this morning on side of the shore where the mud is really sticky . . ." As he embellished his story with hand gestures and frog sounds, Nathan noticed that the lines on his mother's face began to soften ever so slightly. If given a chance, Thad could work his way into anyone's heart. He was proud of his little boy.

Margaret Lange chose to move into her own house that evening. To Nathan's chagrin, he felt almost relieved. When he pulled the buggy in front of the house next to the new blacksmith's, he was expecting another onslaught of complaints. Perhaps she was exhausted from her day of travel, or perhaps she had simply exhausted all of her daily allotment of complaints. For whatever reason, she merely gave a terse "Thank you" to her son when he brought in her luggage. She then dismissed him with a wave, "That will be all. Good night."

Before he crossed the threshold, he asked, "Would you like us to pick you up for church in the morning?"

"Yes, I will be ready."

"Very well, good night, Mother."

The next morning, after the opening hymn, Pastor Kendrick announced, "We'd like to welcome another new guest to our congregation. Mrs. Margaret Lange has just moved from Boston to live near her son Nathan and his family."

Nathan leaned toward his mother and whispered, "You'll find our church members to be very friendly and inviting."

She lifted her nose slightly and replied, "We'll see," in a tone that communicated, "I highly doubt that."

Sundays fell into a familiar new routine. James would sit across the aisle from Emily but never speak a word out loud to her. She would close her eyes and listen when he would speak to his family just to hear his voice. Emily had an unspoken fear that her love for him would diminish with time, but this fear was unfounded. Her love for James was true, and it would not be altered by their circumstances.

As was now his pattern, James was one of the first to make his way toward the door. He hadn't forgotten proper manners, however. Pausing at the pew where Mrs. Lange was standing with a rather stern expression, he briefly introduced himself. Julie and Matthew stepped up, and he politely introduced them as well.

"Hmph. Uncivilized. The children here are having babies, I see." Mrs. Lange mumbled.

Several others filed by to welcome the visitor, and Luke walked down the aisle with Emily. Mrs. Lange took notice of the pair of them with their blonde hair and blue eyes. "Now here's a handsome couple. Are you married, too?" she asked rather abrasively.

Luke's smile twitched almost imperceptibly as he quickly appraised the woman before him. He answered courteously, but concisely, "This is Emily Kendrick, the pastor's oldest daughter, and I am Luke Hamilton. You met my wife Julie and our son a moment ago."

Mrs. Lange looked aghast. "That baby is your son?"

"Yes, he is."

She looked skeptical, "He doesn't look anything like you."

His smile never wavered as he answered without hesitation, "There is a strong family resemblance. He looks just like my brother."

She was aptly silenced. Luke took the opportunity to add, "Welcome to Prairie Hills." Turning slightly toward Emily to let her pass before him, they continued to the door.

Emily whispered, "You handled that perfectly. She took me completely off guard with her frankness."

Luke declared, "My mother warned me about people like

her." At the quizzical look on Emily's face, he continued, "She taught me to answer questions politely, with a smile, but give as little information as possible. Too much information will somehow be misconstrued and will always haunt you later."

"Well, you were brilliant. She got my bristles up when she all but accused you of not being Matthew's father."

"She is obviously experienced at her craft. Mom always said those who wheedle information to gain the upper hand were usually covering up a deep hurt. We'll just have to show her grace and kindness."

CHAPTER 11
Adding to the Herd

The days of summer had begun to transition into the cooler days of fall. With her egg basket in one hand, Emma knocked on the door of the bunkhouse and received a chorus of "Come in."

She opened the door to find her boys eating breakfast after morning chores and asked, "Jacob, would you harness the wagon and drive me into town, please? We need supplies, but it shouldn't take long. We'll still be able to get to the Wilsons' farm before lunch." He did not reply other than his curt nod, but he grabbed his boots and began slipping them on. Emma thought his response was unusual, but dismissed it and turned to visit the hen house once more for any additional egg deposits before their departure.

The ride into town was quieter than Emma had expected. While Jacob did not talk nonstop as Tim was apt to do, he usually carried on a pleasant conversation as he drove. Today, however, he seemed almost sullen. "Jacob, are you all right?"

"I'm fine."

"Are you feeling poorly?"

"Maybe a mite tired, that's all." And that, in fact, was all he was going to say.

Emma was mildly concerned, but she held her tongue. *"Maybe the fresh air and sunshine will lift his spirits,"* she thought.

When they arrived in town, Jacob dropped off Emma at the general store. Before she climbed down, she handed Jacob a piece of paper. "Here is the list for the feed store." Jacob merely nodded as he took the paper from her. Emma's feet had barely reached the ground before Jacob moved the wagon toward the feed store. Her eyes followed him while her heart harbored an unsettled feeling.

At that moment, Emily walked toward her, and Emma was delightfully distracted from her musings. "Good morning, Emma." This simple greeting, conveyed with a smile, instantly brightened Emma's mood. Her attitude was contagious.

"Hi, Emily, how are you on this beautiful September day?"

"This would be the perfect day for a walk with someone." Emily's blue eyes clouded over for just a moment. "But this is a glorious day to get a lot done."

"Are you shopping for kitchen staples?"

"Mostly, but I need more school supplies, too. With three additional students, I've exhausted all of my paper and pencils."

"Susanna had told me you agreed to teach them. You just don't know what a blessing you are to her, Emily. I'm sure nearly doubling your class hasn't been easy, but Susanna is amazed with how much they are learning."

"We've had our growing pains, to be sure. I finally had to split up the boys for a few days. Sitting together, they were too mischievous. Since I have let them sit next to each other again, they have been much better behaved."

"Last week, Susanna told me Anna crawled up in her bed with a book. Assuming Anna wanted her to read, she started to reach for the book. Anna shook her head and sweetly said, 'No,

Mama, I'm a big girl now. I'm going to read to you tonight.' She read the book from start to finish and Susanna had to wipe away a few tears. You have made quite a change in that little girl."

"Anna is such a little sweetheart. She was so embarrassed the first day when she stumbled halfway through the alphabet, but she so desperately wanted to read like Louisa that she caught on quickly. She just needed the tools and guidance. Now she reads on the same level with Beth, and I couldn't be more proud of her."

"I may be expanding my class again soon," Emily added.

"Really? How so?"

"Apparently word has spread that I'm teaching the Carters, and I have had two other families ask me to teach their children after fall harvest."

"How will that work?"

With a thoughtful expression, Emily replied, "Well, I'm not exactly sure. Our kitchen table certainly couldn't hold everyone. I've talked to Dad about the possibility of using the church building, but I would need desks. I had thought about asking Josiah if he would build some, since he's the best woodworker I know, but I didn't know if that would be too awkward since he's James' brother."

Emma placed a gentle hand on Emily's arm. "If you decide you need desks, I'm sure Josiah would be happy to help you. Between you and me, I'm sure he would get some help from someone you both hold dear."

Emily looked down and spoke softly, "I miss him so much."

"I know you do. He misses you, too. Every Friday afternoon, he chops wood for two hours. If he chops much more firewood, I'm not sure where we're going to store it; but one thing's for sure, if we have a two-year-long blizzard, we'll be ready."

Emily's heart was strangely warmed to hear James react to

their separation this way, but she couldn't wait until her dad relented, and they could spend Friday afternoons together again.

The two ladies stepped into the store as the jingle overhead announced their presence. Emma handed her basket of eggs and her list to the storekeeper who nodded and began pulling dry goods for her order. Neither of them had noticed the woman standing near the produce stand outside the store, but Margaret Lange had noticed them and had purposefully listened to every word of their conversation. With a look akin to one of disgust, she thought, *"Only fully certified teachers should ever be allowed to teach in a classroom. I doubt she has had any formal training at all. She may be the Pastor's daughter, but she isn't above the law. I need to make some inquiries."*

Several minutes later, the clerk had Emma's order ready. She paid for her purchase and asked, "Is there any mail for the ranch today?"

The clerk turned around to examine the boxes behind him. "Yes, you have one parcel and two letters." He slid them from the box and handed them to Emma.

"Thank you." She slipped them into the first box of goods and lifted it. "I'll send Jacob in to grab the other two boxes."

"Sure thing, Emma. As always, thanks for your business."

When Emma left the store, she saw Jacob still loading feed and alfalfa into the wagon bed parked by the loading dock of the feed store. She crossed the street and walked down to meet him. Sliding her box down the side of the wagon bed, she instructed, "Jacob, leave room for two more store boxes."

Once more, his only response was a nod.

After Jacob finished loading the last feed bag and procured the two additional boxes from the store, they were headed home. Still hoping Jacob just needed some cheering up, Emma tried another conversation. "The parcel from the Texas Cattlemen's Association came in the mail. I'm thinking dinner and pie for our family meeting might be in order tonight. What kind of pie would you like?"

Jacob knew Emma was just being thoughtful, but he wanted to be grumpy, and he was tired of pretending to be otherwise. "It doesn't matter to me." When he glanced at Emma, he saw that his words had caused a sting. He hadn't meant to hurt her and nearly followed with "All of your pies are good," but the words never made it past his frown.

Emma decided any more effort at conversation would only cause more friction, so she chose to pray silently instead. *"Lord, I have the distinct feeling that something is amiss, but I have no idea what it is. How I wish Daniel were here! He would know just what to do and say. Instead, you chose to leave me here to be the only parent figure these boys can claim. I need You. I feel so inept right now. Please help the other boys to step in and guide him, too. Help me to continue to love him unconditionally, no matter what he hurls my way. Help him to see Your love through me. In the name of my loving Savior, Amen."*

Later that night, the family gathered in the ranch house for dinner, and James asked Jacob to say grace. He seemed to pray comfortably and earnestly and made Emma wonder if she had been concerned for nothing earlier. A lingering doubt still clung to her, for her intuition was seldom wrong. Nevertheless, they enjoyed a good family mealtime. Afterwards, she pulled out the peach pie she had made that afternoon, knowing that it was indeed Jacob's favorite. Her act of kindness was not lost on Jacob, but he pushed away the guilt that was trying to haunt him for his bad attitude on their trip to town.

Julie slipped upstairs to nurse Matthew. When she came back down, she spread a small quilt on the floor near Luke's chair and played with her son who grabbed his toys with his fist and put them directly in his mouth. Teething was bound to begin soon, but she was going to miss his toothless grin.

The family stayed at the kitchen table for their meeting in order to pass around the materials from the Cattlemen's Association and discuss options more easily. Emma opened the meeting in prayer, "Heavenly Father, as we pursue necessary steps for our ranch, our utmost priority is Your will. Please guide us as we investigate our choices and make decisions that will greatly impact our ranch. Thank you for loving us. In Jesus' name, Amen."

Though Emma thought of the ranch as belonging to everyone seated around this table, she understood that technically, she was the sole owner, and as such, directed the meeting. "As I'm sure all of you know, Luke found five of our bulls to be subfertile during his last set of exams. Our remaining bulls are aging, but they should last a few more seasons. This puts us in a good position right now. We have the opportunity to add to our bull herd and improve the meat we produce, but if we do not find the right fit, we certainly have enough time to research other options within the next year and add more bulls then. Take some time to look over the materials we have been sent and voice your thoughts. Everyone's opinion is important."

Not surprisingly, Tim piped up first. "What I'm reading here confirms what I read in *The Cattleman* magazine a few months ago. The meat is leaner and tends to bring higher prices at market."

James commented next, "These Texas longhorns tend to eat more forage, so they won't require as much supplemental feed. That would cut costs on our end."

"The initial birth weights are less than what we have been seeing, but they have statistically higher live calves," Luke added. "That might mean fewer sleepless nights since fewer cows would need my help delivering their big babies."

Josiah chimed in, "Those long horns they are named for look menacing, but this says their temperament is fairly docile."

"What about you, Jacob? Any thoughts?" Emma prompted.

Rubbing his chin thoughtfully, Jacob replied, "All of this sounds too good to be true. There must be some negative aspects to consider."

Discussion continued for another hour before James concluded, "We have a lot to think and pray about. Let's plan to meet again next week to make our final decision, whether that is to buy now, get more information, or to wait altogether. We should all be agreed before we proceed with our plans for winter breeding."

"Now, before we go, let's talk about harvest." Every year, the boys at the Rugged Cross Ranch pulled long hours to care for the ranch and help the farmers living around them bring in their crops. They volunteered their time to be a blessing, and the farming families were deeply grateful. "Tim, Jacob, how's the progress at the Wilsons' farm?"

"I'd guess we're about halfway done," Tim replied and looked at Jacob.

"Yeah, I'd say the same," Jacob agreed.

"Then plan on heading back there until they're done. We need to help them finish while the good weather holds." Turning his head toward the other end of the table, James added, "The Lange farm is starting their harvest tomorrow. Luke and Josiah, plan to ride out with me in the morning after chores."

Luke assented, "Sounds good," and Josiah nodded his agreement.

The meeting was ended with James' dismissal, "All right, let's get some sleep; tomorrow will come earlier than usual."

The group rose from the table and filed out of the ranch house.

As Julie began gathering Matthew's things, she suggested to Emma, "I could come just after breakfast to help you get lunches ready for the harvesters."

"Yes, that would give us enough time," Emma replied. "The Wilsons seemed to have plenty of people bring food today, so let's plan to head over and help Molly at the Lange's farm tomorrow."

Sweeping Matthew up in his arms, Luke agreed, "That's a perfect plan. Then I can see my boy at lunchtime."

Pretending to be offended, Julie planted her hands on her hips and protested, "I see who your favorite is."

With a teasing grin, Luke winked at her, "Oh, will you be there, too?"

Julie laughed, "Emma, do you see how unloved I am?"

Emma shook her head and rolled her eyes. "You two are too much. Now shoo. Go home. Tomorrow will come bright and early."

The following week, Emma's family gathered around the table again. Once the dessert dishes were cleared, the conversation turned to business. James began, "I rode over to Jeb's ranch on Tuesday, hoping to get some general advice on introducing new bulls. Unfortunately, he thinks of our ranch as competition and refused to answer any of my questions. His is the only other large established ranch in greater Prairie Hills. I couldn't think of anyone else with enough experience to ask."

Tim joined in, "I went to the cattlemen's association in town to research some records, but as far as I can tell, no other

Texas longhorns have come to this area. That leaves us with no precedent to follow."

"What are your thoughts, Luke?" Emma inquired.

"My decision could go either way. The thought of introducing better traits into our herd now is alluring. However, with a split herd this year, we really don't need to have new bulls until next winter. We will need new bulls; the question is the timing."

Emma moderated again, "Josiah?"

"If this is the breed we're going to choose, I don't see any benefit in waiting until next year when we could start improving the herd now."

"Jacob?"

"I don't have anything to add that hasn't already been said."

After a bit more discussion, James declared, "We seem to be in agreement. Let's make this official. If you're in favor of pursuing the purchase of Longhorn cattle for this breeding season, raise your hand." One by one, every hand was raised. "All right, the decision is unanimous. I'll send the Texas Cattlemen's Association a telegram in the morning."

CHAPTER 12
Prairie Hills School

The following Sunday morning, Josiah approached Emily after church. "When I mentioned to Emma that I needed a new woodworking project, she mentioned that you might need some desks here in the church."

"Yes, I think turning this building into a classroom during the week is going to be my best option."

"I drew up a couple of sketches for a removable desktop that would fit over the back of the pew when needed but could be easily stacked in the corner on Sundays. Since the pews would never need to be moved, the conversion to a classroom would be much easier." He handed her the paper with his pencil sketches. "What do you think?"

Emily's face lit up. "Josiah, this is an ingenious design. Will it be sturdy enough to hold the students' books and slates while they study and write?"

"Absolutely. If you would like, I can take some measurements and build a prototype for you to test."

"Would you? I'm eager to see how it will work."

"I could have it ready by midweek. Why don't I bring it by

on Wednesday afternoon, and we can discuss any changes you want."

"Thank you, Josiah. Wednesday afternoon would be perfect."

As promised, on Wednesday afternoon, just after school had finished at the parsonage, Josiah pulled the buckboard up to the church. Emily spotted him from the front window of her home and met Josiah at the steps. From the wagon bed, he lifted an odd-shaped object wrapped in canvas and carried it inside, setting it on the floor. "This desk has only had a preliminary sanding. If you like the design, I'll sand it perfectly smooth and stain the wood to match the pews."

He unwrapped the portable writing desk and laid the canvas over the back of the next to last pew. Then he slid the desktop over the canvas onto the pew. "The finished ones will have leather wrapping around the attachment piece here to prevent any scratches on the pew."

Emily sat in the last pew and admired Josiah's work. She tried to wiggle the desktop, but it didn't budge. The fit with the pew was snug. Then she reached for a couple of hymnals to lay on the surface and rested her arms on the desk as if she were writing. The desk was sturdy and stable. "Josiah, you have exceeded my expectations. This design is brilliant."

"Having individual desktops rather than one that runs the length of the pew will give you more flexibility for seating your students. Plus, the lighter weight means the boys can remove and stow them in the corner on Friday afternoons to make it easier for you to change the room back for church."

"You have considered every detail, as I knew you would."

"How many desks will you need?"

"As of this moment, twelve, though the number may be fifteen by the end of this week. Another family told me yesterday that they may enroll their three children, too."

Josiah raised his eyebrows. "Wow! That's a lot of students."

"I know," Emily nodded. "Even the mere idea is daunting. After all, I've never even been a student in a formal school setting. I love to help the families in our community, and I enjoy teaching, and God is opening the doors for me to do both. This seems to be what I'm meant to do right now."

Josiah considered her circumstances, "You have a distinct advantage, though. All of your students have been taught at home, just like you were, and you have plenty of experience teaching Robert and your sisters. You nearly doubled your students when the Carter kids joined in. Now you're just doubling again."

A smile spread across Emily's face, and she laughed. "Thank you, Josiah. I needed that change in perspective."

"Anytime." Josiah raised his first finger to his lips in thought. "Now that I have the pattern pieces made, with James helping me, I should be able to finish all fifteen desks by the end of next week. Would that be soon enough?"

Pausing to consider the timing, Emily replied, "That should be just right. Harvest is well underway. As long as the weather holds, harvest should be finished next week, and the school could open for the fall term a week from Monday. Fred told me on Sunday that his mill will donate the wood for the desks . . ."

"And James and I will donate our time to build them," Josiah interrupted.

Shaking her head, Emily disagreed, "No, I couldn't ask you to do that."

"You didn't ask. I offered. You know James would never let you pay him, and I can be just as stubborn on occasion."

Giving up her argument, Emily raised her hands in

surrender. "As you wish. Thank you, and please tell James 'thank you' also."

"Of course." Josiah lifted the desktop, wrapped it, and departed.

Emily strolled to the middle of the room and slowly turned in a circle. "In less than two weeks, this will be my classroom. Lord, I need you. Thank you for providing the church building and the desks. My mind is spinning. This is happening so fast." She continued her stroll to the front of the room and turned to face the pews. She bowed her head and prayed for each one of her students by name. When she finished, she lifted her head and took a deep breath, "This is really happening."

The next afternoon, Emily visited each of her prospective students' families to inform them when the school term would begin. The eagerness of the parents and the students helped to abate Emily's apprehension.

On the Friday before the transition, Emily spoke with the class around the parsonage dining table. "Next week will be a change for all of us. I am going to need all of you to be a good example to those joining our class."

"Will I have to call you Miss Kendrick?" Robert asked.

Emily pursed her lips in thought. "I had not considered that, though I think the others would understand and expect the four of you to call me Emily as you do here at home and in this class."

"The rest of us will call you Miss Kendrick," Jonathan added.

"Miss Kendrick makes you sound old and grown up," Sarah frowned.

"The Carters have already been calling me that, and you didn't object. Though I'm not old, I am indeed grown up," Emily explained.

A new idea occurred to Sarah. "Grown-ups get married. If you're grown up, why aren't you and James married yet?"

There it was. The question Emily had been trying to avoid for several weeks. She answered honestly, "We're waiting on God's timing."

The look of confusion on Sarah's face was evidence that she did not understand, but to Emily's relief, she refrained from asking further questions.

Continuing to address her students, Emily said, "On Monday, remember to come straight to the church rather than here to the parsonage."

Robert interrupted, "If you come here, only Laura will be here, and you don't want her for a teacher."

Unknown to Robert, Laura was just walking behind him and overheard his comment. In response, she loudly snapped the back of his chair with the dishtowel she was carrying. When the surprised young man jumped, everyone started laughing. With a teasing smile, Laura admonished, "Be sure your sins will find you out." Then to the Carters, she added, "Of course, he is right, you wouldn't want me to teach you, especially when you have Emily, I mean, Miss Kendrick."

Sunday morning had dawned; James was sure of it; but the light coming over the horizon was hidden by the thick, low-hanging, dark clouds. The puddles gave testimony to the rain overnight, but a mere glance at the sky by the dullest observer would persuade him that more storms were yet to come.

After morning chores, James found Josiah. "Let's pull the wagon into the barn and load up the desks. If we work quickly, we can still have time to change and get the desks into the church before the others arrive for the service. If we wait until this afternoon as we had planned, they may get ruined by the storm that is coming."

Josiah agreed, "Good idea. I'll grab a few extra tarpaulins, too, in case the rain comes before we get the desks unloaded."

Overhearing his brothers, Tim piped in, "You two go change now while I hitch the wagon." He called to his other brother, "Jacob, when you're finished milking, bring the stack of tarpaulins from the tack room."

Clapping Tim on the shoulder, James replied, "Thanks, Tim." To Josiah he said, "Let's go." They dodged the puddles as they jogged back to the bunkhouse.

By the time James and Josiah had returned to the barn, the wagon was already hitched and inside the barn, and Tim and Jacob were spreading the first tarpaulin in the wagon bed. Tim directed, "Josiah, why don't you and James get up here since you know how best to stack these things, and Jacob and I will hand them up to you."

Within minutes, the desks were loaded, covered thoroughly, and tied down securely. Luke leaned over the last stall door to inform them, "Don't worry about Emma. I'll stop by the ranch house and let her know we'll be by with the buggy to pick her up for church."

With that, James set the horse into motion. Keeping an eye on the threatening clouds, he urged the horse on to a faster pace, trying to find the balance between protecting the desks in transport and arriving before the downpour began.

Sensing James' thoughts, Josiah reassured him, "The desks are tied down well. They're not moving at all."

Several minutes later, James pulled the wagon in front of the church, with the wagon's tailgate right at the foot of the stairs. The pair of brothers worked quickly and efficiently to unload the desks and stack them in two piles in the back corner of the church. When they reached for the last two desks, the first raindrops began. They had barely crossed the threshold into the dry room when the raindrops changed into a pouring deluge.

At the sound of the sudden roar of water falling, Josiah turned around to look through the doorway at the rain, then looked over at James, "That was close. We finished just in time."

Exhaling a rush of air, James nodded, "Indeed."

Next door, the sudden, loud rumble of wagon wheels had drawn Emily to the front window of the parsonage. There she stood, with her hands loosely folded in front of her, watching James and Josiah scurry to get the desks unloaded. When the last two desks disappeared into the church, Emily realized she had been holding her breath, inwardly cheering them on in their race against the weather. True, her heart was aching, but that ache was not created by the man she loved. In this painful season of waiting, James was telling her in a hundred ways that he loved her without ever saying a word. Before her emotions got the better of her, she turned and made her way up the stairs to ensure her youngest sisters were getting ready for church.

Emily walked over with her family several minutes before the service to start a fire in the wood furnace, but found the warmth already emanating from the lively, crackling fire within. Though the fall air was not that chilly yet, something about being wet brought a chill even in mild temperatures. Her siblings were already in a semicircle before the fire, drawn to it like bees to honey.

The heavy rain kept about half the congregation home, especially the ones who lived further away. Those who had made the journey into town were mostly drenched, despite raincoats and umbrellas. Emily made sure her siblings moved to give the newcomers a turn in front of the furnace to warm up and dry a bit.

After Emily hung her wet coat on the peg for that purpose, she turned to see the neat stacks of desks in the opposite corner, dry and ready for the next day. Her gaze then traveled down the aisle to where James was sitting in his now-usual place on the right side of the aisle. She so wanted to thank him – for the desks, for the timely delivery, for the fire. Once again, the words of her heart were forbidden.

Josiah approached her and interrupted her musings. "Josiah, thank you for finishing the desks in such a short time. The stain on them is a perfect match to the pews."

"You're welcome, but I'd never have finished on time without James' help. He used my design patterns to cut all the wood pieces we needed. Then, after I assembled the desks, he sanded them, so I could stain them. James is the one who suggested that we leave so early this morning to beat the rain because he wanted everything for tomorrow to be just perfect for you."

Emily's eyes glistened with unshed tears, and she whispered, "Please thank him for me."

Giving her a half-smile that communicated his understanding, Josiah assented, "Of course." He walked toward the front of the church and slipped into the pew behind James, sliding down far enough that he could lean forward and talk to James.

Just then, Emma and Julie walked in with Matthew, whose lusty cry declared he was not very happy at the moment. Emily rushed forward to help, "Here, Julie, let me get him warmed by the fire while you take off your raincoat." Emily removed his soaked blanket and held him close to her. His little feet and hands were as cold as ice. No wonder he was voicing his displeasure. She knelt before the fire at just the right distance so he would feel the warmth but not intense heat. Matthew's cry soon turned to a whimper, then he drifted to sleep still stutter breathing after his cry. Time always seemed to stand still when she was holding this little person.

Julie reached for her son, and spoke softly to her friend, "Pastor just entered from the prayer room. You should go."

"Oh, right." Emily released the little boy to his mother and made her way to the piano.

When the service had concluded, Emily looked across the aisle, expecting James to have already slipped away, but he was still sitting there gazing at her. Their eyes met, just for a moment, and Emily mouthed the words, "Thank you," before she could stop herself. James just nodded, but it was enough.

When she rose, Josiah met her and offered, "James and I will hang the desks before we leave if you tell me how you want them arranged."

So that is why James hadn't left. "I think three on each side of the first two rows, with two on the right and one on the left of the third row."

"Will do."

Emily was torn. She needed to get home to make dinner for her family, but she so wanted to stay a few more minutes. Even if she and James couldn't speak to one another, at least they could be in the same room for a little bit longer. After all, shouldn't she be the one to oversee the desk placement? She knew she was just making excuses, and she certainly wanted to protect James' integrity where her father was concerned. In the end, as the last few congregants were filing out, she turned to Josiah to thank him one more time, smiled at James, and departed.

Stepping down the stairs, Emily's tears mixed with the rain. *"Why was this so hard? How long would it take for her dad to reconsider?"* The mere weeks of their separation seemed like years. *"Lord, I'm struggling. Please change Dad's heart. Remind me of Your blessings, so I can be grateful, waiting with a happy heart."* By the time she walked the short distance to the parsonage, her face and hair were dripping so much that no one even suspected she had been crying. She quickly removed her raincoat and began her dinner preparations.

After changing her dress, Laura scampered down the stairs and into the kitchen. "Emily, go upstairs and get into something dry before you catch a cold. You don't want to be sniffling through your first day of school." Emily looked as if she were going to protest, but Laura interrupted before she could speak, "I've got this. Besides, I'll be doing more of the cooking once you start teaching a full classroom of students, so I might as well start now. Go." Laura shooed her away like she was a child, and Emily relented.

"All right, I'm going."

When the brothers had finished placing the students' desks, they moved the table that would serve as Emily's desk to the center of the platform. "Ready to go?" Josiah asked.

"Go ahead. I'll be out in just a minute."

James waited for Josiah to jog down the front steps into the rain before he reached for the canvas-wrapped parcel he had slipped into the building when no one was looking. Stepping up to Emily's desk, he arranged the contents of his parcel neatly on the desktop, and turned to follow Josiah to the buckboard. He was grateful that Seth had helped him purchase this gift for Emily; he only wished he could be there to see her open it.

The heavy rain continued for the rest of the day, so Emily planned to head to the schoolroom early Monday morning to distribute a slate, chalk, paper, and pencils to each desk in order to be ready for her students. Long before breakfast, Emily reached for a muffin and asked, "Laura, would you please be sure everyone gets to the school by eight o'clock? I'm going to head over now."

Laura had just arrived downstairs, dressed but sleepy-eyed. "All right," she yawned and stretched. "Have a good first day."

Filled with fluttering butterflies, Emily turned to exit. "Thank you, Laura."

Stepping carefully across to the church building, Emily was thankful that the rain had finally stopped and many of the puddles had dried during the night. That would make traveling easier for her students. As she climbed the steps to the front door, Emily took a deep breath. "This is it, Lord. I desperately need You today." With that, she opened the door and stepped inside. After setting her books on the back pew, she started a small fire in the furnace to get out the morning chill. "There, that's a bit more cozy. I can't have my pupils shivering, now can I?"

Gathering her books again, she walked to the front, where her desk was just as James had left it. Suddenly, her eyes teared up. There, on the desktop, was a thin white box with a bright yellow daffodil softly resting on it. Emily moved the delicate flower and lifted the lid of the box. She gasped. Within the folds of tissue paper lay a beautiful journal bound in leather that had been dyed a raspberry pink color. What took her breath away, though, was the cover. Embossed there was the outline of a daffodil with gentle scrollwork extending to the corners. Beside the floral outline these words were engraved: "Love bears all things, believes all things, hopes all things, endures all things. I Corinthians 13:7."

Gently lifting the cover, Emily found a short note, written in James' masculine script.

Dear Emily,

Praying for you today and always. Write down whatever you want to tell me later. I don't want to miss a thing.

Yours Forever,
James

"Thank you, Lord. I needed James' encouragement today. Thank you." Emily carefully replaced the tissue and lid, slipping the box carefully into the top drawer of the desk. That singular book had just become her second greatest material treasure, only surpassed by her mother's Bible.

Noticing that her butterflies were all but gone, Emily began distributing the school supplies. Her students would begin arriving soon.

As if on cue, her siblings came through the doorway. "Laura sent us over early in case you needed help with anything," Sarah announced.

Susan rolled her eyes. "I think she was just getting us out of the house."

Emily understood. "Well, whichever it is, I'm glad you're here. Take a look at where you are going to sit. I have names at the top of the paper on each desk. Before any of you say anything, I have you scattered throughout the room to be with other students learning at your level and to help the others know how we do school."

Tipping her head a little, Beth asked, "Will it still be like school at home?"

Knowing her youngest sister did not adjust to change easily, Emily assured her, "Mostly. The only differences will be where we are doing school and who will be joining us. The learning part will be just the same."

Beth seemed to relax a bit. When she saw Anna's name on the desk next to hers, she brightened a little more. "This won't be so bad. I'm sitting by Anna." Emily smiled at her sister, for she had positioned the two together on purpose. She knew Anna would need some reassurance, too.

Soon, the other children arrived, most of them buzzing with the excitement of something new. Miss Kendrick took great patience to get everyone settled in their proper place. "As we begin our new school year together, let me explain my expectations. Academically, I expect your best. Not perfection. Your best. Your best might not be your neighbor's best, and that is all right. All of us have strengths and weaknesses in different areas. Do not compare yourself to anyone else in this room. As your teacher, I am here to help you learn. If you have a question, ask me. As we learn together, remember what Ephesians 4:32 tells us: 'Be kind to one another, tenderhearted, forgiving one another.' Make sure both your words and actions are kind. Why should we give each other grace and forgive? Because Jesus forgave us and died for us."

"Another part of being kind is showing respect to me and the other students in this classroom. If you have a question, raise your hand, and I will call on you. Otherwise, please do not speak out or interrupt our lessons. Any questions so far?"

When no hands were raised, she continued, "Now let's officially begin our day with a short Bible study. We will usually take turns reading verses as we study the lives and character of some of the heroes in God's Word. Today, however, I want to focus on Jesus' answer to a question while He was teaching and see how we can apply His words to our lives in this classroom."

"When a lawyer asked Jesus what the greatest commandment of their many laws was, He responded, 'Love the Lord your God with all your heart and with all your soul and with all your mind. This is the great and first commandment. And a second is like it: You shall love your neighbor as yourself.' These verses in Matthew 22 will be our theme verses this year. If you love the Lord with all your heart, will you complain about your assignment? No. If you love Him with all your mind, will you do your best in arithmetic? Yes. Why? For His glory. If you love your neighbors, will you steal their answers and cheat? No. Will you be kind when another student has a bad day? Yes. Will you be respectful and obedient when I ask you to do something? Yes. Everything goes back to our love for God and others. Let's close our Bible time in prayer."

"Dear Father, having school here is new for all of us. Please help us to be patient with each other as we adapt to this change, and help these boys and girls to listen and learn what they need to learn today. Give me wisdom as I teach, that they might understand the material. You are the Master Teacher. We need You today and always. In Jesus' name, Amen."

"Now take out your slates, please. It's time for arithmetic." Emily turned to set her Bible on her desk, and her eyes rested just a moment on the bright yellow flower. She silently added to her prayer, *"Thank you for James."* Knowing that he was praying for her today warmed her heart; seeing the flower made him feel as if he were there with her – almost.

Just outside the window, the owner of a very keen pair of ears stood quietly scoffing, *"This isn't a school; it's a Bible club."* Mrs. Lange spun around and came as close to stomping off as a lady of her former status would allow. Her eyes were set on the telegraph office, and she would not stop until her mission was complete.

Bursting through that office door with a little too much vigor, Mrs. Lange bluntly declared the reason for her presence. "I need to send a telegram right away."

The telegraph operator was in the midst of sending another message, and responded, "Yes, Ma'am, I'll be right with you."

The portly lady's indignation was rising. "I will not be kept waiting. Do you know who I am? Margaret Lange of the Boston Langes."

Completely unimpressed, yet polite, the operator repeated, "Yes, Ma'am, I'll be right with you."

She mumbled loud enough to be distinctly heard, "Humph. These small-town people are so uncivilized."

After taking a moment longer than necessary to complete his current transmission, the operator stood, taking his notepad and pencil, and approached the impatient person at the counter. "To whom would you like to send your telegram?"

"The Oklahoma Territory school superintendent. Mark it urgent." She carefully dictated her missive, paid the attendant, and ordered, "I want the reply when I return at four o'clock this afternoon." With that, she turned with a swish of her skirt and exited the way she had come.

The operator, not the least bit ruffled by her demeanor, just stared at her over his half-moon spectacles and shook his head in amazement at her blunt rudeness. His only regret was that his oath of confidentiality forbade him from warning the victim of her subterfuge.

CHAPTER 13
Town Meeting

The first few days in the schoolroom had a few bumpy moments, but by Friday, everyone was much more amiable about following the routine of the day. Miss Kendrick had just called the children inside to begin their day as the morning stage arrived across town.

Wearing a well-practiced haughty air, Mrs. Lange greeted the gentleman disembarking from the stage with his briefcase. "Good morning, Mr. Bennet, I am Mrs. Margaret Lange." He had barely reached the ground before she began her diatribe. "The children of this uncivilized town have been educated at home until this week, when the Pastor's daughter took it upon herself to start a school. She has no formal education, no credentials, and no permission from the town council to hold this post. It is scandalous of her to presume to be considered a teacher. She must be stopped."

Mr. Bennet was somewhat nonplussed by her vehemence. "Are you the chairwoman of the town council?"

"I would not stoop so low. I am merely acting as a concerned citizen."

"I see. Fortunately for the accused, as school

superintendent for the territory, I will be the one determining the course of action in this case." Not wanting to waste any more time conversing with this woman, he asked, "Where is the school?"

"She has taken over the church building during the week. I'll walk with you."

Mr. Bennet remained silent until they reached the school. When he realized Mrs. Lange meant to come into the schoolroom with him, he made his position clear. "You may wait outside."

Her attempt at courtesies ended abruptly with a scowl and a "Humph," an expression that seemed to be frequently used when she was displeased, which was, in fact, frequent.

Miss Kendrick was just beginning her Bible study when the superintendent entered. She paused for a moment, but he signaled for her to continue and sat quietly on the back pew. From his briefcase, he removed a notepad and pencil, which he used to jot notes as he listened.

When she had prayed and asked the students to prepare their slates for arithmetic, she walked back to greet the stranger. He stood and spoke softly, "Good morning. I am Anthony Bennet, the Oklahoma Territory school superintendent."

"I am Emily Kendrick."

"Pleasure to meet you. If you don't object, I'll just sit here and observe a typical school day, and we can discuss my notes after class."

"Certainly," Miss Kendrick replied, though she did not feel quite certain about anything at the moment.

As she made her way back down the aisle to her students, she looked down at her hands and noticed they were trembling. Glancing up, she focused on the yellow daffodil that she had preserved in wax on Monday afternoon. That singular flower gave her courage. James was praying for her. She took a calming breath and announced, "All right, class, let's begin arithmetic with addition."

Whether the boys and girls sensed the seriousness of the visitor in the back of the classroom or not, they did obey and participate better than they had all week. Finally, the time for dismissal was at hand. "Before you leave, I have an announcement. If the weather is good, we will be taking a field trip to the forge next Friday afternoon." Delighted cheers surrounded her. "Mr. Carter has agreed to teach all of us about the forge and the process he uses to design and repair various items. In light of that, you will be taking your first arithmetic test next Thursday." Now a few groans replaced the former cheers. "If you are unsure about your math problems, be sure to see me before then so you will be ready for your test. Have a wonderful weekend! Class dismissed."

The pupils gathered their things and chatter filled the room as they left to go home. Only one remained. Robert glanced at the stranger then asked Emily in a whisper, "Do you want me to stay for a few minutes?"

Proud beyond words that her little brother wanted to stay and protect her, Emily replied, "Thank you, Robert. I would appreciate that."

Her brother nodded and opened the book he had been reading, only giving partial attention to it. He didn't want to be rude or eavesdrop, but he also didn't want to leave Emily alone with a man he did not know. At fourteen, he was already five and a half feet tall with broad shoulders. Having all sisters, he didn't have any fighting experience, but as he considered the thin, middle-aged man on the back row, he thought, *I could take him if I had to.*

Emily walked smoothly to the back, where she sat across the aisle from the class visitor. Throughout the day, his expression had been serious, but not unkind. "I must admit that I was impressed. I had been brought here under the pretense that someone incapable was masquerading as the town schoolteacher. What I found was quite the contrary. You keep good order in the classroom, and your students respect you. Your lessons are thorough, appropriate for each age, and sprinkled with fun. By the end of the day, you made me wish I could stay until next week to attend your field trip."

Visibly relaxing, Emily replied, "I'm glad you enjoyed your visit here today."

Mr. Bennet continued, "I need to ask you some questions to determine your qualifications. First, please tell me about your teaching experience."

Emily began with her years as a student, when she would help her mother teach her younger siblings. She explained how she transitioned to her capacity as full-time teacher when her mother died, mentioning her sister Laura's passing the high school diploma examination under her tutelage. "Recently, a family with three children moved to our community because their mother needs medical care. When they asked me to teach their children, I was honored to be a blessing to them. Not long after, news began to spread that I was teaching the Carters in our home, and three more families asked me to teach their children. Fifteen students wouldn't fit around our kitchen table, so my Dad suggested using the church. We just began our fall term on Monday."

"May I say that the design of your students' desks is remarkable."

"Two members in our church volunteered to design and construct them with wood that had been donated by the lumber mill owner."

Based on a reasonable assumption, he asked, "Are they parents of your students?"

"No, just men who wanted to be a blessing."

"To have that much support from your townsfolk says a lot about you. Do you have any formal teacher's training?"

"No, but my mother had her teaching certificate from the Missouri Territory before Missouri became a state."

The superintendent jotted down a couple of notes while Emily waited patiently. When he finished writing, he laid down his notebook and spoke carefully. "You obviously have a passion and talent for teaching. That is undeniable. Your compassion to serve members of your community in this way is admirable. However, according to the statues of Oklahoma Territory, as soon as you moved your students from your home to a public building, your school came under my purview. To be qualified as a formal schoolteacher in this territory, you need to have a teachers' certificate. This certification has two requirements: a practicum under a certified teacher for a minimum of six months and six months of pedagogy courses followed by a certification examination. From what you have already attested, your practicum under your mother was well over six months, and your performance today is evidence to the effectiveness of that instruction. Unfortunately, there is no way to circumvent the didactic teaching instruction or certification examination. The nearest teacher's institute is in Kansas City, Missouri; but the fall session has already begun. Upon evaluating your teaching today, I would certainly be willing to write a letter of extension to the school board to allow you to continue teaching until the next session begins in January as well as a letter of recommendation for your admission to the institute."

Feeling suddenly overwhelmed, Emily whispered, "I had no idea changing our venue would create so many additional requirements." Questions began flooding her mind. *"How much does the teacher's institute and examination cost? Who would teach the students if I am away for the entire spring term? Could I bear to be away from James and my family for such a long time?"*

"These requirements may seem sudden, but they are in place to protect you. From what I have seen today, this town is blessed to have you teach full-time." Handing her a pamphlet from his briefcase, he instructed, "I'm sure you have many questions. This information on the teacher's institute may answer some of them. I would also recommend the convening of a town meeting to discuss these issues publicly and have the town formally install you to your teaching post. That would prevent any naysayers from creating conflict in the future." Of course, he had one particular naysayer in mind. "If the town council is able to meet before I leave Monday morning, I would be happy to moderate on your behalf."

Emily's thoughts were still spinning wildly, but she had the presence of mind to extend hospitality. "Please join our family for dinner this evening, and you can discuss the meeting's particulars with my dad. He is the pastor here as well as a member of the council. If he agrees with your recommendation, he could call a meeting as early as tomorrow evening."

"I never turn down a good meal. Thank you for the invitation."

Emily stood, and Mr. Bennet rose with her. "Dinner's at six. The parsonage is the home next to this building."

The superintendent grasped the handle of his briefcase and prepared to go, "I'll be there."

When he left, Emily walked slowly to her desk at the front and lowered herself into the chair. To say that Robert was observant would be a terrible misjudgment of his personality, but even he could not miss the dazed look in his sister's eyes. He put his elbow on his desk and rested his chin in his hand, "So, what are you going to do?"

Emily's gaze slowly turned toward him, "I don't know. I feel as if my world just got flipped upside-down – again. I really wish I could talk to James."

"Why don't you?"

"Speaking to James is against father's wishes right now. I don't know why, but I will honor him."

Abruptly changing subjects, as he was apt to do, Robert asked, "May I go for a horseback ride before dinner?"

Amused at his short attention span, Emily replied, "I don't see why not. Just don't be late for dinner. Remember, we have company tonight."

"Thanks." With that note of permission, he got up to leave and then realized, "It's Friday. We forgot to put away the desks for Sunday. I'll stow them before I go."

Thinking that two observations in one day must be a record for him, she was nevertheless grateful for his help. "Thank you, Robert, I appreciate that."

While he stacked the desks, she slid open the desk drawer and removed her journal. Each afternoon, she added a note about her day, including a funny moment or a personal struggle. Today, she sat with pen in hand, not knowing where to begin. Once the words began to flow, she filled an entire page before she laid her pen down and fanned the paper to dry the ink. After she collected the rest of her books, she slipped the journal back into the drawer and moved her desk back to the side wall and swept the floor. Satisfied that her schoolroom had been returned to its previous appearance, she stepped outside and paused as the sunshine touched her face. Closing her eyes against the brightness, her heart spoke in silent prayer, *"Lord, I need Your wisdom. I desperately want to follow Your plan for my life, but I am so confused. Please help me know what You want me to do. I love You."* With turmoil still in her heart, she walked next door to speak with her dad and help with dinner.

Meanwhile, Robert was on a mission that carried him to the Rugged Cross Ranch. Luke was unsaddling Dakota in front of the barn when he spotted the rider coming. When the horse approached, Luke greeted the boy, "Hi, Robert, what brings you out to the ranch?"

"I'm looking for James," he replied.

"He's still finishing up in the south pasture. Do you want me to get him for you?"

"No, just point me in the right direction."

Nodding, Luke instructed, "Keep heading straight. The south pasture will be on your right just after the corral ends."

"Thanks." Robert nudged his horse back into motion. When he reached the end of the corral and saw the huge expanse of the pasture, he wondered if he should have taken Luke up on his offer. Being on this side of the fence was one thing. Being in with the cattle was quite another. Fortunately, Tim saw him, got James' attention, and pointed to the perimeter fence. A moment later, James pulled his horse up alongside Robert with the fence between them.

James voiced the first thought that came to his mind, "Is Emily all right?"

"Yes, well, mostly," Robert stumbled. He had James' full attention. Robert explained the visitor at school that day and the conversation that ensued afterward. "Emily looked so confused. I've never seen her that way. All she would say is that she wanted to talk with you, but couldn't."

James winced as the words stung. *"Lord, why can't I be there for her right now?"* To Robert, he asked, "What can I do?" hoping this fourteen-year-old would give him some way to help her.

"I was hoping you would give your advice so I could tell her."

Down deep, James wanted to tell her, *"Elope with me, and let's start our life together."* He pushed the thought aside as he rubbed his forehead. *"God's timing. Remember God's timing."*

"Do you think she enjoys teaching in the new schoolroom?" James felt almost ashamed that he had to ask her brother what he would have already known if circumstances had been different.

"Yes, she's already planned our first field trip to the forge next week, and she's always busy with lesson plans in the evenings after dinner. I know she was nervous about teaching so many, but she's really good at it. Even the superintendent complimented her."

Succumbing to half a smile, James responded, "I'm not surprised." Returning to logical thought, he added, "There are only a few options: return to the parsonage with your family and the Carters, step down and find a certified teacher to teach in the schoolroom, or invest six months to earn her teaching certificate. As much as I would love to choose for her, only she can make that decision. Tell her that I will be praying God shows her the right choice."

"What are you going to do if she chooses to leave for the teaching institute?"

"Miss her like crazy," was James' honest reply. "Would you let us know if they do schedule a town meeting tomorrow? We'll all want to be there to support her."

"Of course."

"Robert, thanks for riding out to talk to me. I really appreciate it."

The young man nodded and turned his horse to leave. He arrived home just as the table was being set for dinner; his conversation with Emily would have to wait.

Anthony Bennet arrived precisely at six o'clock. He was a cordial guest who answered questions when asked, freely told of his travels, but did not overrun the conversation with business. After the meal, Pastor invited him into the study to discuss the school's new requirements.

Robert took this opportunity to get Emily alone. They

went into the back yard as the sun was sinking below the horizon, and Robert told her about his conversation with James. Emily felt she should reprimand him for acting as intermediary, but she just couldn't. She was too grateful for his concern and for James' rational perspective. Unfortunately, his logical options didn't make her decision any easier, but knowing that he was praying specifically for this matter was intensely comforting.

When the two men exited the study an hour later, Pastor Kendrick announced, "I'm going to visit the town councilmen to call a meeting for tomorrow night at seven. While I'm gone, would you prepare some flyers to post around town tomorrow morning?" His kids rang with a chorus of "Yes, Dad" while Emily pulled paper and pencils from the drawer.

From the moment Emily woke on Saturday, she felt anxious, almost as if she were being put on trial. She tried to pray and stay busy, but she couldn't shake her feeling of foreboding. *"This is silly. The superintendent will discuss the requirements, and the council will vote on what they want to do, simple as that."* Try as she might, though, she just couldn't convince herself that the meeting would be as "simple as that."

A quarter hour before seven, Emily and her siblings walked over to the church and found it nearly full. Her dad motioned for her to come to the front. "I saved a seat here for you." He looked around. "Wouldn't it be wonderful to have the church this full tomorrow morning?" Emily agreed. Their church services usually seemed pretty full, but not like this. People were still coming in, but they were filing along the back wall since all the seats were now taken.

James was glad they had arrived early. He and his family were seated in the third row from the back, and he had put Luke next to him on purpose. "Luke, I need you to be Buck tonight."

His brother looked quizzically at him, "What do you mean?"

"If I start to do or say something stupid, elbow me in the ribs."

"Buck would do that?"

"He usually didn't have to. He would just give me 'the look,' you know, like the one Dad would give us if we were up to something mischievous."

"Why do you think you'll be tempted to say something foolish?"

"I don't know exactly. Just a feeling. There's a tension in here I hadn't expected, and Emily's face is as white as a sheet."

A few minutes later, Pastor Kendrick brought the meeting to order. "Let us pray. Lord, we thank you for the families You have brought to Prairie Hills, and we pray that as our town continues to grow, we will never stop depending on You. Guide us tonight as we make decisions about the school here. In Jesus' Holy Name, Amen."

"Thank you all for coming on such short notice. The meeting tonight was necessary for our guest must leave on the stage Monday morning. May I introduce Mr. Anthony Bennet, the Oklahoma Territory superintendent of schools? He will explain the reason we are gathered here and will answer any questions you have. After questions, the town council will vote on our course of action. Mr. Bennet, you have the floor."

"Thank you, Pastor Kendrick. I received a telegram on Monday, informing me of the opening of your school. Since

Prairie Hills is under my jurisdiction, I arrived yesterday morning to observe classes and perform an evaluation. You have great reason to be proud of this new school. I found the teaching to be exemplary."

Mrs. Lange indignantly rose from her seat in the middle of the room, "But the teacher is unqualified."

Pastor quickly took charge. "Mrs. Lange, you do not have the floor. There will be time for questions when Mr. Bennet is finished."

With her "Humph," she plopped back into her seat.

James was gripping his knees so tightly his knuckles were white. Luke whispered, "Take a breath." James nodded that he had received the message.

Mr. Bennet continued, "On the contrary, Miss Kendrick is partially qualified. She has already met and exceeded the minimum practicum with a formally certified teacher, and she has excelled in my evaluation. In addition, she has several years of teaching experience with all grade levels, and has graduated one student with the completion of the high school diploma examination. The only requirements to be completed are a six-month pedagogy instruction course and the completion of a certification examination."

"That brings me to our purpose here tonight. If your council votes to continue the school as it is here in this building, I recommend that they also vote to officially install Miss Kendrick as the teacher. This formality will qualify her for a partial scholarship at the teacher's institute in Kansas City, Missouri."

Mrs. Lange could hold her tongue no longer, "This is absurd. She should be removed from her post at once!"

Pastor Kendrick again moderated, "Mrs. Lange, please be seated."

"This town should consider itself blessed to have such a caliber of teacher among them. My position takes me to schools all over the territory, and I assure you she excels the vast majority of the teachers I visit."

Again Mrs. Lange stood, "That is a sad commentary on your district, Sir."

James was fit to burst. Luke leaned in, "Anything you say right now would only hurt Emily. Keep your mouth shut." James pursed his lips tightly to comply. At least this superintendent fellow wasn't backing down.

Thankfully, Pastor kept his head, "Mrs. Lange, if you refuse to stop interrupting Mr. Bennet, I must ask you to leave so we can conduct this meeting with order and civility."

Her emphatic "Humph" could be heard throughout the room as she sat dramatically.

Mr. Bennet resumed, "No, Ma'am, it is a testament to Miss Kendrick's talent." When he finished his statements, Pastor Kendrick called for questions. To everyone's surprise, Margaret Lange kept her seat, realizing that her devious attempt to humiliate Emily had failed miserably. Instead, the questions came primarily from parents in the room.

Seth Carter rose to his feet. "May I make a comment rather than ask a question?"

"Certainly," Pastor agreed.

"Miss Kendrick has been teaching my children since June. Because of my wife's illness, they were behind in their studies. In these few months, Miss Kendrick has enabled my children to attain their grade level in every subject. More importantly, she has instilled in them a renewed love of learning. I highly recommend that the board retain her as the teacher here."

Mr. Horne, father of Millie and Opal, stood. "If we approve the school, would we be required to send our children here?"

Shaking his head, Pastor replied, "Not at all. The education of our children is an important matter, but one that each family must decide for themselves. Until this week, all of my children have been taught at home, and they received an excellent education. For some families, a classroom is a better fit. If the board approves the continuation of this school, the only change in this community will be the addition of a second educational choice."

Another hand was raised, and Pastor called on Mrs. Cooper. "I enjoy teaching my children at home, but one of them really struggles in math. Will there be any opportunity to participate in just one class?"

Pastor gestured toward his daughter, "Miss Kendrick, would you like to answer that?"

Emily stood on shaky legs and turned toward Maddie's mom. "I think having a student come in for one subject would be rather disruptive, but I have been planning to add a short class one day a week after school for those who need a bit more explanation and practice. If you're interested, I'd be happy to inform you when those classes begin."

"Thank you, Emily, I would be interested."

Margaret Lange sat quietly fuming. *"How could these people be so accepting of this incompetent child?"*

Across the aisle and back a few rows, James was finally starting to relax.

When the questions had all been asked, the town council voted unanimously to continue the school and officially offer Miss Kendrick the teaching post. Now she would have two weeks to decide whether to continue teaching and commit to the teachers' institute or to resign her post.

CHAPTER 14
Church Social

The time for the fall church social was drawing near. This was the annual celebration of the end of harvest. James knew he would not be allowed to escort Emily, and he debated about whether or not to go at all. In the end, he decided he wanted to see Emily, even if it was from afar.

The day of the town meeting marked two weeks before the social. The following morning after church, James slipped out of the building while the rest of the congregation was still milling about inside for a few more minutes of fellowship. Josiah was standing near the back with Jacob, when he overheard two young men, both with a reputation for being troublemakers, arguing over which of them would ask Emily to the dance.

"Emily is the prettiest girl in the church. If James is too much of a fool not to ask her, I will."

"You're not good enough to take the pastor's daughter anywhere. I'll ask her."

"You get into more trouble than I do. Which one of us should take her?" One rolled up his sleeves, getting ready to throw the first punch.

"We're in a church. If we fight here, we'll get tossed out on our hide. Let's flip a coin to decide."

Knowing he had to hurry, Josiah deftly slipped around people to get to the pew near the front where Emily was standing. Slightly out of breath, he arrived to find Emily speaking with Laura. "Excuse me for interrupting, but I need to ask . . . Will you go with me to the social?"

Emily was too surprised to speak. Suddenly, a brash young man with unkempt hair and a wrinkled, soiled shirt arrived and blurted, "Emily, go to the social with me."

Understanding and relief washed over Emily. She gestured toward Josiah and replied, "I'm sorry, but Josiah has already asked me."

The new arrival glared at Josiah, who merely nodded back. The unsavory fellow turned and left. Emily whispered, "Thank you, Josiah."

"You're welcome. Now to explain to James why I'm taking his girl to the social."

Hearing Josiah call her "James' girl" brought a smile to her face. "Good luck."

"Thanks. I may need it."

That afternoon, James entered the bunkhouse to hear Tim and Jacob discussing the social. "So, have either of you gathered the courage to ask a girl?"

Tim answered first, "I'm taking Laura Kendrick."

"She actually said 'yes'? I thought she was smarter than that," James teased.

"Of course, she said 'yes.' I'm a very charming fellow," Tim replied with a mock haughty air.

James cocked his head in serious consideration. "Laura, huh? She'll be good for you. She has enough spunk to keep you in line."

With a tone of disapproval, Tim jerked his thumb toward the younger brother beside him and reported, "Jacob asked Mandy Evans."

Surprised, James crinkled his brow. "Why Mandy? I don't think I've ever seen her without a sour expression."

With an edge to his voice, Jacob replied, "Maybe that's what I like about her."

Before James could respond to Jacob, Josiah came in from stabling his horse and distracted him. "So, what about you?" James asked. "Have you asked anyone to the social?"

Josiah turned a shade paler and responded, "Yes."

"Really? Who did you ask?"

Josiah hesitated and answered quietly, "Emily."

James voice cracked, revealing the shock he felt, "What?"

"Don't be upset with me. I heard those two troublemakers from the back row arguing over who was going to ask her, so I asked her first. I didn't want her having to dance with them just because she couldn't dance with you." He was desperate for James to understand. "I'm only filling in as your substitute, you know. That's what brothers are for."

When the shock wore off, James realized Josiah was only doing what he could for him and Emily, and he was grateful. He reached over and put his hand on Josiah's shoulder. "Thank you."

Josiah nodded with a sigh of relief.

The following Friday afternoon, Emily's dad entered their home holding a telegram. Heading to his chair by the fireplace, he said, "Emily, come talk with me."

Emily looked over at her sister Laura, who was cooking dinner. "Go ahead, Emily, I'll finish here."

When she had walked over and sat on the sofa near her dad, he began, "Next Saturday is your deadline with the town council. Have you made a decision yet?"

"No, not yet. I telegrammed the institute for their tuition and the value of my scholarship. If I save every penny my school families are paying me, I can cover the balance of my tuition and books, but I would have no money left for room and board."

"It sounds to me as if you are seriously considering the teachers' institute, so I'll share the news I just received. A pastor friend who mentored me when I first entered the ministry lives in Kansas City with his wife. Their home is only four blocks from the institute, and they have graciously agreed to let you stay with them if you decide to go." He handed the telegram to Emily.

She reached for the parchment and read "John and Deborah Witherspoon. I remember you mentioning them on occasion."

"Their children are grown now, so you would have a bedroom to yourself. I have no doubt you would help around the house while you are there, and I know that would be a blessing to Deborah."

Emily held the telegram almost reverently. "This is the last piece of the puzzle. Every detail is in place. It seems the Lord is really directing me to do this." Tears threatened to overflow.

Her dad reached over and placed his hand on her arm. "Pray about it for a few more days. Whatever you decide, I'll be proud of you."

"Thank you, Dad." Though inwardly, Emily felt fairly

certain what her decision should be, she thought, *"Oh, what I wouldn't give to be able to talk to James about all of this."*

Before the church service two days later, James studied the face of the one who held his heart. She was still polite and smiling to those around her, but her eyes were sad. He knew the weight of her decision must be wearing on her. Wishing again that he were allowed to speak to her and longing to wrap her in his arms were almost too much to bear in this moment. *"God's timing. Pray for grace and wisdom and comfort. Wait for God's timing."* Truth be told, he was tired of waiting, but the Lord knew that. *"Lord, give me the endurance to continue waiting. This is so hard."*

Pastor's message that morning seemed to penetrate deep into the hearts of the young man and woman sitting across the aisle from one another. "Did you know you can talk to your soul? In Psalm 42:5, David records a conversation he has with his soul. 'Why are you cast down, O my soul, and why are you in turmoil within me? Hope in God; for I shall again praise him, my salvation and my God.' He spends the next few verses encouraging himself, but he has to repeat the exact same words to his soul in verse 11."

"There are seasons in life when for one reason or another, we are 'cast down.' That phrase means discouraged or weighted down. May I challenge you to talk to your soul? Tell your soul, as David did, to 'hope in God' and praise Him, not just because he saved you from sin and gave you eternal life if you have accepted His gift of salvation, but because He is your God every minute of every day. He loves you more than you can imagine, and He promises never to leave you. Ever."

Emily felt the gentle prod of conviction. *"Lord, have I been hoping in other things than You — my family, my home, my teaching, James? These are all wonderful things, but help me to place my hope in You."*

A few feet away, James was having a similar conversation with his Savior. *"Yes, I have definitely been 'cast down.' Lord, I want my soul to praise You. I want to put my hope and trust in You, not just for my salvation, but each and every day. When I trust You fully, I will wait for You."*

Just before the service ended, Pastor reminded everyone about the upcoming social. After he closed in prayer, James turned around to Josiah, "Don't forget to tell Emily when you're picking her up on Saturday."

"Already done. Don't worry, James. I will take good care of your girl."

James clapped him on the shoulder, "Thank you."

As they rolled along in the buggy on their way home, Luke asked Julie, "Will you go to the church social with me this year?"

She responded without thinking, "Of course."

"Since this would be the first time you weren't going with Buck, I wasn't sure if you would want to go."

Now he had her full attention. "Oh," the whisper came. After a moment of quiet reflection, she answered again, "Yes, I would like to attend the social . . . with you," adding a bit of emphasis on the 'you' so he would understand her heart's intent.

Luke's blue eyes smiled. "Would you wear your cream dress?"

"Why that one?"

"Do you remember your first social after you came back to the ranch?"

Julie smiled, "Yes. I still can't believe Emma had to teach Buck to dance."

"We found the one thing he couldn't do, but he even learned to dance well. What I remember about that night was the moment when you and Buck came through the door together. You were so beautiful; you took my breath away. I had to work very hard not to be envious of Buck that night. If you remember, all of us took turns dancing with you throughout the evening."

Looking wistfully, Julie responded, "Yes, I remember."

"One of the hardest things I've ever done was let you go after we danced."

"I never knew."

"No one did. My feelings were well covered. I had dreams of dancing with you in that dress, but my love for you and Buck far outweighed my own wishes." Luke looked over and sought Julie's soft brown eyes, "Other than my mother and Emma, you are the only woman I have ever danced with."

Julie spoke sincerely, "I feel honored. I'd be happy to wear your favorite dress." She had a fleeting feeling of sadness, remembering that it had been Buck's favorite, too.

Pulling up in front of their home, Luke gently tipped up his wife's chin for her lips to meet his kiss. "Thank you."

On Saturday evening, Luke brought the sorrel mare and buggy home after chores. He got cleaned up and changed while Julie was feeding their son. When Matthew had a full tummy and a clean diaper, Luke took him so Julie could get ready. Several minutes later, Julie stood in the doorway to their bedroom. Her cream-colored organdy dress had loose ruffles around a modest scoop neckline and three-quarter sleeves with a soft flowing ruffle at their hem. An azure blue sash was tied into a bow at the back of her waist. Luke was in awe. If she had been glowing, he would have been certain he was looking at an angel.

He stood and walked slowly to her, thankful that he did not have to hide his feelings tonight. With Matthew in his left arm, he reached out his right hand to lift her left hand to his lips. "You are so beautiful, my wife." He added, "How is it that I can even call you my wife? I am beyond blessed." Releasing her hand and offering her his arm, he asked, "Shall we?"

Emma rode with James and Jacob in the buckboard, and they dropped Jacob off near the Evans' home, which was run-down from neglect. As James and Emma pulled away, James muttered to himself, "I don't know what has gotten into that boy's head."

Emma heard him. *"So, James has noticed something amiss, too."* That was both comforting and troubling.

They soon arrived at the venue; the barn had been beautifully decorated for the event. Ribbons and greenery wound around each post, and the food and punch tables were covered with matching tablecloths and lace table runners. A platform had been placed along one wall for the musicians, and the center of the barn was open for dancing with chairs lined in rows around the perimeter.

James helped Emma down from the wagon, and she asked him, "What are your plans for tonight?"

"I'm just going to blend into the shadows and watch Emily."

Emma rested her hand on his arm. "I'm so sorry the two of you are having to go through this."

"At least Josiah will be there for her tonight."

Tim and Josiah rode their horses to the Kendrick home and tethered them to the hitching post out front. Since the parsonage was not far from the social and the weather was lovely, they planned to walk to the event. The brothers were approaching the front door when a girl's voice from inside yelled, "Emily, Laura, they're here!"

Tim rubbed his upper lip and said to Josiah, "I think we've been announced." A moment later, the door opened and there stood Laura in a deep violet dress with tailored seams. Tim handed her a small bouquet of purple pansies, inwardly pleased that he had guessed the right color. "Good evening."

"Thank you, Tim, they're lovely. Just a moment, and I'll put them in water." When she returned, Emily came to the doorway in a dark blue dress with a lace collar.

Josiah handed her a colorful bouquet of wildflowers and Gerbera daisies. "These are for you." Lowering his voice to a whisper, he added, "They are from James."

Laura looked from Josiah to Emily and raised her eyebrows. Emily blushed. "Thank you, Josiah, that is most kind." She brought them close to her face and filled her nostrils with the wonderful fragrance before she turned to also put her flowers into a glass of water.

Tim offered Laura his arm, and they talked and laughed while Josiah and Emily walked side by side several feet behind them. After strolling in silence for a moment, Josiah commented, "It's a beautiful night, isn't it?"

"Hmm? Oh, yes, it is a pretty evening," she returned, obviously distracted from her thoughts.

Josiah tried to lighten the moment. "Other than the fact

that you'd rather be with a man four inches taller and seven years older than I am, what is on your mind?"

Embarrassed at her rudeness, Emily apologized, "I'm so sorry, Josiah. Under the circumstances, I am very thankful you asked me to join you tonight. My thoughts just wandered off."

Trying to guess the reason for her wandering thoughts, Josiah ventured, "Are you still trying to decide what to do about teaching?"

Emily gave a little sigh. "No, I think I've made my decision. I think God wants me to go to Kansas City for the teacher's course. He has provided everything I need to go. The only thing remaining is to announce my decision to the town council after the social tonight."

"If you've decided, then what's wrong?"

Shaking her head, Emily replied, "It's silly, really."

"If something is bothering you that much, it certainly cannot be silly."

Realizing Josiah truly was concerned, Emily answered, "There is something weighing heavily on my mind that I wish I could discuss with James. My heart is craving James' blessing. I know I have no right to ask for it, nor could I ask him if I did have the right. My dad has given his approval for me to go, of course, but James is the one who holds my heart. Kansas City is so far away, and six months seems like forever. I don't think I could endure going if James wanted me to stay."

Josiah gently replied, "Emily, I hate to state the obvious, but James will not want you to leave. He will, however, want you to follow God's path for your life, even if it means you will be separated for six more months."

Tears welled up in her eyes, and she nodded, "I know. I just wish I could hear him say it."

"I'll see what I can do. Now, dry your tears before we go in, or James will box my ears for making you cry." Emily dabbed the corners of her eyes and regained her composure. Josiah offered her his arm just before they entered the barn. "Let's have fun tonight and enjoy the dancing."

James immediately noticed when Emily entered with Josiah. He would periodically move around the perimeter of the dance floor to another chair, but his eyes never left the one he loved. He appreciated the way Josiah kept her close and protected her from the two scruffy boys who tried in vain to cut in.

During the intermission, Josiah retrieved glasses of punch for him and Emily, and instructed closely, "I'll be right back. If anyone asks, you've promised all the rest of the dances to me, all right?" Emily smiled and nodded. She, too, had appreciated his protection tonight.

Josiah sat down next to James, "You are hard to find; you keep moving."

"I'm trying not to make it obvious that I'm here alone watching Emily dance."

Following James' gaze right to Emily, Josiah replied, "You are obvious, but that's not why I'm here." He shared what Emily had told him on the way over from the parsonage. "So, I was thinking, if we sat near you for a moment, you could talk to me. If Emily happened to overhear our conversation, well, that wouldn't be breaking any rules, would it?"

For the first time tonight, James' gaze left Emily. He planted his hand on his leg and looked directly at Josiah. "You're not usually the one to bend the rules."

"No, I'm not, but desperate times call for desperate measures." Josiah looked over at Emily, who was being approached again by one of the troublemakers he was trying to protect her from. "Speaking of which, I've got to go. You must be more imposing than I am. I can't get these fellows to take a hint."

Josiah approached Emily and turned her away from the approaching imposter. "Shall we get some dinner?"

"Yes, please. All this dancing has made me hungry."

When they had served their plates, Josiah commented, "Follow me. I saw a few seats over here earlier." He sat two chairs down from James – close enough to have a conversation, but far enough away that James and Emily could not be accused of sitting together. As they ate, James waited patiently in silence, leaning forward with his elbows on his knees and his hands folded in front of him.

Josiah wiped his mouth with his napkin, wondering what his brother was waiting for.

As if on cue, James sat up and looked right at the woman he wanted to make his bride. "Josiah, please tell the one I love that I will miss her like crazy. God has prepared her for this moment, and if she feels His hand guiding her to earn her teacher's certificate in Kansas City, she has my blessing." Emily stared down at her plate, listening to every word and the camber of his voice as he spoke. A single tear fell on her cheek. "And tell her to please come back home when she finishes, or my heart will be broken forever."

To finish the conversation, Josiah replied, "I'll be sure she knows." James nodded, stood, and walked out of the barn as if he needed some fresh air.

From Josiah's right, Emily whispered, "Thank you, Josiah."

"You're welcome."

Across the room, Emma approached Julie. "The next volunteer just relieved me at the cake table. Let me hold Matthew for a while so you two can dance." She reached for the little boy.

Luke bowed gallantly to his wife and extended his hand toward her, "May I have the honor of this dance?"

Returning his invitation with a curtsey, Julie placed her hand in his, "Yes, you may."

Emma just rolled her eyes and shook her head. She looked down at the infant in her arms and told him, "Those two are so in love; you are blessed to have them as parents."

Julie let herself get lost in Luke's striking sky blue eyes as they danced, blue eyes that saw only her. One song after another, they moved as one across the floor, as if they had danced together forever. When the last strains of the final waltz vanished into the air, Luke pulled her close and whispered into her ear, "Thank you for making all my dreams come true, My Love."

Emma looked around for her boys. Luke, Josiah, and Tim were on the dance floor. She spotted James leaning against the barn wall near the door and kept scanning the crowd before she finally found Jacob and Mandy sitting in the back corner looking sullen. Her mama's heart ached for both James and Jacob, but for very different reasons. *"Lord, please change Pastor's mind about blessing Emily's marriage to James. They are both hurting so much, and he seems utterly oblivious to their pain. Give them the courage to wait for his blessing."* Looking back toward Jacob, she continued in silent prayer, *"Please work in that boy's heart. His attitude is only an outward symptom of a much deeper hurt. Only You know what that hurt is, but I pray you would heal that hurt, whatever it is, before he makes a decision that ruins the rest of his life."*

Earlier that evening, the Carters were enjoying dinner together when Louisa inquired, "Dad, what is a social?"

Seth rubbed his chin and looked over at his wife, thankful she was feeling strong enough to join them, and thought aloud, "How would you describe a social? Well, it's a gathering of friends, rather like a party, with food, music, and dancing. Socials often celebrate an event or a time of year."

"Like harvest," Jonathan interjected.

"Yes, this social celebrates the end of harvest."

"Did you and Mama ever dance?" Anna asked.

"We loved to dance before your Mama got so sick." Seth reached over and wrapped his fingers around Susanna's hand.

"Yes, I miss it," Susanna admitted.

Louisa summoned the courage to ask her dad, "Would you teach me how to dance?"

In response to Seth's raised eyebrows, his wife remarked, "Our little girl is growing up."

"Yes, she is." He stood and walked over to Louisa, holding out a hand to her. "May I have the honor of this dance?"

Louisa's face lit up, and she put her hand in her dad's. He led her to the open floor and gave her simple instructions. At first, Louisa was embarrassed that she kept stepping on her dad's toes, but he assured her, "You're not the first one to step on these toes of mine."

He looked over at Susanna and winked. She had been watching the scene with misty eyes, but at Seth's wink, she rolled her eyes and hid her smile behind her hand.

After several minutes, Louisa gave her dad a big hug. "Thank you."

"You're welcome, my dear." As Louisa returned to her chair, Seth approached Susanna with an outstretched hand. "Dance with me?" He knew she wanted to say yes, but she hesitated. "Just put your feet on mine, and I'll dance for both of us. Please."

"Go on, Mama. Dance with Daddy," Anna implored.

Susanna stood and Seth led her a few steps from the table. "Are you sure?" The twinkle in his eyes gave her the answer. She carefully placed her slippered feet on his, and Seth wrapped her in his arms. He hummed a tune and swayed back and forth to the music. Susanna laid her head against her husband's chest, and he rested his cheek on the top of her head. After a few minutes, Seth felt her knees start to buckle in weakness. He stopped and lifted her into his arms.

"Thank you, Seth. I enjoyed that very much."

"As did I." He carried her into the bedroom and tucked her in with a kiss before returning to their children.

CHAPTER 15
Decisions

A s the social ended, Josiah walked with Emily over to where the town councilmen had convened, then excused himself to go stand by James, whose gaze was locked onto Emily. He watched from afar as she addressed the council, knowing that the time of his waiting had just been extended until at least June. To passers-by, James looked relaxed, leaning casually against the wall with his arms folded. His clenched jaw was the only clue of the emotions that were threatening to erupt at any moment. His thought was nearly overwhelming. *"These last three months have been torture. How will I survive another nine?"*

Josiah sensed the turmoil within the brother standing next to him, especially after hearing his impassioned plea for Emily to come home again. The rumors that had been circulating about them splitting up or taking a break from one another were completely untrue. James and Emily deeply loved one another. Josiah knew there were no words he could say in this moment to bring comfort, so he just stood there, hoping his presence would speak his support and solidarity.

Emily was thankful Josiah had escorted her over to this meeting. True, he wasn't James, but he was a good brother, one of four additional brothers she hoped to claim for her own one day. Her own brother Robert looked up to Josiah, and her sister Sarah adored him. Now she stood before six men, her father among them, who were waiting for her to officially declare her intentions.

Mr. Wilson spoke first, "Good evening, Emily. Have you come to a decision?"

"Yes, I have." She took a deep breath and listened to James' words play in her mind one more time. "I have decided to pursue the training in the teachers' institute and sit for my certification examination. The term will begin the fifth day of January, and my examination will be on the twenty-third day of June. All of the details have been arranged but one. I do not know who will teach in my place during the spring term."

Another councilman assured her, "We still have three months to figure that out. On behalf of the entire council, let me say that we are proud of you for taking this big step. Having a school in Prairie Hills will help this town grow, and we could not imagine anyone else more suited to the teaching post."

"Thank you. You are most kind."

"Knowing what a burden this must be for you, we have decided to send you a monthly stipend to help offset your expenses. That is, of course, assuming you will commit to returning here to teach in Prairie Hills."

Emily again thought of James' last words to her – or rather, Josiah – and stated resolutely, "I will return to Prairie Hills.

This is my home. My heart is here, and I couldn't live anywhere else."

"Well then, the matter is settled."

The men shook hands and dismissed the meeting. Emily turned to find Josiah and found James watching her. Her gaze met his, and she stood planted where she was, unable to look away. After a moment, she noticed his lips moving. Josiah looked over at him, nodded, and started walking toward her. Their gaze remained unbroken until Josiah appeared before her, asking, "Are you ready to head home?"

She glanced at Josiah for a split second to respond, then back over to the man against the wall, but he was gone.

James drove with Emma to the Evans' house, picked up Jacob, and traveled home in silence. Emma knew James was struggling and needed to be alone with his thoughts, so she sat next to him and again prayed silently for him and Emily. Once he had dropped Emma off at the ranch house and she had gone upstairs to ready for bed, she heard noise coming from direction of the barn. Emma went to the front window and pulled back the lace curtain. What she saw brought tears to her eyes. James was at the chopping block, splitting firewood with a vengeance; but the slice of the axe was not the only sound she could hear. Her mother's heart could hear his agony in every swing.

The distinct reverberations of chopping wood continued throughout the night. After morning chores, Emma answered a knock at the front door to find James with his eyes bloodshot, whether from lack of sleep or tears, she wasn't sure. "What can I do for you, son?"

"Do you have any of that blister salve on hand?"

"I'm sure I have some in the medicine cabinet. Come on in." Emma went to the kitchen to procure the salve. When James pulled off his leather gloves, tears welled up in Emma's eyes again, for his hands were raw and bleeding. "Oh, James."

He winced when she gently applied the ointment and wrapped his hands in soft gauze. "They will heal. My hands don't hurt like my heart does."

Emma reached up to cradle his unshaven cheek in her hand. "I know. You may not be my son by birth, but you are my son, and a mother's heart hurts when her children's do. I feel so helpless and powerless to do anything about it, but I will keep praying."

"Thank you, Mama." James turned to leave and gingerly pulled his gloves back on. He had work to do.

Later that week, a courier from town brought a telegram from the Texas Cattlemen's Association to the Rugged Cross Ranch. Emma read through the message and walked over to the barn where Tim was stacking hay bales. "Tim, we just received a response about the longhorns. Tell the boys we'll have a family meeting at the house. I'll make a roast."

"And apple pie?" Tim hinted.

Emma laughed, "All right, Tim. And apple pie."

"Yes!" He lowered his voice, "If I happen to forget to let the others know about the meeting, do I get the whole pie?"

"If you come alone, you won't get any pie."

"All right, all right." Tim called up to the rafters, "Hey, Luke, there's a family meeting at Emma's tonight. With apple pie."

Luke peered over the edge of the hayloft, "We'll be there."

"One down, three to go." Tim tried to look angelic, but failed miserably.

Emma just shook her head. She pointed her finger at him for emphasis and reminded him, "I'm counting on you."

Once dinner was finished and the apple pie had been served, Emma pulled out the telegram. "The information I received today may change our plans. Because of the demand for the longhorn bulls this fall, the price is fairly steep. If we are willing to wait until just after the spring drive, the cost is projected to drop by half." She handed the telegram to James.

His response mirrored her initial reaction, "This is a dramatic price cut. You have said yourself that we're not in a rush here. Based on this information, I think we should wait until spring." One by one, the brothers all voiced their agreement. The quest for new bulls would have to wait.

CHAPTER 16
Remembering

J ulie couldn't sleep. Moving very slowly and smoothly so she would not wake Luke, Julie slipped from their bed and donned her robe against the autumn chill. She paused for a moment at Matthew's cradle and stared at the sleeping face that seemed to glow in the soft moonlight filtering through the window. A solitary tear glided down her cheek as she was reminded of just how much her son looked like his first father.

Stepping quietly from the bedroom into the living area, Julie walked first to the fireplace. Above the mantle, mounted on the wall, was an Indian bow – Buck's bow. She reached up with a reverent hand and touched the leather handle. Though he had never been fully accepted in his village because his father was white, Buck had been respected for many things among his people, his skill with the bow and arrow among them. When Matthew was older, she would teach him how to fashion a bow and arrows. Perhaps one day he would have the accuracy and confidence his father had. Julie lingered one more moment before moving toward the wooden chest sitting against the wall to the left of the fireplace.

There she knelt and studied the design on the colorful

blanket that laid folded across the surface of the wood. She and her adoptive Kiowa mother had made this covering when she was still living in the village. Tormented emotions filled her heart. Julie felt compelled to lift the lid, but she honestly wasn't sure she could bear it. Within this chest were stored Julie's most treasured possessions.

Slowly, resolutely, Julie pulled the blanket off the chest and laid it across her lap. With shaking hands, she reached for the top corners of the chest, wavered a few seconds more, then lifted the lid. Her tears now coursed down her cheeks as she gently caressed the beaded moccasins her mother had secretly made for Buck's betrothal gift to her. Next to them were her buckskin tunic and split riding skirt, with a beaded headband and two beaded braid ties lying on them. The last time she had worn these things, she had been visiting her parents' village with Buck. Just in time, Julie covered her mouth with her hand to stifle the sound of the sob that was threatening to erupt.

After closing her eyes for a moment to regain her composure, Julie lifted the tray that held the clothing of a cultural heritage she had shared with Buck. Setting the tray aside, she peered into the box again and brought out a small once-white Bible. This Bible had been brought to her from her family's wagon train by one of the braves in her village. For many years, this book had been her only link to the English world. After a riding accident that took her sight, Julie had not thought to ask about her Bible. What she had not known was that her best friend Morning Song had given it to a brave visiting from another village, a young man who was trying to learn English. Many years later, she found this Bible again in the hands of her beloved Buck. She caressed the worn leather. This is the Bible that had pointed Buck to the Savior. Knowing that he was in Heaven was the comfort that got her through the painful days. Days like today.

Once again Julie reached into the chest. She pulled out her

first love's buckskin tunic and lifted it to her cheek. The soft leather still smelled like him. Sorrow engulfed her. She buried her face in its folds and wept.

Luke rolled over in his sleep and his arm found only empty linens. Instantly, he was awake. One of the joys or curses of veterinary medicine was that he could sleep soundly, yet be completely awake and alert when his eyes opened, ready to handle any emergency. As he listened, he first heard the soft breathing of their son, so Julie wasn't awake on his account. Then he heard another sound coming from the next room.

He padded softly to the doorway. There he could see Julie on the floor in front of the chest, but he remained mostly obscured from her view. Luke knew Julie's heart was breaking anew today. Part of him wanted to immediately wrap her in his arms and just let her cling to him, but he sensed that right now, in this moment, she needed to be alone with Buck. He had not forgotten what day this was; he had already arranged to spend the entire day with his wife and son. Luke leaned against the doorway, quietly observing his Love, protectively waiting until he was invited to join in her grief.

The hours passed. Finally, the sun began its ascent and the first few rays of light brightened the horizon. Julie looked over to the window, but the sunlight seemed to taunt her with its joy. She didn't know how long she had been hugging Buck's tunic. She didn't want to let go, yet she knew she must. Ever so carefully, Julie folded the tunic and laid it gently in the chest.

A slight movement from the corner of her eye caught her attention, and she turned her head to find Luke watching her. In a sudden jumble of emotions, Julie felt protected, hurt, vulnerable, ashamed, broken, loved. Though the other chest contents were still lying around her, Julie stood and went to him, laying her cheek on his chest as he wrapped her in a comforting embrace.

A fresh wave of tears washed over her. "I loved him so much." In the fog of sorrow, she suddenly realized that she had just told her husband she loved another man and felt embarrassed, almost ashamed. "I'm sorry, Luke, I didn't mean . . ."

"Shh. You do not need to apologize. You loved Buck. You still love him. That is as it should be. Allow your heart to grieve, for tears will bring healing." His last words were meant for himself as well, and a tear dripped from his lashes onto her hair.

Julie knew that sunrise was when Luke would leave for morning chores in the barn, but she pleaded in a whisper, "Luke, please don't go."

He responded gently, "James understood completely when I told him I would not leave you alone today."

"You remembered."

"Yes. This day changed my life forever, too. Today is not only the anniversary of Buck's passing; it is also our first wedding anniversary."

Julie winced slightly. She had forgotten. "I guess it is, isn't it?"

"I hope you don't mind, but I asked Emma to make us a picnic lunch so we could spend the day with Buck."

Julie crinkled her brow in confusion until she realized, "Do you mean on the Hill?"

Luke nodded. "We can head up there mid-morning and stay as long as you like."

"Thank you, Luke."

"Anything for you, my Love." Luke continued to keep Julie wrapped in his arms, held securely against his chest.

Here she felt protected and loved. That her thoughts were so conflicted bothered her. How could her love for Luke be true when she was so deeply mourning another man? Her renewed grief was too raw to make sense of it, but she clung to Luke with sheer desperation, willing him to share this burden with her, knowing she could not bear the weight of it alone.

Luke understood. He was thankful that God had chosen him to take Buck's place, though he would never be able to fill the moccasins Buck left behind. Buck had had the greatest influence on the man Luke had become, was still becoming.

Recently, Luke had wondered why losing Buck seemed more painful than the loss of his own family. He had been close to his parents and brother, after all. When he remembered back to those first months after his family had died of cholera, he realized how hurt and abandoned he had felt. What was the difference now? Time. He had been only thirteen then. Now he could enjoy pleasant memories of his first family.

That recollection was oddly comforting. Time. Luke would still catch himself expecting Buck to walk silently past him in the stable on his way to saddle Wind Dancing or give him a bit of wisdom in as few words as possible. That had been Buck's way. No word was ever wasted. In those few words and by his godly example, Buck had shaped Luke's character.

Luke rested his cheek on Julie's lavender-scented hair. Now Luke understood what it meant to love someone so deeply that your very souls seem intertwined. That is what Julie had ripped from her one year ago today. His own sorrow must pale in comparison to what she was enduring at this moment. He would gladly carry part of her grief on his shoulders. He would do anything to make this day easier for her.

A soft whimper in the bedroom quickly turned into a lusty cry. Luke was reluctant to let Julie go. "He can wait another minute or two if you need to stay where you are."

Julie tried to take control of her tears with a shaky breath.

She leaned back just enough to be able to look into Luke's blue eyes. "Our son needs me."

Luke kissed her on the forehead before he released her. "While you're feeding Matthew, I'll make breakfast."

Half an hour later, Julie exited the bedroom carrying their son. His broad toothless smile was evidence that he was oblivious to the sorrow attached to this day. Luke turned in response to his happy squeal, and the little boy stretched out both arms and opened and closed his fists in a gesture that begged his dad to hold him. Luke grasped his torso with both hands and lifted him high into the air. Matthew's laugh filled the room. After flying him in a huge circle, Luke held his son against him with his left arm. "Hey, big guy, do you want to help me finish breakfast?" Lowering his voice to a whisper, he added, "Your first dad taught me to make this frybread on our first cattle drive together. This was his favorite breakfast. Today, we're making it for your mama. Give her extra smiles today. She's going to need them." Plating with his right hand, he announced, "Breakfast is ready." Turning toward the fireplace, he observed her replacing the interior tray, closing the lid, and draping the blanket over the chest. Her movements seemed slow and sluggish, as if each task were a heavy weight. Perhaps it was.

Lingering a few more seconds before the chest, she took a deep breath and responded, "I'm coming," before turning toward the kitchen table. Now the little boy in Luke's arms reached for his mama, who scooped him up and hugged him close.

When they were seated at the table, Luke reached for Julie's free hand and rubbed the back of her hand with his thumb. She looked from her son's face to her husband's eyes and saw his pain veiled there. "I love you, Julie."

Julie could not find her voice, so she simply nodded.

Luke bowed his head in prayer, "God of Comfort, please

surround our hearts today as we honor a man we both held dear. Though we know with certainty that he is in Heaven with You, we miss him greatly. Please be especially with Julie, as the wounds of her broken heart are hurting again. Thank You for allowing Buck to be a part of our lives, and thank You for allowing Julie to be a part of mine. Thank You for Matthew. Help us to rear him to be a godly man like his father. Thank You for this food and for being able to spend this day together as a family. In my Savior's name, Amen."

Quiet tears were again falling down Julie's cheeks, but she managed, "You are Matthew's father. Buck chose you to rear his son. He knew you shared the same godly character. Teach Matthew to be like you, and you will have taught him to be like Buck."

With his voice catching a bit as he spoke, he responded, "Thank you, Julie."

Julie's gaze finally dropped to her plate. "You made Indian frybread. This was Buck's favorite."

"Yes, I know."

"I love you, Luke."

After breakfast, the trio made their way to the barn. James had just mounted Trigger for his morning ride, but when he saw Julie, he dismounted and enveloped her in a brotherly hug. When he released her, he put his hands gently on her shoulders. "I have been praying for you today."

"Thank you, James. I know I'm not the only one hurting today. You miss him, too."

"Yes. Yes, I do. Little did I know when Buck first came to this ranch that he would become my best friend." He took a step backward. "Okay, I'm going to go before my eyes start watering." James pointed at his brother, "Luke, take good care of her today."

"Always."

James rode toward the north pasture, and Tim led his

saddled horse from the barn and approached Julie, fidgeting with the reins in his hands. "For once, I'm not quite sure what to say. You're family, and we are all hurting with you. If there is anything I can do, let me know."

"Thank you, Tim."

Julie entered the barn and led Cinnamon and Spice one by one to the pasture while Luke and Matthew were saying hello to Wind Dancing. Returning from the pasture, she met Josiah, who asked, "Are you all right?" Flustered, he added, "Of course you're not all right. What a thing to ask!"

Knowing his heart was in the right place, Julie laid a hand on his arm. "No, I'm not all right, but I will be. Thank you for your concern." He gave her a bear hug, too. When he released her, he had tears in his eyes.

Turning quickly to hide his tears, he spoke, "I need to saddle up and check the perimeter fence." As he walked away, Julie could see him wipe his eyes with his sleeve.

She had the fleeting thought that Jacob was the only one of the brothers she had not seen this morning, but she dismissed any concern, assuming he was already out with the herd.

Julie looked back over through the rails of the pasture fence and watched Spice frolic around her mama while Cinnamon calmly grazed. They seemed so free and happy while her heart felt bound with sorrow; Wind Dancing would understand. She walked back toward the stall where Luke was holding Matthew, stroking the horse's neck. Buck's horse turned his face toward Julie as she approached, and she laid her forehead against his long face. Yes, Wind Dancing understood. Once more, her tears began to fall.

Luke seemed to sense what she needed. "Would you like me to saddle Wind Dancing, so you can take him for a ride?"

"Yes, please."

He handed Matthew to Julie and made his way to the tack room. On the very last saddle rack sat the saddle his brother had treasured as one of his only possessions. Luke grabbed a rag and wiped it down. The polished leather shone in the sunlight streaming from the window. Buck had been quite protective of this saddle, not even allowing anyone else to touch it, that is, until Julie. Even now, the brothers still honored his wish, letting Luke be the only one other than Julie to handle it. He lifted the saddle and carried it to Wind Dancing, who seemed to nod his approval. When Luke had secured the saddle, Julie passed Matthew back to him, slipped the bridle over Wind Dancing's head, and led him from the barn. Luke walked beside her.

"Take as much time as you need, My Love," Luke instructed softly. "We'll be at Emma's when you return."

"Thank you." Julie looked from the blue eyes of her husband to the big brown ones of Wind Dancing. "Would you like to run with me?" The horse snorted and dipped his head as if nodding. In one smooth motion, she lifted herself into the saddle. She waved at Luke and Matthew as she set Wind Dancing into motion. Julie guided him past the south pasture where there was a huge expanse of grassland. Leaning into his side with her left leg and gently kicking him with her right urged him into the smoothest canter. They rode as one, with the wind flowing through his mane and her hair. Memory after memory of riding Wind Dancing with Buck came with a rush, but the wind wiped the tears from her eyes.

After a time, Julie led him up Ridge Hill. Buck had brought Julie here for a picnic for their first outing together, an outing that had not ended as he had planned. She brought Wind Dancing to a stop at the crest of the hill near the spreading oak tree and looked out to the horizon. The deciduous trees had started their annual transformation, so she saw little pockets of gold and crimson among the green. Here in this spot she felt so small, so insignificant, yet the majesty of God's creation around her reminded her of His love. He didn't have to make the world beautiful, but He did. He could have made everything black and white, and no one would have known the difference, but His world abounded with colors just for everyone to enjoy.

Wind Dancing shook his head and broke her reverie. "Yes, I'm ready to go home, too." Julie turned him, and he stepped gracefully down the rocky trail. At the bottom of the hill, Julie bent low and gave him his head. He read her cue and sped faster and faster until he was in a full run. Not until he reached the edge of the south pasture did he slow his gait. Julie brought him back to a walk to cool down before she led him to the barn to unsaddle him. Once Wind Dancing's saddle was returned to the tack room, Julie led him to the pasture to be with his family. "Thank you for the ride, Wind Dancing." He shook his mane in response, for he had enjoyed it, too.

Luke and Emma had seen Julie return and now met her as she exited the barn. Luke had his hands full. One held Matthew, and the other held a picnic basket. Emma reached for Julie and hugged her tightly. "Julie, I know how much you are hurting today, for I've been there. There are no right words to say. Just know that we love you and are praying for you, especially today."

"How did you ever make it without Daniel?"

"If these boys had not been here to daily remind me of God's love and comfort, I don't think I would have survived. They kept me going when I had no emotional strength left. I'm so thankful that you have Luke and Matthew. I've packed some of Buck's favorites in the basket. Talk about him. Remember the good memories and the bad ones, even if they bring tears."

Emma turned and headed back toward the ranch house. Luke spoke quietly, "Take a walk with me." Since both of his hands were occupied, they walked slowly, side-by-side through the garden toward the back of the ranch house where the path to the Hill began. No words were spoken, but Julie could feel his strength and reassurance without them.

A few minutes later, they reached the crest of the Hill. A small cluster of poplars and oaks dotted this grassy area. Beneath the largest tree sat a wooden bench facing north. When Emma's husband Daniel had placed this bench, he would often come here after dark to pray. During times that he felt discouraged, he would look at the North Star and remember that the same God who created the star that guided ships across the open water would also guide him. His sons after him come here to pray, just as Luke was praying now. Praying for wisdom. Praying for comfort for the woman he loved more than life itself.

Julie reached for the blanket tucked between the picnic basket lid and handle and spread it on the grass in the shade of the poplar's branches. Luke laid Matthew down on his tummy on the blanket and sat on the bench, putting his arm around his wife sitting beside him. At the base of the Hill behind them stood the ranch house. Before them, the graves of Daniel, Buck, and Buck and Julie's daughter were in a neat row. Beyond them, the Hill sloped down toward the river. Julie could just make out the top of the tepee in the trees below, with their house a short distance to the left. This spot was so peaceful, soothing to Julie's troubled heart.

Breaking the silence, Julie whispered, "I don't know how you can be so sweet to me when my heart is aching for another man."

Luke gently rubbed his hand on her upper arm as he held her close beside him. He looked from Buck's gravestone to Julie's face. "I do not feel threatened by your love for Buck. Quite the opposite, in fact. Love is an amazing thing. It cannot be divided; it can only multiply. The intensity of your love for him shows how great your capacity for love really is."

"The crazy thing is that I love you just as much, maybe more, if that's possible."

"I know." He leaned in and kissed her hair. "Now for stories. Shall I begin?" With Julie's nod of encouragement, he started with the time he first met Buck and told story after story. "By the time we were on our first cattle drive together, I had already learned to admire him. On our second morning, I woke early to find Buck already stoking the fire. 'What are you doing?' I asked. 'Making breakfast. Do you cook?' 'No, not really.' 'Come. I will teach you.' With simple ingredients like flour, salt, baking powder, and water, Buck taught me to make Indian frybread. That was my first cooking lesson, and I've never forgotten the recipe."

"That would explain why your frybread this morning tasted just like his." Luke nodded his response to Julie's observation.

"In those early years, I would follow him like a puppy. Looking back, I'm surprised he never got tired of me hanging around. There were many times I asked to ride with Buck just to learn from him. Daniel mentored me, too, but Buck was the one who really understood me."

"Probably because you are so much alike," Julie acknowledged.

"Except the one day I saw a side of him I'd never seen before."

"Tell me."

Gesturing toward the middle gravestone with his free hand, Luke continued, "The day you were attacked and your little girl died, I saw the warrior in him. He was broken-hearted, but never broken. He was fierce, resolute. When he changed into his buckskin, drew the war paint on his face, and held his bow, he was terrifying. There had to be anger within him, but he never let it control him. I've never been more proud to be his brother or more determined never to make him cross."

"What I remember about Buck on that day was that he carried me in his arms as though I were as light as a feather. He brought me here first, to the grave of our daughter, then he carried me home." A sudden realization hit her, "You carried me that day, too, didn't you?"

"Yes, from the river trail to the ranch house. Dakota has never run so hard as I pushed him that day to get Doc. I . . . We were afraid we were going to lose you."

Sensing everything that Luke had just left unsaid, Julie laid her head on his shoulder, communicating her love and trust in one simple movement.

They continued telling stories, both sad and happy, and paused to feed Matthew and enjoy their picnic lunch of Indian stew, yeast rolls, and apple pie. Finally, Julie signaled that she was ready to go by packing up the basket and picking up their sleeping son. Luke stepped closer to Buck's grave for a moment. Speaking softly to the gravestone, he said, "Even if you had not asked, I would have gladly taken care of Julie and Matthew. Thank you for entrusting me with them and for giving our marriage your blessing. I am honored to be your brother and your successor."

Luke carefully took Matthew from Julie so he wouldn't wake him. She lifted the mostly empty basket, and Luke enveloped her free hand with his. The three of them arrived home just as the sun was beginning to set. Julie got her son ready for bed, and they tucked him in. Her lack of sleep the night before was catching up with her.

"Why don't you crawl in bed, too?" Luke prompted.

"I haven't even fed you dinner yet," Julie replied with a yawn.

"Don't worry about me. There are still a couple pieces of frybread left. I won't starve."

She changed into her nightgown and slipped between the sheets. She was sound asleep before Luke even made it back to the kitchen. After his light dinner, he crawled into bed, too, and fell fast asleep.

CHAPTER 17

The Christmas Program

The chill of the autumn nights was a signal that winter was on the way. One day after school, Emily finished her daily journal entry, describing in detail the chaos that ensued when one of the boys let a frog loose in the schoolroom. She looked at the penned words and shook her head. "Boys." After placing the journal in the drawer, she pulled her heavy shawl around her shoulders, reached for her basket, and strolled to the general store for more paper and pencils.

The jingle above the door announced her arrival. To the clerk, she greeted, "Good afternoon," and headed down her most frequented aisle for school supplies.

Margaret Lange observed her entrance and purposefully spoke loudly enough to her companion that Emily could distinctly hear her. "When I taught at the preparatory school in Boston, we performed a Christmas program every year. It's too bad the school here is too backward to put on a program. The event was always loved by all."

Emily's first thought was to sternly tell Mrs. Lange that if she wanted a program, she should plan it herself. Knowing that wasn't very charitable, Emily stayed rooted where she was and took a calming breath. Then she had an idea. She might live to regret it, but only time would tell. Stepping from the shadow in the aisle, Emily ventured, "Mrs. Lange, a Christmas program is a wonderful idea. Would you help me plan it?"

The portly lady looked aghast, "Me?"

"Certainly, you just told everyone you have experience with school Christmas programs, and I wouldn't know where to begin. The children would love it. We could invite the parents to attend. Will you help me?"

"We should invite the entire town," Mrs. Lange amended.

"Absolutely, we could invite everyone. Is that a 'yes'?"

"Well, I suppose it would give me something constructive to do. Yes, I will help you."

"Wonderful." Emily was a little unsure just how wonderful it would be to work with Mrs. Lange, but a Christmas program really did sound like a fun idea.

That night at the Kendrick dinner table, Emily told her family about her conversation. Laura exclaimed, "What were you thinking? That woman hates you!"

"Well, I think 'hate' is a bit strong. Despises, maybe."

"Still, what made you ask her?" Laura implored her for a logical explanation.

"Something Luke said to me right after we introduced ourselves to her that first Sunday. He said that people working to find fault in others are often just trying to cover up a deep hurt. Maybe, just maybe, she needs a friend."

"The Bible does say to love your enemies," their dad remarked.

Laura raised her eyebrows and looked sideways at Emily, with an expression that said she seriously doubted Emily's sanity at the moment.

. . .

Despite Laura's misgivings, plans for the Christmas program progressed much more smoothly than anticipated. Mrs. Lange strode into school the following afternoon with a file full of copious notes. "If we're going to do this right, we need to get started today." Though surprised at her abruptness, Emily was certainly willing to begin the planning. Mrs. Lange opened her file and began to discuss the list of things they would need. "How many students are there?"

"Fifteen."

"Only fifteen? We cannot put on an adequate production with only fifteen students," insisted Mrs. Lange.

"There are quite a few school-age children who are still learning at home. Perhaps we could invite them to join us for rehearsals," Emily suggested.

"Yes, that would be fine." Pulling another few pages from her file, Mrs. Lange continued, "Here are the costumes."

Realizing that Mrs. Lange's former students must have been from affluent families to afford these costumes, Emily attempted to convey the changes necessary for Prairie Hills. "These costumes are beautiful. The families here won't have access to these elaborate trims and laces, so we might need to simplify these designs. Many of the mothers will be stitching by hand, and we want to be sure to have the costumes ready in time."

"Good thought. Now, about the sets." Again Mrs. Lange pulled several detailed drawings of set designs for each act of the nativity play.

"How big was the stage where you performed in Boston?"

Mrs. Lange scanned the front of the church. "Probably three or four times as wide as this building and about twice as deep as the platform."

"Since we don't have as much room, let's choose the most important set pieces. We'll need the manger and the outline of a stable. Perhaps we could raise the left side of the platform and place the stable and manger there for everyone to see. On the right, we could make some rocks from papier-mâché for the shepherds and a ladder draped in dark fabric for the angel."

"What about the wise men? Where is their scenery?" Mrs. Lange simply had to fix this obvious omission.

"Hmm. Would it work to bring them in from the back and slowly down the center aisle as if they were traveling a long distance?"

Emily was expecting a retort, but instead, she turned and looked back down the aisle before nodding, "Actually, that just might work."

"How much rehearsal time do you think we will need?" Emily inquired.

"Two afternoons a week should do, but the last week we should rehearse every afternoon."

"How about Tuesdays and Thursdays until then?"

"Yes, that would work well."

Though Emily had written the lines, designed the simple costumes, and coordinated the stage props, she knew Mrs. Lange was going to take all of the credit for the program. In her heart, Emily was all right with that, for she had seen a change in Mrs. Lange, however subtle, for the better. She barked far less frequently, and was even heard to utter a compliment on rare occasions.

Emily prepared packets for each of the children with their script and the details for their costume. When Seth came to pick up his children, Emily asked, "May I speak to you for a moment? Knowing that your wife will be unable to make your children's costumes, I'll ask Laura to help me sew them. In lieu of costumes, I was wondering if you might be willing to help me with the building of the stable and manger for the stage."

Somewhat relieved, he replied, "Of course, I'd be happy to

help. Trust me, I'll be much better at building than I would be at sewing."

Julie met Emily for brunch at the café the following Saturday. After a hug, Emily admitted, "Thank you for suggesting this. I've been needing an excuse to take a break."

Once they were settled at their table, Julie remarked, "You've caused quite a buzz around town asking Mrs. Lange to help you with the Christmas program. How is that going?"

"Surprisingly, better than expected. The moms are sewing the costumes; Seth is building the sets; and the children are helping me decorate and make the props. As long as Mrs. Lange thinks she is in charge of the production, she's happy. I take care of all the behind-the-scenes details and keep the rehearsals running smoothly. Mrs. Lange needed a purpose, and the program seems to have filled that need."

Julie spoke sincerely, "I'm proud of you for taking the risk with Mrs. Lange, but it sounds as if you have a lot going on right now with teaching and the program. Have you been able to plan for your trip yet?"

"No, not really," Emily replied honestly. "I expect the weight of it all will hit me the day after school dismisses for Christmas."

"I'll come over after Christmas and help you pack," Julie reassured her. Emily released a soft sigh and looked almost fearful. "Emily, what's wrong?"

"What if I fail?" Emily's question revealed another concern on her mind.

"The teachers' certification examination?" Emily nodded. "Nonsense. Your classes will more than adequately prepare you for the exam. Just take an hour each night the week before the test to review over your class notes so they are fresh in your mind. Get a good night's sleep the night before and resist the temptation to study the morning of the exam."

Emily was surprised. "You sound like you're speaking from experience."

"I am. I took my certification examination after my second year at the blind school and taught a couple of classes my last two years to save for my return trip to the ranch. This counsel was given to me before my exam, and I, in turn, gave the same advice to all of my students. None of them ever failed, and neither will you."

Emily smiled, "Thank you so much. You don't know how I needed to hear that today." When she considered her words, she asked, "How did I not know you were a teacher, too?" A sudden thought occurred to her, "You could teach my students while I'm away!"

Julie raised her eyebrows and reached over to rest her hand on Emily's arm, "Along with my responsibilities at the ranch, and being a wife and mother? Adding full-time teaching responsibilities might be a little much. Besides, I think you are overlooking the obvious choice."

Crinkling her brow, Emily asked, "Who?"

"Mrs. Margaret Lange." Julie laughed at the shock on her friend's face. "Think about it. She is a seasoned educator who already knows your students and desperately needs something to do besides gossip, cause dissension, and meddle in other people's affairs. You said so yourself."

Letting the thought sink in, Emily replied, "Mrs. Lange. She is certainly qualified, but how would my students react?"

"They will want you back, but in the meantime, they would be getting a sound education, whether she teaches like you or not."

The following day, Emily stopped by the Carters' home to drop off two books Louisa and Anna had asked to borrow. When she had exited the gate of the picket fence out front, Emily took a deep breath and resolutely walked next door. During a brief meeting after church that morning, the town council had approved her recommendation for the substitute teacher. The responsibility to ask now fell on her shoulders. If she were being honest, Emily was rather intimidated by the matron who lived in the next house. Nevertheless, she approached the front door and lifted her hand to knock, pausing for one more inward word of encouragement before she rapped on the wood.

One moment later, Mrs. Margaret Lange opened the door and sized up the woman standing before her and asked curtly, "Yes, what do you want?"

"There is a matter I wish to discuss with you," Emily responded simply.

"Very well. Come in so I can close the door."

Emily stepped into Mrs. Lange's home and looked around to see velvet covered furniture in a neat arrangement and tapestries hanging on the walls. An ornate rug covered the floor, and rich draperies framed the windows. She felt as if she had gained a peek into this woman's prior life in Boston.

"Stop your gaping and tell me about this 'matter you wish to discuss,'" Mrs. Lange ordered.

"Forgive me. Your home is beautiful, Mrs. Lange." Realizing the most direct approach would be the best, Emily continued, "On behalf of the town council, I am here to ask if you would consider teaching my students while I am away next term."

An expression that was almost a smile played on Margaret
Lange's face. "I was wondering if you would have the sense to
ask me." She gestured toward her dining table. "Well, lay off
your things and join me for tea while we scrutinize the
particulars."

Emily removed a notebook from her basket and sat at the
mahogany table. While they sipped tea, Emily reviewed her
educational goals for each grade level. She turned to the next
page, "As you can see, I have detailed information on each
student including their current grade level and their strengths
and weaknesses. Robert, for example, detests writing
assignments, but he will exceed your expectations if you give
him a gentle word of encouragement. Millie needs to sit near
the front, where she will wiggle less and listen more. Jonathan
will need some extra help with his math, but he will rarely ask
for it. Louisa reads far above her grade level; she may need
your guidance to find books that will challenge her. Anna and
Beth sit side-by-side, for they bring out the best in each other."

"You have forgotten that I am the only truly qualified
teacher at this table."

Determined not to back down, Emily replied, "I may not
yet be qualified in your sense of the word, but I do know my
students, and I care deeply about them and their education.
Sharing this information with you will enable you to teach
them more efficiently and will improve their learning
experience."

The corner of Mrs. Lange's mouth twitched with a smile
that wanted to come. She reached for the notebook and turned
page after page. "Well, you are indeed thorough." Emily
waited patiently while the elder woman read. When she had
finished, she asked, "May I keep this notebook for reference?"

"Certainly."

"You may tell your students that I will begin classes on the
fifth of January."

Emily breathed a sigh of relief and smiled, "Thank you. I will let them know."

Seth was present for the final week of rehearsals for the Christmas program in case he was needed to alter set pieces or repair props. Sitting quietly in the back, he listened to several of the students discussing their family members who would attend. Then he heard Anna's little voice, "I wish my Mama could come." The words were spoken with such sadness. Seth leaned forward to rest his elbow on the back of the pew in front of him and put his chin in his hand. He had to find a way to get Susanna to the program for Anna.

After rehearsal, he waited until he could speak with Emily privately. "Please don't say anything to my children, but may I reserve a spot on the back row near the center aisle in case Susanna can come?"

"Certainly. I'd be happy to save a place closer to the front, if you wish," Emily replied.

"Thank you, but no, the back is better. Anna's part is near the beginning. If Susanna cannot stay, we could easily slip out without disturbing anyone."

Emily nodded in understanding. "I'll prepare a reserved notice so no one else will sit there."

"Thank you again." Seth turned and walked to meet his children standing near the door. "Are you ready to head home?" The trio crowded around him, and they departed.

That night after the children were asleep, Seth divulged his entire plan to Susanna. "Uncle Caleb will let me borrow his buggy. I'll have it hitched and ready before I leave work. Since the kids need to be at the school early, I'll drop them off and swing by the livery for the buggy. Then I'll come pick you up. Literally." He smiled mischievously. "We'll have a seat reserved on the back row so we won't need to be there until just before the program starts, and we can leave quietly if you need to return home and lie down. What do you think?"

"You have thought of every detail. I'm sorry my illness is creating so much trouble for you, but I'm happy we can do this for Anna. Louisa and Jonathan will be pleasantly surprised, too."

"I wouldn't mind carrying you all the way to the school, but I figured you wouldn't want that much attention." Seth winked at his wife.

Susanna laughed softly, "You are right about that."

"Which dress will you want to wear?"

"My dark green one."

He found a green dress and held it up. "This one?" At Susanna's nod, he added, "I'll hang it on the line tonight so it will be fresh for tomorrow."

The night of the Christmas program arrived, and the church building was full with some of the audience standing along the back wall. About five minutes before the program began, Seth entered carrying Susanna. Fortunately, everyone had honored the reserved sign on the back pew.

When Anna stepped forward to say her line and join the choir of angels, she spotted her mama. Her sad expression transformed into a beaming smile. She even remembered to say her line loudly enough for her mama to hear. When Anna's part was finished, Susanna looked up at Seth, who met her gaze, and they smiled. She rested her head on her husband's shoulder.

Seth crinkled his brow and asked softly, "Do you need to leave?"

Susanna shook her head. She did not want to miss even a moment.

Susanna found Jonathan in the group of shepherds and watched Louisa, as Mary, hold baby Jesus for the shepherds and wise men to see.

Other than a couple of shepherds missing their cue and a wise man tripping over his long tunic while walking down the aisle, the program was a success. During the closing prayer, Seth gathered Susanna in his arms and carried her out.

Several people came up afterwards to congratulate Mrs. Lange, and Emily saw something she had never seen before. Margaret Lange smiled.

CHAPTER 18

A New Home

T he day after Christmas dawned with sunshine glistening off the thin layer of snow on the ground. Julie was in awe of the beautiful morning as she dropped Matthew off at Emma's and rode Cinnamon to the Kendricks' home to visit Emily and help her pack. Laura opened the parsonage door, "Julie, I'm glad you're here. Emily is upstairs going crazy. I'm not sure anything has stayed packed in the trunk for more than five minutes."

Julie lifted the hem of her skirt and ascended the stairs. Laura was right. Emily, usually so poised and neat and organized, looked almost panicked. There were small piles of clothing and books all over the bed, desk, and floor, but the trunk was nearly empty. Julie removed her coat and winter scarf and was hard-pressed to find anywhere to lay them.

"Oh, Julie, I have so much to do. How will I ever be ready in time?"

Julie carefully stepped over piles to where Emily was standing and put her hands on Emily's upper arms. "Take a breath and relax. You will be ready in time. You still have a week." She pulled her friend in for a hug. "I remember feeling just like you do before I left Emma's for the blind school. Remember, you don't have to pack for six months. You'll be able to do laundry, and if you run out of something, you can replenish in Kansas City."

"Now, let's think about your trunk. Any books or heavy items need to go in first." Julie cleared a place in front of the trunk and knelt down. Emily handed her two books and her Bible; Julie packed the books and said, "Lay your Bible on the desk. You will want to keep it with you, so we'll put it in your valise." Emily carefully laid her Bible on top of the white box that held her journal.

"What toiletry items are you taking?" Emily reached for the appropriate pile and gave the items to Julie, who placed each carefully like puzzle pieces. "The key is to fill in all available space so things don't shift and break."

"What's next?" Emily inquired.

"Clothes. Choose a nightgown, seven dresses, two Sunday dresses, seven undergarments, and stockings. Your Sunday shoes can go in the night before, and you'll be wearing your everyday shoes." In no time at all, the trunk was packed, the remaining piles were put away, and the two friends sat on the edge of the bed.

"Julie, what was I thinking when I agreed to this?"

"I know you're overwhelmed. The preparation is the worst part. Once you get there, you will get unpacked and settled; then you'll be too busy to notice the days passing. Before you know it, you'll be studying for your certification exam and packing to come home."

Laura peeked around the doorway and exclaimed, "Julie, you are a miracle worker! I thought I was going to have to sleep on the sofa downstairs until next week."

To Julie, Emily said, "You see, she's not going to miss me at all."

"Are you kidding? Do you know how much work you do around here? How will I get everything done without you?"

"You will delegate, like you always do. Something I've never been good at. Besides, you should get used to it. Someday, I'll . . ." All three in the room heard the unspoken words "marry James." ". . . move away. Well, anyway, Julie, what else do I need to do before I leave?"

Laura leaned against the doorpost and folded her arms. Reading Emily's heart, Julie reminded her, "James misses you as much as you miss him. Though I think all the brothers will be counting the days until your return."

"Why do you say that?" Laura asked.

"After the church social, James stayed up all night chopping wood."

With compassion in her voice, Emily repeated, "All night?"

Julie nodded. "Emma said his hands were bleeding by the next morning." Tears were brimming in Emily's eyes. "None of the brothers in the bunkhouse or Emma got any sleep, and my, were the boys grumpy the next day. Jacob was so angry he threatened to move the chopping block to the other side of the south pasture if James ever did that again."

"Is Jacob all right?" Laura asked. "He seemed so surly at the social."

"Truthfully, I don't know what is wrong, but something definitely is," Julie replied. "Emma used the situation with James to remind him that the attitude of one member of the family affects all of them."

"I'm sorry they all had to suffer for James' actions, but somehow I am comforted knowing he is hurting as much as I am."

Laura interjected, "Why don't you just ask Dad to change his mind?"

Emily's look implied she would never consider such a thing. "I would never want to cause a rift between me and Dad."

When Laura started to refute her reasoning, Emily held up a hand, "God will change Dad's heart in His time."

"What if he doesn't?" Laura countered.

"He will," Emily responded with a certainty that surprised even Laura.

A week later, on the second day of January, Julie and Luke stood with the Kendrick family as the morning stagecoach pulled in front of the general store. After the mail bags were exchanged and the passengers disembarked, Pastor Kendrick loaded Emily's trunk onto the back of the coach. Emily had spotted Trigger tethered in front of the telegraph office, but she didn't see James anywhere. Surely, he would come. With many tears, Emily hugged every member of her family, then hugged Julie with a desperation only she understood. Julie whispered, "Look behind me at the corner of the store." Emily lifted her eyes to see James standing there. When their eyes met, he respectfully touched the brim of his hat and nodded to her. Emily worked to engrave this scene in her mind, for she would not see him again for six months.

While still clinging to Julie, her dad touched her shoulder. "Sweetheart, the coach is ready to leave." She released Julie, and her dad offered his hand to help her climb aboard the stage. Using another piece of advice from Julie, she sat so she would be facing forward when the coach started moving. Emily waved her gloved hand at those standing near, but as the coach wheels began to move, her gaze returned to the one she loved most, and she kept her eyes fixed upon him until the coach turned out of sight.

Two days later, when the coach stopped in Kansas City, an exhausted Emily was greeted by Pastor and Mrs. Witherspoon. Deborah Witherspoon was kind and motherly, just what Emily needed in that moment. She covered Emily's hand with both of her own. "Come, child, let's get you home and settled. After dinner and a cup of hot cocoa, you can turn in early for a good night's rest."

"Thank you, Mrs. Witherspoon. That sounds lovely."

Pastor Witherspoon pointed out the teachers' institute on their ride from the station. It was a two-story stately brick building with mullioned windows surrounded by carved stone. The grounds were extensive. His wife interjected, "The gardens there are just breathtaking in the spring." Emily caught herself gaping at the sight, and closed her mouth to avoid being impolite.

Their home was a modest three-bedroom dwelling on a small lot. The street in front of the house was lined with trees currently bare, but Emily could imagine this lane once the trees sprouted their leaves, and she was mesmerized.

After the three alighted from the carriage and entered the home, the matron showed Emily to her room. When she stood in the doorway, the wrought-iron bed with a sage green spread was against the wall facing her. To her right was a window overlooking the street with a small writing table and chair before it. Wispy ivory curtains framed the window, giving the spot a very inviting feel. On the left wall was a wardrobe with a small mirror on the wall beside it.

"Do you like it?" Mrs. Witherspoon inquired.

"Oh, yes. This is just perfect," Emily replied.

Pastor Witherspoon entered and set her trunk at the foot of

the bed, and his wife instructed, "Take your time unpacking, my dear. There is a bath in the room next door, if you would like to use it. Dinner will be at six o'clock."

"Thank you so much. You are most kind."

When the door had clicked softly closed, Emily set her valise on the bed and opened it. Gingerly, she removed a rectangular box. When she had lifted the lid, she carefully removed her wax-dipped daffodil and a small narrow-stemmed vase and set them on the writing desk. Now the room felt like home.

Emily took Mrs. Witherspoon's offer of a bath, and she arrived at dinner feeling clean and refreshed. She entreated her hostess, "Please allow me to be of help to you while I'm here. I am so accustomed to caring for the needs of an entire household, I would miss it if you refused."

"Very well, my dear, though you needn't feel obligated. You will have much studying to do." To her husband, she remarked, "This will be like having our daughter Sally home again."

The next day, classes began, and Emily found herself lost among a sea of people her own age. Thankfully, she found her way to her classes without too much difficulty. The days began to blur one into another, just as Julie had predicted.

On the Lord's Day, Emily donned her Sunday dress and accompanied her host couple to the church they attended. Pastor Witherspoon had retired, and his son preached in his former pulpit. The service itself felt more formal than what she was accustomed to, but those around her greeted her warmly, and the preacher's message resonated in her heart. After the service, Mrs. Witherspoon introduced Emily to her grandson. "This is John Witherspoon, named after his grandfather, you know. He's also attending classes at the institute. I have invited him over for dinner, for I thought you might have a lot in common to discuss."

The young man standing before her reminded her of

Josiah. He stood only a few inches taller than Emily with brown, wavy hair and hazel eyes, though he was missing Josiah's dimples. His clothing was the highest fashion of the day. Bowing toward her formally, he said simply, "How do you do?"

Emily felt compelled to curtsy in response, "Very well, thank you."

"Well, come along. The two of you can get better acquainted at dinner." Mrs. Witherspoon guided Emily away. "He's a fine young man. We're very proud of him."

Having the distinct feeling that Deborah Witherspoon was trying her hand at matchmaking, Emily wished to delicately make her position clear. "Thank you for making me feel so welcome, but I must tell you that I have a young man waiting for me at home."

"Oh, your father said you weren't courting anyone," intoned Mrs. Witherspoon.

"I have been courting a young man for four years."

"But you're not courting now?"

"No, not at the moment," Emily answered honestly.

A smile returned to Mrs. Witherspoon's round face. "Well, then, perhaps a new friend is just the thing for you."

John Witherspoon was much more casual at the dinner table. "Which courses are you taking?" Emily listed her classes. "I'm taking several of the same ones. Perhaps we could study together on occasion."

"What are your plans after graduation?" Emily was attempting to make polite conversation.

"My dream would be to perform concerts on either the pianoforte or the cello, but my 'responsible and stable' plan is to further my education and teach music to aspiring musicians."

"My mother taught me to play the piano when I was

young, and it is still one of my favorite pastimes," Emily admitted.

"You both enjoy both teaching and music. See, I knew you two would find some common ground," Mrs. Witherspoon asserted. On the other end of the table, Pastor Witherspoon cleared his throat as a signal to his wife not to interfere.

After dinner, Emily cleared the table and prepared to wash dishes, glad for the excuse to leave the room. To her chagrin, John appeared at her right hand. "May I dry the dishes for you?"

Trying to be polite, Emily answered, "Yes, that would be fine."

John lowered his voice now that he was out of earshot. "Please forgive Grandmother. She has been, shall we say, 'encouraging me' to find a lovely young lady worthy of my courtship. You are a lovely young lady, and I'm delighted that we have some similar interests, but I sense that your courtship might be worthy of someone else."

Looking up from the sudsy water, she affirmed his suspicions and pleaded for him to understand. "Please do not think me rude. There is a young man that I love with my whole heart waiting for me in Prairie Hills. It is true that he and I are not courting at the moment, but that was a decision not made by either of us."

"Can you tell me what happened?"

Yearning for a listening ear, Emily briefly explained their situation, then added, "James is kind, thoughtful, and giving. He loves his Savior above all. He's a diligent worker; in fact, he's the foreman of the largest ranch in our area. Even as a grown man, he is very respectful to his mama and loyal to his brothers."

"And I'm going to guess he's handsome, too?"

Emily blushed, "Yes, he is very handsome."

"I am happy for you. I'll tell you a secret. For the next few years, I want to devote myself to my studies. Courting a lady means preparing for marriage, and it wouldn't be fair to her when my priorities are elsewhere. So, for the sake of amiability, could you and I be friends? Grandmother would be happy, and it seems both of us could use a friend right now. What do you say?"

"Just to be clear, you do understand that my intentions are to return to Prairie Hills and marry James, right? We would only be friends?"

John suggested, "Think of me as a brother, if you wish."

"You actually remind me of James' brother Josiah."

"Excellent. Our plan is settled then." He extended his hand, and Emily shook it with her soapy one, and they laughed. Their conversation was very relaxed and included many topics from family to music to school.

From the dining room, Deborah Witherspoon smiled at her husband. "See, I told you they would make a handsome couple."

John would meet Emily a couple of times during the day and carry her books between classes. Occasionally, he would come over to his grandparents' home before a big test and study with Emily at the dining table. Their friendship was amiable, nothing more.

One day, Emily was walking to her first class of the day and spotted colorful blooms making their spring appearance and was surprised to realize that the end of March was upon them. The thought warmed her heart, *"I'm halfway home."*

When John met her after her second class, he had a surprise for her. "Now that we're halfway through the term, I thought we should celebrate." He reached into his pocket, withdrew two tickets, and showed them to Emily.

She read the inscription and stifled a squeal, "The Symphony? I've always dreamed of hearing a symphony orchestra in person."

John was thrilled at her reaction, "Now your dream is coming true. Does that mean you will allow me to escort you?"

"Yes!"

He carefully inquired, "Forgive my impertinence, but am I correct in assuming you do not have a formal gown?"

Emily's excitement deflated instantly, "No, I don't. There is no need for a formal gown in Prairie Hills."

"Do you trust me?"

Hesitating, she crinkled her brow and answered, "I think so."

"There's a vote of confidence," John laughed. "A delivery will arrive for you tomorrow."

The next afternoon, Mrs. Witherspoon was in a tizzy when Emily arrived home from the institute. "Emily, a box was dropped off for you. I laid it on your bed." She couldn't contain her excitement. "It's from John."

Emily wordlessly strolled to her room and set her books on the writing table. The referenced box was rather large. She looked up to see her hostess in the doorway, about to burst with anticipation. Emily's own response was curiosity as she snipped the twine, unwrapped the brown paper, and lifted the lid of the white box within.

Before her lay a gown made of emerald green satin. She reached for the shoulders of the dress and lifted it. Mrs. Witherspoon gasped, and with good reason; this was the most beautiful dress she had ever seen. The bodice was fitted with a sweetheart neckline bordered with intricate lace of the same color and tapered three-quarter sleeves also hemmed in the same lace. The A-line skirt was full, covered with a layer of organza, dyed the same shade of green. Emily was speechless.

"You must try it on," Mrs. Witherspoon persisted.

Shaking her head slowly, Emily disagreed, "No, this dress must have been very expensive; I cannot accept it."

"That's just silly. John's father is a wealthy and influential businessman here in Kansas City. The women in his family have closets full of gowns, though this is the prettiest one I've seen. Even his cousins, the pastor's daughters, own gowns." She insisted again, "Try it on. Please."

When Emily finally nodded and her hostess closed the door, she changed into the gown. When the folds of the satin skirt fell limply, she peeked again into the box and discovered a crinoline underskirt and low pump shoes of satin dyed to match. After slipping on both of these additions, she opened her door to find Mrs. Witherspoon patiently waiting.

The older woman clasped her hands together and rested them on her chin. "Emily, I have no words. Come." She led Emily into her bedroom, where there stood a long mirror. Emily just stared in wonder, barely recognizing the woman in the reflection.

"The dress is beautiful," Emily breathed softly.

"You make the dress beautiful, my dear," assured Mrs. Witherspoon. "Do not give another thought to the cost, for suitors here often give such gifts."

Emily had nearly forgotten that John's grandmother thought of them as more than friends. As she admired the new gown, she reminded herself that she needed it for the concert; she could always return the gown to him afterwards. Satisfied with that line of thought, she returned to her room to change and hang the gown in the wardrobe.

The following morning, John was waiting for her as usual after her second class. He reached for her books and asked, "Did you get my delivery?"

"Yes, I did. The gown is beyond beautiful, and it fits perfectly. How did you know the size?"

"I figured you were about the same size as my sister. I placed an order at her dressmaker's two weeks ago and told her to use my sister's measurements."

"Two weeks ago? You only asked me to the concert two days ago."

"Yes. It was a risk, I'll admit; but if I had waited until I had procured the tickets, there wouldn't have been time to make the dress."

"What would you have done if I had said 'no'?"

"Given the dress to my sister for her birthday or something."

Hearing him say the dress could have been a gift to his sister was oddly comforting. So, he was still thinking of himself as a brother rather than a suitor. Her concerns about Mrs. Witherspoon's comment vanished.

"May I pick you up tomorrow evening at seven?" John asked.

"Yes, I will be ready."

CHAPTER 19
The Symphony

At precisely seven o'clock, a knock sounded on the front door. Emily was sitting at her writing desk. She laid down her pen and wafted her hand over her journal page to keep the ink from smudging. Mrs. Witherspoon appeared in her doorway and exclaimed, "The image of you sitting there is one that should be painted. Emily, your young man is here."

"Thank you." Emily reached up to check the pins in her hair one more time, rose to her feet, and moved smoothly toward the front door, the folds of soft satin rustling as she glided across the floor. John looked very debonair standing there in his tuxedo.

When John first saw her coming toward him, he was struck dumb. The beauty of this young woman before him shone from the inside out, and this gown made her simply radiant. Emily was so much more beautiful than the stuffy and conceited women his station typically tried to pair him with. Finally recovering, he extended a tussie-mussie of yellow roses to his companion. Rather than the traditional paper cone, however, the stems were wrapped in green satin ribbon. "These are for you, My Lady."

Emily smiled and reached for the roses, lifting them to her nose to inhale the sweet fragrance. "Thank you. Allow me to put these in water." As she turned, she was suddenly overcome with the memory of sweet wildflowers and Gerbera daisies. Though the roses were lovely, she personally preferred the latter, more so because of their giver rather than the flowers themselves. Nonetheless, she was grateful for these roses and the friendship she shared with this young man.

John opened the stole he held in his other hand. At Emily's questioning look, he explained, "I borrowed this from Kay, my sister. The night air is quite cold." She allowed him to drape the stole around her shoulders. He offered his arm, "Shall we?"

Outside, an open, horse-drawn carriage was waiting for them, the driver sitting with rigid posture, having both reins and a crop in hand. John lifted her hand from his arm and held it for support as she climbed aboard. Once they were both seated, he spread a thick blanket over both of them for warmth. "All right, kind sir, we are ready." At John's cue, the driver pulled away.

John looked at Emily, "Did you know there is a 'language of flowers'?"

"No, I did not."

"Neither did I, but my sister informed me that floriography should be an intrinsic part of my education. Every kind and color of flower has a meaning, apparently. Having said that, you may be wondering what yellow roses represent. They stand for friendship, and I am deeply grateful to have you as my friend."

"I am also thankful for your friendship. Without it, I would have been homesick and lonely beyond remedy."

A few moments later, the carriage stopped in front of the theater, brightly lit with gas lanterns. The façade was made of white stone with marble steps leading to the front portico, held by twenty-foot columns. John stepped down and made his way around the back of the carriage to her, extending his hand to help her down. She was too enraptured to notice.

With merriment in his voice, John instructed, "Miss, you have to disembark the carriage in order to see the symphony."

"Oh, I'm sorry." She held her hand to him and stepped down.

"No need for an apology. Looking at your face, I was transported back to my first time here. My reaction was quite similar." He gently rested her hand on his arm. "Be careful of the stairs. They can get quite slippery in dress shoes."

Thankful for his insight, Emily lifted the hem of her skirt a couple inches above the ground and stepped very cautiously. The doors that offered entrance into the theater were at least eight feet tall. Emily had the amusing thought that Tim would appreciate not having to bend down for this doorway.

Inside, the floor was covered in regal red carpeting, and the gas-lit chandeliers emitted a scintillating light. The effect was magical.

John stopped at the cloak room to check Emily's stole, then led her to the secondary entrance doors to present their tickets and receive performance programs. Their seats were in the middle section, ten rows up from the stage. "In my experience, these are the best seats in the house. We are high enough to see every musician, but close enough to literally feel the music." Pointing to the program, he continued, "Tonight will feature Bach, my favorite musician from the Baroque era. Just after the intermission, the principal cellist will be performing the best-written cello music: Bach's 'Cello Suite Number 1'."

Hearing his description, Emily realized, "I have never heard you play the cello."

"And I have never heard you play the piano. We should rectify both sometime soon."

Feeling somewhat embarrassed, Emily replied, "You would be disappointed. I play hymns, not concertos."

John assured her, "I guarantee that I will not be disappointed."

Emily studied her surroundings, trying to memorize them in order to describe them in detail in her journal. Her eyes moved to the people around her, especially the ladies, dressed in elegant gowns and dripping with jewelry.

Her friend seemed to read her thoughts. "These ladies around us must be envious; you are lovely through and through. I'm sitting next to the most beautiful lady in the room."

Emily looked a bit skeptical, but kept her peace. Soon, the musicians came to the stage and began to tune, and all of Emily's attention was focused upon them. When the music began, Emily mused, *"This must be what music in Heaven will sound like."* She could feel every crescendo and decrescendo. The melodies were expertly performed and inwardly moving. After the intermission, the cellist came centerstage and enraptured Emily's soul with the excerpt from Bach's 'Cello Suite.'

All too soon, the concert ended, thunderous applause erupting from the audience. While waiting for those around them to exit, John inquired, "Did you enjoy the cello solo?"

"Honestly, I enjoyed every note tonight; but, yes, the Cello Suite was beautiful."

"If you would honor me with your presence at my recital in June, I will play the prelude for you."

"As long as it is before I travel home on the twenty-fourth, I would be happy to attend."

John's smile wavered almost imperceptibly, but Emily didn't notice. "My recital is on the sixteenth. Representatives from the Boston Academy of Music will also be in attendance. Their conservatory focuses mostly on vocal repertoire, but they encourage all musical talent. I am hoping to gain entrance there to further my training in musical education after I graduate from the institute."

Emily spoke confidently, "They will accept you. I have no doubt."

"You sound very certain for someone who has never heard me play."

"Remember, you said you would rectify that soon."

"Indeed."

Emily thanked John again for the wonderful evening and returned the stole when he delivered her to his grandparents' door. She briefly told Pastor and Mrs. Witherspoon about the delightful evening before retiring to her room. After changing into her nightdress, she carefully folded her evening's attire into the box from which it came, having every intention of returning the dress to John the next time he came over to study.

Sitting at her writing desk, she reopened her journal and imagined James sitting in front of her. With painstaking detail, she described everything from her evening from her gown to the theater to the concert itself. "The music was a glimpse of Heaven," she wrote, "but it was part of a world where I do not belong. My heart longs for a waltz with you in the Wilsons' barn."

After her journal entry, Emily pulled two pieces of paper from the drawer and began a letter to Julie. The letters she had received from her friend were treasured words from home. Emily was unaware that those letters had been carefully crafted to omit what James did not want her to know. She described the events of the last few weeks, unwittingly mentioning her friend John several times. In closing, she commented, "We have just finished our midterm examinations, so I am now officially halfway home. My heart cannot wait. Your Friend, Emily."

She addressed the envelope and leaned it against the vase holding her precious yellow flower, purposing to mail it on the morrow.

A week passed before John came to his grandparents to study with Emily. When they felt sufficiently prepared for their test, Emily excused herself, returning with the box. "What is this?" John asked.

"Here is the gown you lent me for the concert."

His expression showed the hurt he felt. "The gown was not lent to you; it was a gift. Besides, you will need to wear it to my recital, remember?"

She had not meant to hurt her friend. "Oh, I did not realize the recital would require formal attire." Drawing the box to her chest, she spoke softly and sincerely, "Thank you for the gown."

The days blurred into weeks. Emily had accompanied John's grandparents to his home for the family celebration of his birthday. She had been overcome with the opulence around her juxtaposed with his family's simple warm welcome. After dessert, John led Emily into the music room, where he played his cello for his audience of one. She was impressed, though not surprised, by his exemplary performance.

When he finished, he asked if she would play the piano. "You'll be disappointed, for I haven't played in several months."

"Music never leaves you. Please play for me."

Emily lowered herself reverently onto the bench, for she

had never before fingered the keys of a grand piano. The music started slowly with a few stumbles here and there, but soon the strains of "How Great Thou Art" rose with smooth arpeggios to the majestic proclamation of God's greatness. As the last note faded away, John remarked in awe, "If that doesn't make your heart want to worship, nothing will."

By the end of the evening, John and Emily were seated side-by-side at the piano, attempting to sight-read duets together. The music seemed to have more laughter than notes, as they would mess up and start again. When Emily departed with his grandparents, he finally admitted to himself that he was really going to miss her when she went home.

The week of final examinations had come. Emily studied and fretted and studied more. One test score at a time was posted with excellent marks. By Friday evening, she was exhausted but happy. Her course exams were over, and tonight was John's recital. In one week, she would take her teachers' certification exam and travel home. Emily slipped into her formal gown, noticing that it no longer felt so unfamiliar. Since John had to be at the hall early to prepare, she would be riding with his grandparents.

Mrs. Witherspoon doted on her. "My dear, you do look lovely. Tonight is the culmination of many years of practice. Only the best musicians are offered a recital." Emily was excited for John and thankful the recital was scheduled before her departure home.

The recital hall seated about three hundred, but the front row had been reserved for Emily and the Witherspoon family. At the appointed time, John entered the stage to polite applause and performed a full repertoire. For his last piece, the pianist excused himself, and John looked at Emily right before he began the lovely melody of the prelude to Bach's "Cello Suite Number 1" as promised.

The room roared with applause, and the audience congratulated him with a standing ovation, but John's attention was focused only on one young lady. The members of the admissions board from the Boston Academy of Music met him after the recital and offered him an acceptance pending the submission of his final grades and certification from the institute. This had been his goal. Why wasn't he more pleased?

His family surrounded him with heartfelt congratulations. When they turned to go, he asked his grandparents if he could escort Emily home. His grandmother, of course, was quick to offer her approval. John shook the hand of his pianist and thanked him for being his accompanist before he reached for his cello and returned it and his wood bow to its padded case.

With his cello in one hand, he offered his other arm to Emily. "Walk with me." She rested her hand on his arm as he guided her from the recital hall and into the flower garden. When they reached the fountain in the center of the garden, John set down his cello case and turned toward Emily. "You are planning to leave next week?" Emily nodded. John searched her blue eyes and pleaded, "Please don't go." Emily's face revealed her shock. "You have become the best friend I have ever had. Somewhere along the way, I fell in love with you. I want to spend the rest of my life with you, making music together."

Emily spluttered, "But you were accepted to the Boston Academy of Music. That has been your dream."

"Dreams can change. I would turn them down in an instant if you would accept me and become my wife." He knelt down on one knee and pulled a ring from his vest pocket. "Please say 'yes'."

Tears started streaming down Emily's face. "John, if I have given you a false impression of my affection for you, I am so sorry. I cherish our friendship. I never meant to hurt you." She turned and ran as quickly as she could in her dress shoes toward his grandparents' home. At the edge of the garden, she stopped to remove her shoes. She did not stop again until she was safely in her room, lying face down on her bed, sobbing into her pillow.

John was still kneeling next to his cello case, clutching the ring in his hand, realizing that his dream had just slipped away.

For the next week, Emily remained secluded in her room, coming out only for preparing meals. She would study until her brain felt full, then take a short packing break before diving into her studies again. On Thursday night, Emily closed all of her books for the last time and resolved to get a good night's rest. Between her emotions and her concern about the examination, she tossed and turned for hours before succumbing to sleep.

Whispering a prayer for mental clarity, Emily sat in her assigned place, staring straight ahead at the chalkboard lest her eyes might find John in the room. Once the signal was given, she gave her full attention to the test and was pleased that she felt confident of her answers. When the students were dismissed, she rose and quickly exited the room.

Later that afternoon, Mrs. Witherspoon knocked on her bedroom door. "Emily, John is here to see you."

Pleading with her to understand, Emily responded, "I just cannot see him. Please tell him that I am busy packing."

"Emily, please," her hostess entreated.

Emily could not very well reward her hostess' sweet hospitality with a refusal, so she rose slowly and walked to the foyer. "John, I . . ."

John held up a hand to stop her. "Please, let me speak. Let me congratulate you for graduating with honors and having a certification exam score near the top of our class. More importantly, please forgive me for surprising you with my proposal last week. You are the most wonderful woman I have ever met. Please know that I was not trying to be deceitful. I never meant to fall in love, but I did. My broken heart is no one's fault but my own. I hope James knows how blessed he is to have your heart."

Not knowing what to say, Emily asked the only think that came to mind. "Do you wish to have the gown back now?"

Shaking his head, he replied earnestly, "No. Keep it. Remember me." He handed her an envelope with a long-stemmed red rose tied to it.

"What does the red rose mean?"

He spoke softly, "I think you already know. Good-bye, Emily." His eyes glistened with unshed tears as he stepped over the threshold and closed the door behind him.

Three days later, Emily alighted from the stagecoach in front of the general store in Prairie Hills and wept tears of joy as she hugged every member of her family, saving Julie for last. Emily looked up at the corner of the general store, expecting to see James where he had been standing when she left in January, but he wasn't there. She whispered to her friend, "Did James come?"

"No," Julie admitted.

The sparkle in Emily's eyes vanished and sudden feeling of dread filled her heart. "Why? Is he all right?"

"Physically, he's fine. It's a rather long story. A lot has happened since you left."

Emily requested, "Please, come and help me unpack." The two friends walked silently arm in arm while Robert and her dad carried her trunk down the street and up the stairs, setting it precisely where it had been six months ago. When the men had left the room and descended the stairs, Emily implored, "Tell me the story from the beginning."

Julie sat quietly on the edge of the bed for a moment, deciding how she would begin. Emily was poised beside her, ready to hang on every word, a nagging foreboding feeling in the pit of her stomach. Finally, Julie spoke, "The morning you left, James watched you until the coach was out of sight. He stood there a moment too long, for your dad spotted him. He marched right up the steps and sternly admonished James for being there at all. James gritted his teeth and said not a word. When your dad was finished, James descended from the boardwalk and stormed to Trigger, mounted, and rode away. Your dad was quite miffed."

"That was only the beginning of trouble . . ."

CHAPTER 20
The Blizzard

J ames pushed Trigger for speed. He needed to get home. He needed to go to the Hill and talk to God. After tethering Trigger to the hitching post in front of the barn, James ran up toward the bench on the Hill. He wanted so badly to pray, but no words would come. Inside him was a turmoil of anger and hurt and resentment and loneliness – a turmoil he wanted to get rid of before it rooted in bitterness. His lungs burned from the run in the cold air, but he didn't notice. He paced, and shivered, and paced some more. Finally, he let out a loud cry of anger and anguish. The tension subsided, but only slightly. "Lord, I want to love and serve You, but why are You making my life so hard?" He was reminded of several of the Psalms when David asked God the same question, but he couldn't get his heart to an attitude of praise like David was apt to do.

The following week, the gray clouds that had been dusting snow from time to time since November began to release the fury of winter snow. The emergency ropes had already been hung between the house and the bunkhouse and the barn in case of sudden blizzard. Between storms, the brothers would regularly check on the herd and ensure they had enough hay.

One winter morning, Julie and Matthew came up to the ranch house to do laundry with Emma. By afternoon, the dark ominous clouds rolled in and completely blocked the sun. Within minutes, the snow began to fall in earnest and soon escalated to a blinding blizzard. Emma went to the front window, "That blizzard came out of nowhere." With a note of worry in her voice, she whispered, "I hope the boys all made it back to the barn."

Buck's father had died in a blizzard, so from the time he came to live at the ranch, the boys would only travel in pairs once the first snows began. Unfortunately, since his death, there was an odd number of boys, usually leaving James out on his own since he had always paired with Buck.

One by one, the boys arrived on the porch, stomping the snow from their boots before entering the ranch house. Luke was the fourth brother to arrive, and Julie ran to him and hugged him out of sheer relief. Luke commented, "Though we rarely need that connecting rope, I'm glad we had it today." He looked around the room. Only James was missing.

"Has anyone seen James?" Luke asked. "I haven't seen him since we rode out this morning."

Around him, the chorus of "neither have I" turned Julie's relief to one of dread. Luke strode to the fireplace, where the rifle hung above the mantle. "Emma, where's your ammunition?" She was already on her way to him with several boxes of bullets. "Jacob, when I fire, give me a signal every two minutes." Luke wound an extra scarf around his neck and went back out to the porch. He aimed the rifle at an angle high in the air and shot three times before he lowered the gun and looked at Jacob through the front window. At his signal, Luke again fired three times. When Luke had been outside for twenty minutes, Tim bundled up and took his place.

Every two minutes, three shots. With every cycle, Emma was closer to tears. She loved all of her boys, but James was her first, and he was the only one who still consistently called her "Mama." He had taken Daniel's place in the running of the ranch when Daniel died, and Emma still depended greatly upon him. She was blessed to have him as her son. Another two minutes, three shots. Finally, just before Josiah was going to bundle up and take his turn with the rifle at the forty-minute mark, there was commotion on the porch.

Tim yelled over the wind, "Open the door!" When Josiah complied, Tim mostly dragged James inside. He was literally covered in snow. If the moment had not been so serious, Julie would have laughed that he looked like a living snowman. Instead, Luke grabbed James' feet while Tim had a firm grip of his torso and they carried him toward the fireplace and laid him down on the floor.

Emma delegated, "Tim, warm some water, but don't get it too hot. Josiah, bring the small bucket from beside the sink. Jacob, grab the stack of washcloths from the linen closet."

Emma was removing James' hat and scarf, so Julie helped Luke gently pull off his boots. James was awake, and pulling the first boot off brought a groan to his lips. Luke took courage, "At least he still has some feeling in his feet." They removed his second boot with the same response. They removed his socks, finding that he had worn three pairs of wool socks on this day. Luke spoke softly to his wife, "That may just be his saving grace."

Luke assessed his brother's feet, while Julie scooted over to remove his gloves and check his fingers. "James, the skin on your toes is freezing cold, but still white rather than shiny and waxy. Your frostbite here is still in the early stage."

"My feet itch," James reported.

"Another good sign. Julie, how do his fingers look?"

"About the same. Cold and white." She reached up to move

the hair that covered the tips of his ears. "Your ears and nose are just red from frostnip. Are they sore?" James nodded.

Luke addressed Tim, "Help me sit him up a little so we can get his coat off and get the warmth of the fire to his chest."

Josiah brought the bucket, and Julie bent James' knees and gently rested his feet on the bottom. Julie double-checked the temperature of the water before Emma poured it over James' feet. When Jacob handed her the washcloths, she handed Luke half of them. They dipped them in the warm water and wrapped James' hands and ears, and Julie folded a warm one and draped it across the tip of his nose.

The water and warm cloths were changed at thirty-minute intervals. By the second change, James was beginning to squirm. "Ooh, my feet and hands feel like pins and needles."

"Good," Luke expressed his pleasure. "That means they are thawing out." After the third set of warm-water wrappings, Luke allowed James to get up and sit on the sofa. Emma brought a thick quilt and wrapped it around him as if he were her little boy.

"Thank you, Mama."

Emma gently admonished him, "Don't ever give me a scare like that again. From now on, you need to stay with two of them." She gestured around the room to his brothers.

James looked around at his family. "Thank you for firing the rifle when you did. I was heading the wrong direction when I heard the shots in regular intervals and followed the sound home."

Now that the entire family was present and accounted for, Emma wanted to keep them safe in the house until the blizzard ended. She only got half her wish, for the barn animals still needed to be cared for. The four non-frostbitten brothers followed the rope lifeline to the barn and back. For Emma's sake, they all agreed to spend the night in the house. Trying to lighten the mood, Emma remarked, "Thanks to James' chopping, we have plenty of firewood." James rolled his eyes, and the others laughed.

Emma gave Luke, Julie, and Matthew the first bedroom upstairs, and the other brothers grabbed a pillow and blanket and found a comfortable spot on the floor near the fireplace. When Emma checked on her boys later, they were all sound asleep, their faces lit by the lingering flicker of the firelight. Her boys were safe; her heart was full.

Three days later, the storm had still not abated. James sat in the chair by the window, with his elbow resting on the back of the chair and his chin in his hand. He stared out into the swirling wall of white snow. "Mama, have we ever had a blizzard like this one?"

Emma replied, "One this intense, yes. One that lasted this long, not that I can remember."

"I'm worried how the cattle are going to fare," James admitted.

Tim piped up, "There's nothing we can do but wait and see."

"Waiting. My best quality," James said sarcastically.

"James, let me see your feet," Luke insisted.

"Not you. Where's your pretty nurse?" James teased.

"Julie, come check James' feet, please."

"Okay, okay, you can check my smelly feet. Julie can check my fingers." Julie walked over, glad that James was feeling better. Luke carefully assessed his brother's feet and toes, pleased that they were warm and pink. Julie found the same condition in the fingers hidden inside his knit gloves.

"Your frostbite is healing better than I would have expected. You may not even have any scarring from it," Luke reported.

"That's something to be thankful for," James responded.

Emma called from the kitchen, "You are someone to be thankful for. I'm glad you're still with us."

Finally, on the fourth day, the blizzard ended as abruptly as it began. By mid-morning, the sun was shining. James gathered his brothers, "All right, boys, let's saddle up and check on our cattle."

Following Emma's admonition, James rode with Luke and Josiah, even though it would take more time to cover the ranch. They soon realized the snow drifts beyond the corral were too high for the horses, and the brothers returned to the barn for their snowshoes. James admitted, "I've got a bad feeling about this." Luke grabbed a shovel.

When they had climbed to the top of the snow, the view was white as far as the eyes could see, but where were the cattle? Luke knew, for he started digging. "Here's one," Luke said dejectedly.

James groaned, "Oh, no." The cattle hadn't left, they were buried in the snow.

Tim rode to the edge of the corral and called to Luke, "There are some cattle over in the north pasture that need you."

Luke handed his shovel to Josiah and started snowshoeing back toward Tim. James followed him. "Tim, grab Jacob and a couple of shovels and help Josiah find our cattle. Try to keep a head count, if you can."

James and Luke moved to the other side of the bunkhouse

where their manmade windbreak and bed of hay seemed to have saved some cattle by keeping them warmer and fed. They huddled together and mooed mournfully. Luke examined them one by one. "Most of them have frostbite on their ears and tails, but that just alters their appearance; it won't be fatal. These two have frostbite on their feet. We need to try to warm them up."

"With warm water?" James asked.

"No. We need to gently warm some towels and wrap their legs with them. Warm air would be better, but building a fire would scare the cattle." Luke moved over to the next cluster of cattle and found a calf that had succumbed to hypothermia. "This is going to be a rough day." All of the cattle seemed to have frostbite in some approximation, but only a handful had their entire legs affected, mostly those with arthritis that had laid down in the snow. Luke knew these animals wouldn't make it very long. Fortunately, almost all of the expectant cows in this pasture were near the windbreak. That was going to be the only good news of the day.

When Matthew was laid down for a nap and Emma was busy making coffee and stew for her family, Julie bundled up and walked over to help Luke. "James, while Julie is helping me, could you get some more hay?"

Julie later returned to the ranch house, but the brothers worked through until dinner. After Luke and James treated the cows in the north pasture as much as they could, they joined their brothers in the south pasture. James inquired soberly, "How many live cattle have you found?"

Tim looked gravely at his older brother, "None."

"None?" James was incredulous. "Not even along the windbreak?" Tim just shook his head.

Looking up into the late afternoon sky, James ordered, "Let's split up and check the windbreaks in the outlying pastures. If any cattle are still alive, that's where they should be." Trudging through the snow on snowshoes took precious time, but it was their only option. Most of the outlying pastures were buried in feet of snow, but the southernmost pasture that bordered and expanse of evergreen trees provided the most shelter from the blowing snow. There they found another cluster of cattle huddled between the windbreak and the fence along the tree line. Several of these were heifers, but there were some expectant cows among them. Luke began his assessments right away. James delegated, "Josiah, stay with Luke. Tim and Jacob, come help me get some hay out here."

They trudged in heavy silence until they reached the comparative warmth of the barn. Tim removed his snowshoes and climbed the ladder to the hayloft. James noticed the grimace on Jacob's face right before he erupted. Jacob threw down the shovel in his hand as hard as he could, creating a clatter that reverberated through the barn. When Jacob turned to face his older brother, James could see the fire in Jacob's eyes as he seethed with anger.

Tim peered over the edge of the hayloft and saw Jacob and James remove their gloves and carefully unbuckle their snowshoes without ever taking their eyes off each other. *"Here it comes,"* he thought.

Jacob confronted James. When his face was mere inches from his brother's, he screamed, "How are you not angry?"

With a forced calm, James replied, "Angry about what?"

"Angry about what?" Jacob yelled. "We invested years of hard work. For what? Our herd lies dead in the snow."

"God never promises that hard times won't come, just that He will be there with us when they do."

Jacob continued his tirade, "God? God doesn't care about us, and neither do you." In one smooth motion, he threw the first punch toward his brother's jaw. James was ready for him, for he blocked the punch and landed his right fist in Jacob's gut. The punches flew for several minutes, but James had a distinct advantage, for he was both taller and stronger than his brother. Jacob, however, had more fighting experience from his days protecting Josiah from bullies at their first orphanage.

Jacob's uppercut connected with James' jaw just as James' left hook reached his brother's nose with a crunch and a gush of blood. Jacob's surprise gave James the opportunity he needed to pummel a series of punches into Jacob's gut until he doubled over and crumpled to the floor. With their chests still heaving from the fight, the older brother asked, "Are you done yet?" Jacob finally admitted his defeat, and James tossed him an old rag to wipe his bloody face.

James lifted his eyes to the hayloft as he rubbed his jaw, "Tim, throw down three bales of hay."

An hour after they departed, the trio arrived at the seventh pasture windbreak, each carrying one bale of hay. Because their faces were wrapped in scarves against the blowing wind, their brothers did not notice anything amiss. Luke and Josiah took the bales of hay and began spreading them on the ground while Luke gave his report to James. "Like the cluster in the north pasture, all of these cattle have at least some frostbite, but only one has frozen legs. She's one of the expectant cows, but her calf is too young to deliver early. We're going to lose both of them."

Knowing they had done all they could for one day, the five brothers trudged back to the barn together. James approached Luke as they walked, "When we get to the barn, you're going to need to straighten Jacob's nose."

Luke raised his eyebrows, "What happened?"

"Just helping Jacob with an attitude adjustment."

Once their snowshoes were removed, Luke found Jacob. "All right, let's see it."

"What?" Jacob asked evasively.

"Your broken nose." Josiah heard Luke's words and looked at his brother. Jacob unwound his scarf to reveal a black eye and a bruised nose bent at an unfamiliar angle. "Yep, it's broken all right. Have a seat."

"Why?"

"Unless you want a crooked nose for the rest of your life, I need to straighten it now. Have a seat," he repeated. Luke ungloved his hands and gently placed the sides of his thumbs against Jacob's nose. "Sit on your hands. This is going to hurt." As soon as Jacob complied, Luke pressed hard against the bone and cartilage until it moved back into alignment.

The brothers moved to finish up the evening barn chores and walked across to the ranch house. As they entered one by one, Emma saw the pain in their eyes and did not need to ask the severity of what they had found. "Take off your winter things and come warm up by the fire and get something warm to eat and drink." When James removed his scarf, she noticed his bruised jaw, but he met her gaze and shook his head in a silent plea for her not to ask. One look to his younger brother behind him answered her question. Jacob had obviously borne the brunt of their fight.

The men were exhausted, both mentally and physically, and all but collapsed into the sofa and onto the floor around the fireplace. Julie passed out handled cups and poured coffee. Emily followed behind with bowls of steaming beef stew. Other than a few muttered thank yous, the boys did not say a single word.

When they had finished eating and the ladies had collected the dishes, Emma came up behind James where he was sitting on the sofa and placed a hand on his shoulder. In a whisper, she asked, "How bad is it?"

James took a deep breath and exhaled through pursed lips before he responded, "Five of the seven pastures are completely buried in snow drifts to the top of the windbreaks. We have only found live cattle in the north pasture and the seventh pasture. Our headcount currently stands at fifty-two, but Luke says we may lose a few of those to severe frostbite."

Emma's face turned pale, "Fifty-two? Out of five hundred?" She paused to let the shock of the number sink in. "Were there any bulls among the fifty-two?"

"No." James informed her, "We will dig along the windbreaks of the other pastures tomorrow, but I'm not hopeful that we will find any more cattle alive."

Julie sat down on the floor next to Luke and reached for his hand. She held it gently in hers and laid her head on his shoulder, quietly communicating her love and concern.

The expedition the next day confirmed James' prediction. Every frozen bovine they found seemed to take a bigger toll on the ones digging. They lost two frostbitten cows from the north pasture and one from the seventh pasture, bringing the cattle headcount to forty-nine.

The winter seemed to have expended all of its snow in one fell swoop, for in the weeks following, only light flurries dusted the landscape from time to time. As the snow melted, more and more of the ranch's buried herd was exposed, until the cattle were all accounted for.

One afternoon, a lone rider entered the ranch. Seth's horse struggled walking in the deep snow, but Seth did not push him. Eventually, he arrived at the hitching post near the barn, relieved to see the area between the house, bunkhouse, and barn shoveled to a shallow ground covering. Here was at least some sign of life. He walked into the barn and called, "Hello! Anybody here?" There was no response. He walked over to the bunkhouse, but his knock received no reply. He was heading over to the ranch house when he spotted three heavily-garbed men coming toward the barn and went over to meet them.

Tim, Jacob, and Josiah were removing their snowshoes as Seth approached and addressed Tim, "Is everyone all right?"

Tim answered wearily, "The people, yes; the cattle, not so much."

"Where is James?" Seth inquired.

"He and Luke are still in the seventh pasture bedding the cattle there."

Seth laid a hand on Tim's shoulder in silent support. "May I borrow a pair of those snowshoes and get directions to the seventh pasture?"

Josiah handed Seth the shoes he had just removed. When Seth had buckled them over his boots, Tim walked with him out of the barn and pointed. "Can you see the line of trees in the distance?" Seth nodded. "The seventh pasture ends at that tree line."

"Thank you."

As he set off across the field, Seth surveyed the landscape. The blanket of white seemed almost polka-dotted, for there were holes scattered around with brown heads showing through. Seth swallowed hard, for he understood more than any of these brothers realized.

In time, Seth arrived at the seventh pasture, guided by the sound of the only mooing around him. James looked up, expecting to see one of his brothers and surprised to find Seth standing there.

Not mincing words, Seth asked, "How bad?" James gravely gave the report. Seth nodded his head slowly. "How many of the forty-nine are expecting, Luke?"

"Forty," Luke replied. "Eight are heifers, and one cow is barren."

"How bad is the frostbite?"

"The three worst cases have died. A few are recovering

from frostbitten feet, but most of them just had frostbite on their ears and tails. Barring infection or another blizzard, the ones still living should make it."

"Good."

"Good?" James exclaimed. "How could a blacksmith see anything good in this?"

Understanding James' reaction, Seth asked, "Have you heard of the Rafter C Ranch in southern Kansas?"

Puzzled by the change in conversation, James answered, "Yes, they are known for Angus beef."

"Right. That was my ranch," Seth explained.

"Your ranch?"

"Yes, the one I started fifteen years ago and left behind when Susanna became so ill. The 'C' stood for Carter, and we chose the rafter because it seemed to symbolize to us that our ranch was under God's protection."

Feeling embarrassed at his earlier accusation, James repented, "Seth, I'm sorry. . ."

"You have only known me as a blacksmith. I would have reacted the same way. During the fifth winter at our ranch, we had a blizzard that decimated our herd, too. With some careful planning, the ranch was able to come back better than it was before. Your ranch will be able to do the same."

Luke had been standing to the side leaning on his pitchfork while listening to their exchange. "That is the first glimmer of hope we have had in weeks."

James wanted the particulars, "Where do we begin?"

"Let me help you finish up here, and we can all discuss it together somewhere warm."

Two hours later, Emma and her sons were seated with Seth around the kitchen table. Julie filled their cups with hot coffee as Seth discussed his recommendations. "When the snow melts enough to move the cattle from the seventh pasture to the north pasture, do so. Your immediate concern is keeping the cattle, especially the expectant ones, supplied with nutrient-rich hay and protected from disease. With forty-nine cows and heifers and up to forty live calves coming, your ranch may nearly double in size in the next few months. Plan to keep the female calves and fatten the males for the cattle drive to Kansas City in the fall. They won't fetch as high a price as they would if you let them grow over the winter and drive them in the spring, but you will need the capital to cover the cost of winter feed."

From the head of the table, Emma queried, "What should we do about our imminent need for bulls?"

"One step at a time. You won't need bulls until the end of May." Seth had a plan for the acquisition of bulls for the Rugged Cross Ranch that he could not divulge it until the details were finalized.

The palpable tension in the room had abated with these few encouraging words. Yes, their ranch had endured a terrible hardship, but there was hope for the future. James felt as if the weight of the ranch had been lifted from his shoulders, at least temporarily, and was deeply grateful to have found an experienced rancher to guide them in the days ahead.

CHAPTER 21

Losing Hope

B y the following Sunday, the height of the snow had decreased enough that the horses could pull the sleigh to church. The family had missed four Sundays of worshipping with their friends. The older brothers had taken turns giving a devotional in the ranch house on Sunday mornings, but a devotional just was not the same as meeting in God's house. When the family arrived, Jacob chose to sit in the back row rather than with his brothers. Though the bruises on his face had faded, the bruises on his heart remained.

When Julie played the piano for the hymns, James was reminded again of how much he missed Emily. According to the calendar, this was only the second Sunday in February. The end of June still seemed an eternity away.

When the service ended, James stood and stepped into the aisle to leave, but Mrs. Margaret Lange was blocking his way. She was turned away from him talking to the lady beside her as if divulging juicy details, "Well, it seems as if I may need to consider teaching here in the fall. My cousin Violet, who lives in Kansas City and attends the same church our Miss Kendrick has been visiting, wrote me a letter. Apparently, Emily has earned the affections of a young man, the son of a wealthy, prominent businessman, and member of a very influential family. Violet has seen them together quite frequently. I believe he is attending the same college where she is taking her teachers' courses."

James refused to hear another word, "Excuse me." His low baritone voice indicated his desire to pass.

Mrs. Lange turned slightly and looked up at him, momentarily startled that he had been within earshot. To ease her own conscience, she noted, "At least you are hearing this sooner rather than later."

Julie had also heard the exchange between Mrs. Lange and her confidant and hurried after James. She caught up with him at the foot of the stairs and touched his arm, "James, do not listen to that woman." When he turned his face toward her, she could see the pain in his eyes. He began to walk again, but she stayed with him. "James, Mrs. Lange is a gossip. Her cousin probably saw them speaking to each other and jumped to dramatic conclusions. You know Emily. She loves you whole-heartedly."

"I'm not a fool. Any man would be drawn to her beauty and gentle manner. She has been gone for six weeks. Anything could happen."

When the Carters were on their way out of church, Seth spotted Jacob still sitting on the back row. Speaking softly, Seth directed his children, "Why don't you walk home together. I'll come in a few minutes." Seth sat down next to Jacob. They were silent for a few moments, but Jacob's body language was screaming. He sat straight and rigid with his jaw tightly clenched. He never flinched as his family filed past on their way to the door. Seth did look up at them and saw the hurt on their faces, most pronounced with Josiah and Emma.

When they were the only two left in the building, Seth asked, "Why did you not sit with your family this morning?"

Jacob nearly growled, "I don't belong with them."

Answering dogmatically, Seth said, "Yes, you do. They are family."

Another growl, "Only Josiah is my family."

"You may not be related to them all by blood, but God has strategically placed you together as a family. They are hurting because they love you."

"Good for them," Jacob replied without compassion.

Seth took a deep breath and prayed silently for wisdom. "Do you recall the story from Matthew 18 about the good shepherd?" Jacob continued to stare straight ahead. "He had one hundred sheep that he loved, but when one went astray, he left the ninety-nine to rescue the one. Do you know what a shepherd would do with the sheep who had wandered off?" Silence. "He would break the leg of that sheep and carry him around his neck until the leg healed. Once free, that sheep would never leave his shepherd's side again, for he had known his saving grace, chastisement, protection, healing, and unconditional love."

"Listen for the voice of the Shepherd, Jacob, before He has to do something drastic to get your attention." Seth rose and prepared to leave. "I'm always available if you need me."

A few days later, Julie entered the foreman's office in the barn without knocking. James glanced up from the ledger he was writing in and noticed her look of determination. Before he could ask what she needed, she thrust four neatly penned pages at him. "Here, read this," Julie commanded.

James set down his pencil and reached for the papers, "What is this?"

"The letter Emily wrote to me. Emma picked it up in town this morning. Read it," she repeated.

Dear Julie,

Our first set of tests are finished, and I feel one step closer to home. As you predicted, my days are so busy, they are passing quickly. My classes are difficult, but interesting, and I am learning many valuable methods to improve my teaching.

Pastor and Mrs. Witherspoon are the sweetest older couple, and I am glad she is letting me help with her domestic duties. She is, I have discovered, a matchmaker at heart, for she tried to pair me with her grandson John. Fortunately, he is just as averse to her intentions as I am, so we have agreed to be friends, only friends, during my term here. He reminds me so much of Josiah, which is perfect, for he told me to consider him as a brother.

He often asks about my life in Prairie Hills, even knowing he will hear a lot about James in the bargain. If the two of them should ever meet, I think they would be great friends.

The letter went on to generally ask about everyone at home, then specifically ask about James. She described her classes and the characteristics of each teacher and what her daily schedule was like.

> *Please write soon. I so long to hear from home.*
> *Your Devoted Friend,*
> *Emily*

James laid the letter down when he finished reading.

"See? Emily is a friend of her host family's grandson. That is all. Now trust her over the meddling Mrs. Lange."

"Thank you, Julie," he said sincerely as he handed the missive back to her. "Do me a favor. When you write Emily, please don't tell her about her dad's admonition or the frostbite or the blizzard."

"Why ever not?" Julie asked.

"Emily admitted that her studies are hard. The last thing I wish to do is distract her with problems here." He hesitated, "Promise me."

"If it means that much to you, then yes, I promise; but I'm not sure how I will find anything to write about."

"Tell her all about Matthew; he is her favorite little person."

"Good idea." Julie smiled, confident that she had achieved her purpose, and went to bring the horses in from the pasture.

Reading Emily's words in her own feminine script was a comfort to James' soul. Julie was right. Emily's love was true; he had to trust her, even from afar.

The last week in February, Emma called a family meeting. Tim entered the back door and scanned the kitchen counter for a pie, but he did not see one. They each grabbed a cup of coffee and settled at the table before Emma began, "We are family. Daniel and I always believed in sharing everything about the ranch with you. Today is no different." Her sons waited patiently for her to continue.

"I wanted to start by thinking about all the things we have to be thankful for. All five of you are still safe and here with us. James didn't lose any fingers or toes to frostbite. Our homes and the barn faired the blizzard without damage. Despite the terrible losses, we still have forty-nine cattle with the promise of more in another month. Remembering that Daniel and I started with twenty-five cattle seems to put the numbers in perspective. God has also blessed us with a successful rancher who can give us advice from his experience. Since God gave us the wisdom to wait on the purchase of the Texas longhorn bulls, we still have some savings in the bank."

"Unfortunately, our savings doesn't compare to the income we usually receive with the spring cattle drive. We are going to have to work together to make our money stretch at least until the fall drive, maybe until next spring. I have some ideas, but I want your input as well."

"If Josiah would be willing to help me expand the garden, we could grow more vegetables to offset our reduction in beef for meals. I know you enjoy making many of your meals in the bunkhouse, but we could conserve a bit more if we eat here in the house again like you did when you were younger. That excludes Luke and Julie, of course, though you may join us as often as you like."

"I would also like to enlarge the chicken coop and keep more setting hens. Our dinners could include more chicken, and the general store is always asking me for more eggs. That could be another source of income. What else could we do?"

Tim suggested, "Several farmers have asked me if we would train their horses at our ranch. The horses Buck and Julie trained have given us a good reputation. If Julie would be willing to train us, maybe that is a service we could offer for a fee."

Emma nodded, "That is a good idea. We have plenty of pasture land available right now; we might as well put it to good use. Julie, what do you say?"

"I'd be happy to help. Would you help me with Matthew while the horses are in training?"

"Of course." Emma reached over to touch Matthew's arm. "He is always welcome to stay with me."

"Is there a market for hay? We could always plant one of the pastures this year," James offered.

"I'll stop by the feed store and ask the next time we're in town. If there is a need for hay, we could certainly fill it." Emma responded. Knowing the hayfields were Jacob's responsibility, she asked, "What do you think, Jacob?"

Jacob responded dryly, "Sure, we don't need the outlying pastures for anything else."

Ignoring his brother's sarcastic remark, Josiah recommended, "What about the shooting contest in Kansas City? Every year, James says he cannot go because of calving, but this year, we'll be done in plenty of time for him to get there. I spotted a flyer in town; the prize this year is $300."

James dismissed this option. "Thousands of the best sharpshooters from several states around travel in for that event. I may be a good shot, but I'm not that good, and we can't afford the registration fee or the extra ammunition for me to practice."

His brothers were not so quick to reject the idea. Josiah commented, "If each of us contributed $2, we could cover the cost of the entrance fee and ammunition."

"That is $2 we cannot afford to waste," James replied.

"Think of it as an investment," Tim rebutted.

"Look, I don't want the future of this ranch resting on my shooting ability when I know there will be marksmen there far better than I am," James countered.

"How do you know they are better if you never compete against them?" Josiah wanted to know.

"Here I thought you would jump at any excuse to travel to Kansas City this spring," Tim declared. James tilted his head and stared at Tim. "Yes, I win," Tim smiled and pumped his fist.

"James?" Emma asked.

"All right, I'll go," James replied to a chorus of cheers.

"All right, these are a great start, but keep the ideas coming over the next days and weeks. Meeting dismissed."

"Shall I assume the first cutback was no pie for the meeting?" Tim guessed.

"Sorry, Tim. No pie tonight," Emma replied.

"James, you've got to win that contest. I need pie."

James clapped his taller brother on the back, "Tim, you are incorrigible."

"Thank you, I think." To Luke he whispered, "What does *incorrigible* mean?" Luke just laughed.

Spring calving season was usually such a busy time on the ranch, that comparatively speaking, James felt as if he were twiddling his thumbs. Thanks to the tender loving care the forty soon-to-be mothers had been faithfully receiving, the calves that were born were strong and healthy. A few of the larger calves needed a helping hand from Luke to enter the world. Of the forty calves, only one was stillborn; and his mother had been the most severely hypothermic of the now-living animals.

Seth visited often, and he was impressed with Luke's knowledge and assessment skills as well as his gentle touch with the animals. He told James, "You don't know how blessed you are to have a veterinarian like Luke on the ranch with you. I'm envious."

In seemingly no time at all, the calving and branding were finished. The time for James to leave for Kansas City was at hand. When Julie was in the barn tending to her horses, James approached her, "Do you still have Emily's letter?"

"Of course," answered Julie puzzled.

"May I see it again?"

"Sure. I'll get it from home and bring it this evening."

That evening, Julie met James in his office and handed him the envelope. "Thank you, Julie, I'll give it back to you tomorrow."

She looked at him curiously, but turned to go. When she had left, he pulled a piece of paper from his drawer and copied the return address. He folded the paper neatly and put it in his pocket.

Tim gathered Luke and Jacob for a meeting. "I don't know about you two, but I need something constructive to do. Here's my plan: James has had that load of lumber wrapped in tarpaulins all winter. Why don't we start on his house while he and Josiah are in Kansas City?"

"Does he have blueprints or scale drawings somewhere?" Luke inquired.

"He keeps them in his desk drawer," remarked Tim.

Luke advised, "We should talk with Emma before we plan too far ahead."

They ambled over to the ranch house to find her. Hearing their intentions, she cautioned, "All things considered, this isn't the kind of thing we should surprise James with. Let's suggest your plan to him and follow what he says."

The three brothers strolled over to the foreman's office to find James. Tim leaned down, putting both hands on the edge of the desk, and blurted, "We'd like to start working on your house. Is that all right with you?"

James looked hesitant. "I've been trying to come up with a way to sell the lumber to get some money for the ranch, since I can't return it for a refund."

"What's done is done. Let's keep the lumber and build. We certainly have plenty of time to devote to the construction right now, and staying busy will be good for us. What do you say?" Tim countered.

James understood their need to be doing something, so he agreed to let them get started. He rode out with Luke to set the stakes for the corners of the house and described the orientation of the home, referring to the scale drawings as he spoke. He knew Luke was the most detailed of his brothers and would make sure everything was done right. James clapped Luke on his shoulder, "All right, I leave our home in capable hands. Thanks to all of you."

Two days later, James and Josiah left at dawn with food and bedrolls packed. The journey to Kansas City was two hundred miles. They knew it well from their annual cattle drives. Riding without the cattle would cut their travel time in half, but the trip would still be seven days each way. The stagecoaches could travel much further each day since they could change out the horses at regular intervals along the way, but that was a luxury they could not afford. The brothers were both thankful that the rain fell only on one day. The rest of their route was in good weather, and they arrived in Kansas City the day before the big contest.

A banner over the sponsoring hotel read, "Registration for the Kansas City Marksmanship Competition Here." James looked at Josiah and asked, "Are you sure about this? Last chance to change your mind."

Without hesitation, Josiah replied, "Yes, I am sure. I know you will win."

The pair of brothers walked inside and waited in line. As they inched toward the registration table, James studied the crowd of men holding their new-model shiny rifles. The sight was a bit intimidating. He looked down at his own rifle, old and scuffed. James shook his head and muttered, "I feel like I'm just giving this $10 away."

When his turn came, James stepped up to the table and completed the registration form. The man behind the table asked to examine his rifle, which he inspected carefully. He placed a wide checkmark next to "Pass" in the inspection column on the form and requested the fee, which James paid. The registrar handed him a copy of the form. "You're all set. Meet in the competitors' queue at nine o'clock tomorrow morning. Good luck to you. Next."

The next morning, James bathed in the creek next to where they were camped just outside town and donned clean clothes. Josiah had already made griddle cakes for breakfast. After they ate and extinguished their fire, they rode into town for the event.

Josiah asked, "Are you nervous?"

"Nope. I know I'm going to lose," James replied matter-of-factly.

"Why do you say that?"

"Did you see all of those new Winchester rifles yesterday?"

Josiah was unimpressed. "Those shiny things haven't been tested, not the way your rifle has. You have to know your gun from experience to find all the idiosyncrasies and aiming adjustments. They were just showing off. You're the real thing. I've never seen you miss a shot."

"It doesn't happen often," James admitted.

"See, I'm telling you, you're going to win this competition."

When they arrived at the venue, James was the only one allowed in the competitor's area, along with the nearly five hundred other men with rifles, so Josiah found a seat in the stands to watch. Twenty bales of hay were lined end-to-end in a long line at each contest distance: 25 yards, 50 yards, 75 yards, and 100 yards. Each bale had a target pinned to it, allowing twenty men to compete at a time. The judge would give a signal to indicate they could fire at the first line of targets. Once all twenty rifles had been fired, the judge would call a "Cease fire!" while the target judges would evaluate each shot and hang new targets. Any shot that did not find the bullseye was disqualified. The same pattern continued with each consecutive line of hay bales.

When the competitors lined up for the 75-yard target, fewer than fifty competitors were left, James among them. The marksmen took longer to line up their aim and fire at this distance. James was in the third wave. Like he had done before, he got down on his belly, anchored his elbow in the dirt to support the rifle with a steady hand, licked his first finger to feel the direction of the breeze, lined up his target, held his breath to eliminate movement, and fired. The target judge called, "Bullseye!" Josiah cheered.

There were only three men left on the firing range. The judge picked up a megaphone and addressed the crowd. "For the 100-yard target, we have never had a bullseye, so the marksman who shoots closest to the bullseye will win. For the concentration of the competitors, we ask that you kindly remain quiet for this final event."

They spaced the targets and the three men further apart. The signal was given. Two shots were fired. James was feeling the breeze that was variable at the moment. He waited, holding his breath, with his finger on the trigger. The instant the breeze stopped, he pulled the trigger. Josiah was holding his breath, too. The three target judges walked together to evaluate each paper. The first target was read as "first ring." The second target was read as "second ring," and the marksman belonging to it groaned. The judges moved to the third and final target, belonging to James, and the judge yelled, "Bullseye!"

Josiah jumped up and pumped his fist in the air as he whooped as loudly as he could. He watched as three well-dressed men approached James, assuming they were coming to congratulate him.

The first man spoke, "Before we declare you the winner, we must give your rifle a final inspection." James opened his rifle so it would not fire and handed it to the gentleman. He reached for it and commented, "This is an old rifle."

"Yes, it belonged to my grandfather," James replied.

The men examined the rifle and looked at each other. "This is a fine firearm," joined the second inspector, "unfortunately, it is not one of the approved models."

"What?" James asked incredulously. His jubilation immediately turned to dismay. He pulled the registration form from his pocket and presented it to them, the "Pass" on the rifle inspection clearly marked. "My rifle was approved yesterday."

The third and oldest man in the trio finally spoke, "I'm sorry, son. That was the finest shooting I have ever seen. I cannot explain why your rifle passed inspection yesterday, but it does not pass today."

James gritted his teeth. He could feel the sting of tears of anger in his eyes. Seeing he could not change their verdict, he rubbed his upper lip with his thumb. "May I at least get my registration fee back?"

"Unfortunately, no," the first man replied. "The fees are nonrefundable." He handed the rifle back to James, who took it, nodded, and turned to go.

The second-place contestant that had just become the winner stopped James and inquired sincerely, "What would you have done with the winnings?"

"The prize money was going to save my ranch."

Josiah was still in the stands wondering what was happening. He saw the expression on James' face right before the judge announced, "Due to a technicality, the contestant with the bullseye has been disqualified. The first-ring shot has become our champion."

James walked toward Josiah, who met him halfway. "James, what happened?"

"Apparently, I needed one of those shiny new rifles after all." James just kept moving straight toward Trigger.

After dinner at their camp, James declared, "Only one thing could redeem this day. Josiah, come with me."

"Where are we going?"

"You'll see," James assured him.

They rode their horses into town, gaslights lining the main thoroughfare. A large, brick edifice appeared on their right, and Josiah read, "Kansas City Teachers' Institute." They were both in awe of the campus. "James, is this where Emily is taking classes?"

"Yes, it's much bigger than I imagined," James replied.

James turned to the right, down a tree-lined side street. He pulled out the folded address from his pocket and noted the house numbers as they passed each one. Finally, he spotted the house he was searching for, a small home with a manicured yard and stone foot path. There was warm, yellow light coming from the front windows. He pulled Trigger to a stop. He knew he was not allowed to knock on the door and say hello, but just knowing he was this close to Emily was a balm to his heart.

James and Josiah heard the rumble of wheels and turned to see an open carriage stop in front of the very same house. His heart all but stopped when he saw the face of the male occupant in the tuxedo as he climbed down and approached the front door carrying a small bouquet of roses. "Oh, no. It's him."

"Who?"

"Emily's 'friend'."

"How do you know it's him?" Josiah asked.

"He looks just like you."

Josiah was puzzled, but remained silent. They maneuvered their horses so they were partially obscured by the trees. Other than the light from the windows and the singular lantern hanging on the carriage, darkness shrouded them and hid them from view.

A few moments later, the door opened, and John exited with Emily on his arm. The sight of her took James' breath away. She was dressed in a beautiful dark green dress with her hair softly pulled up. Emily was smiling and laughing as John helped her into the carriage. James thought she looked like one of the princesses from Beth's fairy tale books. As the carriage pulled away, James' heart broke.

Josiah looked at the anguish on his brother's face, "James, I'm so sorry." James turned around and headed back for camp, regretting that he had ever left home in the first place.

The following morning, James sent Josiah into town for the supplies they would need for the ride home. He couldn't take the chance, no matter how remote, that he might see Emily again. When Josiah finished his purchases at the general store, he heard the newsboy proclaim the morning headline, "Read all about it! James McAllister shoots first 100-yard bullseye in competition history!" Josiah handed the boy a penny for the newspaper, then departed to meet James.

Emily had not noticed Pastor Witherspoon's newspaper lying on the dining table. She remained blissfully ignorant of James' troubles.

The brothers' week-long ride home was mostly silent. Knowing there was nothing he could do or say to comfort his brother, Josiah simply rode in quiet comradery. When they arrived on the ranch, James stabled Trigger and closed himself into his foreman's office. Josiah stabled his horse as well, then walked over to the ranch house and found Emma pulling clothes off the line. He showed her the newspaper and told her the entire story. Her mother's heart hurt so much for her son. "Oh, James," was all she could utter.

Over the next few weeks, the brothers took turns hunting and fishing, trying to add variety to their meals. Near the end of April, another letter arrived for Julie. This time, James refused her pleading for him to read Emily's missive. Not understanding why, Julie kept persisting. Finally, James stood and all but snapped at her, "Julie, I was there. I saw Emily with her 'friend' that was much more than a friend. He brought her roses; they were dressed like they were headed to a royal ball;

and they rode off in an open carriage. I saw her face as she smiled and laughed with him. She is enjoying a new life that I would never be able to offer her. The test of my love for her is that I love her enough to let her go. Please, do not taunt me with her letters anymore."

With tears in her eyes, Julie replied, "James, you don't know the whole story. Don't stop loving Emily. If you change your mind about reading her letter, just ask; otherwise, I promise not to pester you about it."

The following week, Seth rode out to the ranch and found James. "After I explained how the blizzard had all but destroyed your herd, the man who bought my ranch offered to give you two Angus bulls, with the offer of more next year at a reasonable price. The only hitch is that we need to ride up and bring them home."

James actually almost smiled, "That's the best news we've had in quite a while. Let's get everyone together to discuss it." Since the bulls would need to stay separated, they decided that James, Tim, Jacob, and Josiah would accompany Seth to the Rafter C Ranch. James was reluctant to leave Luke at the ranch since he most trusted him with the health assessment of new animals, but Luke had responsibilities here caring for the calves, and Seth assured him he knew how to evaluate good bulls.

Two weeks later, two Angus bulls were welcomed to the Rugged Cross Ranch. They would have just the right amount of time to acclimate before breeding began.

One afternoon in May, Luke returned home from errands in town to find Julie preparing dinner. He took off his boots by the door and saw that their boy was sleeping, so he came up behind his wife and wrapped his arms around her. "Doc stopped me in town today," Luke began. "He had heard about our trouble on the ranch and asked if I had any extra time to help him with his patients. He's willing to pay me for my time."

"And you love medicine," Julie added.

"Yes, I do. Medicine is fascinating, and it gives me an entirely new way to help people."

"What did you tell him?"

"That I needed to talk to my beautiful wife before I gave him an answer."

"I love you," Julie responded. "If you would like to work with Doc, you should do it. You read medical textbooks for fun; I know you would enjoy using some of that knowledge in a practical way."

"Thank you for understanding me and supporting me. You really are the best wife ever." His sky-blue eyes twinkled in adoration.

By June, the ranch had fallen into a new rhythm. Construction on James' house was nearly complete. Luke and Tim helped Julie train three horses for local farmers. Luke also helped Doc in town a few days each week. Josiah was busy with the expanded garden, and Jacob managed the enlarged hay fields and tried his hand with growing alfalfa. Emma sold eggs and chickens and watched Matthew when Julie was working with the horses. James organized everything on the ranch and took personal responsibility for their growing herd.

After a routine Saturday morning meeting with Emma, James was reminded again of how tight money was on the ranch. He was sitting in his office when Emma came to see him. James was thoughtfully holding a trio of rings in his hand; one was filigree with small diamonds imbedded in the motif; the other two were wedding bands. Reading his mind, Emma commanded, "Do not even think of selling those rings."

"The money I could get for them would help us make ends meet," James explained.

Emma spoke with conviction, "Those three rings belonged to your parents, and they will soon belong to you and Emily. Family heirlooms are priceless, and you will not sell them for this ranch."

"Mama, what if Emily doesn't come home?"

"Emily will come home. I am confident of that, despite what Mrs. Lange says. As for our needs here on the ranch, God will provide. Look at those two bulls in the pasture if you have any doubts. He has never abandoned us, and He never will."

James turned to look out the window at the pastures where the bulls roamed and was encouraged by Emma's words.

Emma continued, "I came over here to tell you that Emily is scheduled to arrive on the afternoon stage on June 26." James winced slightly. He was not as convinced as Emma that Emily would really be on that stagecoach.

The next day after church, Mrs. Margaret Lange was giving her delicious tidbit of news to anyone around her who would listen. "My cousin Violet saw John Witherspoon purchasing an engagement ring for our Miss Kendrick. I guess she won't be 'Miss' for much longer."

The knife she had stabbed James' heart with before had now been twisted for full effect. He looked down at Julie, his eyes mirroring his internal pain. The only words she had to give were, "Remember the source." Unfortunately, James did not find that comforting in the least.

The twenty-sixth day of June finally arrived. Julie found James after lunch. "Are you coming to town to be there for Emily's stagecoach?"

"No," James replied.

Julie's question had been meant as more of a reminder than an inquiry, and she was surprised at his response. "Why not?"

James explained, "I'm highly doubting she will be on that stage at all. Even if she is, I couldn't handle seeing her wearing another man's engagement ring."

Julie continued his thought, "Or risk another railing from Pastor if he sees you there."

"Or that," he acknowledged.

An hour later, Julie rode alone to meet Emily's stage. Now she was sitting with Emily finishing her long story. The only part she had omitted was about the construction of the house, for if Emily was indeed engaged, that knowledge would only hurt her.

A single tear spilled onto Emily's cheek as she thought of what James had endured while she was away. Emily had been sitting quietly, absorbing Julie's story with rapt attention. The telling had brought a weariness to Julie's face as she spoke.

Emily had to add one final detail. "James was nearly right. John did propose to me, but I could never accept. James is the only one I wish to spend the rest of my life with." She rose slowly and opened her valise that she had set on the desk, removed the box containing her treasured daffodil, and set the small vase on her desk. The wax on the petals seemed to gleam in the afternoon sun. She reached into her bag again and removed the box holding her journal and handed it to Julie. "James needs to hear my words, but I am apparently still not allowed to speak to him. Please ask James to read this. All of it."

"I will ask, but I cannot promise he will. He would not read your last letter."

"Tell him I am home, and my heart still belongs to him. He will read my journal." Julie stood and hugged her friend.

When Julie arrived back at the ranch, the sound of chopping wood told her where to find James long before she could see him swinging the axe. Hugging the white box to her, she approached him and waited patiently to be acknowledged. He plunged the blade of the axe into the chopping block and wiped his sweaty face with his shirt. His one remaining glimmer of hope was well guarded as he gave his attention to Julie.

"Emily asked me to tell you that she is home, and her heart still belongs to you. She desperately needs you to hear her words." She extended the box toward him. "Since she is not allowed to speak to you, she wishes for you to read this. All of it."

James immediately recognized the white box and knew what it held. He stared at the box in Julie's hand for a moment before he slowly reached for it and held it gently in both of his strong hands. "Thank you, Julie."

James' glimmer of hope burned a bit brighter as he made his way to the bench on the Hill. Emily came home. Once settled on the bench, he lifted the lid and removed the leather-bound journal, reading the verse embossed on the cover. "Love bears all things, believes all things, hopes all things, endures all things."

"Father, thank You for teaching me how to put my hope in You and You alone. Please give me the grace to trust You as I read what is written on these pages." He did not say "Amen" because he did not want to close this conversation with God; he wanted Him right there with him as he read.

James opened the front cover. His note to her was still there, along with an envelope simply addressed to "Emily." He decided to save that note until last. When he turned to the next page and saw her perfect feminine script, he allowed himself to be immersed in her words. She wrote directly to him as if the journal were one long letter. The first entries covered her time teaching in the new schoolroom. He laughed at the antics of the students and felt sad about her struggles.

He read how much it meant to her to have his blessing for her journey and how difficult the decision to go had been. Upon her arrival in Kansas City, he added what he had seen of the town to her descriptions and felt as if he were right there with her. She freely talked about John and how grateful she was to have a friend to talk with about James. When she described the night he had seen her in the green gown, he realized her excitement was much more about the symphony than her companion.

The sun had begun to set, but James tilted the journal toward the remaining light and continued reading. He came to the evening of John's recital and felt Emily's surprise and anguish as she refused her friend's proposal, agonizing over the hurt she had unwittingly caused him. Her final entry, written the night before her arrival home, was filled with anticipation of seeing James again.

James took a deep breath and closed the journal, sliding out the envelope with her name. Though he was reluctant to read the personal note, Emily had insisted that he read everything. He opened the envelope and pulled out the folded pages.

> Dear Emily,
>
> I am writing these words in case I lack the courage to speak them when I see you this evening. Please forgive me for surprising you with my proposal last week. You are the kindest and most beautiful woman I have ever met. Please know that I was not intending to be deceitful. Our friendship has been a treasure to me. I never meant to fall in love, but somewhere along the

way, I did. My broken heart is no one's fault but my own. I hope James knows how blessed he is to have your heart."

  Your Friend,
  John

James sat back against the bench, his heart full of gratitude. God had brought him to the place where he was willing to let her go forever. Now He was giving her back to him. If only her dad would change his heart.

CHAPTER 22
Repentance

On Sunday afternoon after dinner, Pastor Kendrick sat in his favorite chair near the fireplace and pulled Beth and her dolly up onto his lap. "June 29 is a special day. Twenty-four years ago, your mama and I were married on this day."

Beth looked up at him, "Papa, tell me about when you asked Mama to marry you."

Her Dad smiled as he reminisced, "Your mama was so beautiful, inside and out. From the very first time I met her, I knew she was the only one for me." He chuckled, "Why her Dad ever let me court her is beyond me. We were both so young. I was barely nineteen, and she was eighteen. After we had courted for a year, I finally had the courage to propose."

"Did you have to ask Grandpa for permission to marry Mama?" Beth wanted to know.

"Yes, I did. I don't think I've ever been so nervous in my life. I knew Grandpa liked me well enough, for he had let me court his daughter. What concerned me most was that I still had not yet been called by a church. My odd jobs were fine to get along as a bachelor. But as a husband and provider for my family? Grandpa would have every right to say 'No.' When he said 'Yes,' I was overjoyed. I don't know what I would have done if he hadn't said 'Yes.' I would have been utterly devastated." As he spoke those last words, he looked down into Beth's big brown eyes. He felt as if someone had just jolted him from a deep sleep. His gaze moved from Beth to where Emily was tidying the kitchen, and with a sudden realization of the import of his conversation with James, he whispered, "But I said 'No.'"

He sat for a moment more as the weight of his former decision cleared his mind and strengthened his resolve, spurring him to action. He kissed Beth on the forehead and rose from the chair. As he made his way into the kitchen and looked into his daughter's face, he realized that the sparkle was missing from her eyes. How long had it been gone, and he hadn't even noticed? Feeling rebuked again, he spoke softly, "Emily, please forgive me. My decision to reject James was selfish, and I have hurt you. You have honored me even when my choice was wrong. I am so proud of you." He wrapped his arms around his oldest daughter.

Emily's eyes filled with sudden tears, and she whispered, "I forgive you. I love you, Daddy."

After he released her, he spoke again, "I need to go for a ride; I'll be home later this afternoon." Emily nodded, and he turned to go.

After Pastor saddled his horse, he rode out to Emma Taylor's ranch. On the side of the barn, he noticed a huge stack of firewood beside the chopping block. He tethered his horse to the hitching post in front of the corral and made his way into the barn. There he met Luke.

"Good afternoon, Pastor. May I help you?" Luke greeted him.

Pastor had to ask, "Are you expecting a summer blizzard?"

Luke laughed, "If you're referring to the woodpile, that is James' doing. He has been chopping wood like crazy every Friday since your meeting. He says it clears his mind and adjusts his attitude."

Once again, Pastor was reminded that one decision can affect many people. He nodded, "Actually, I am hoping to speak with James."

Luke pointed a thumb over his right shoulder. "He just rode in. He's stabling his horse in the fourth stall."

"Thanks." Pastor took a deep breath and walked purposefully toward the indicated stall. He watched quietly as James cared for his horse. When James hoisted the saddle to the stall wall, he saw his Pastor standing there.

Immediately, James steeled his features, not in anger, but in defense against the onslaught of criticism he was expecting. He slowly exited the stall, standing face to face with Emily's father.

Pastor Kendrick reached out to grasp the top of the stall wall and began, "James --"

James interrupted, "Sir, I have honored your wishes. Since leaving your house the night of our meeting, I have not spoken even one word to the woman I love more than life itself. What more do you want from me?"

Pastor swallowed hard and began again, "James, I want to ask your forgiveness." James' face showed the shock he felt. "You are a better man than I to have honored my command, even when it was wrong. You are a godly man with strong faith, a hard worker who doesn't quit when the way gets tough, a perfect gentleman to my sweet girl. You are exactly the kind of man I want her to marry."

"Then why did you say 'no'?"

"Because -- because I didn't want to lose her. You never

knew my Eloise before she became ill, but Emily is exactly like her in many ways. When God took Eloise Home, I found great comfort seeing Emily in her place. When you asked to marry her, I suddenly felt as if I were losing Eloise all over again. God used the words of a child to bring me to my senses."

Pastor thoughtfully added, "I can't imagine what I have put you through this last year. To be honest, I don't know what I would have done if Eloise's father had said 'no.' Eloped maybe."

James admitted, "That thought had crossed my mind, but it wouldn't have been fair to Emily, nor would it have been right to marry without your blessing."

Pastor reached up and placed his free hand on James' shoulder, "You're a good man." With a smile, he asked, "Do I presume, then, that you would still like my permission to marry Emily?"

With the enthusiasm of newfound hope, James responded, "Yes, sir."

"Then you have both my permission and my blessing." He extended his hand, and James returned his firm handshake.

"May I see Emily today?"

"Yes, you may." Then he added with a chuckle, "Just be sure I get home first."

James looked down at his sweat-soaked shirt, "I'll need to clean up first anyway."

Pastor turned and began moving toward the barn exit, and James called after him, "You are forgiven."

Pastor turned his head enough to reply, "Thank you, son." He mounted his horse and departed for home, his smile revealing that the heavy weight on his heart had been lifted.

James passed Luke on his way to the bunkhouse and asked, "Could you cover my afternoon ride with Tim to inspect the herd in the north pasture?"

"Of course," Luke replied with a nod.

When James had taken a quick bath and donned clean clothes, he bounded down the bunkhouse steps to find the horse and buggy already tethered to the hitching post. He thought to himself, *"I'll have to thank Luke later."* With a smile on his face and only one lovely woman on his mind, he climbed up and soon had the horse cantering toward the parsonage. When he arrived, his heart was thudding in his chest.

Inside the parsonage, Pastor was sitting by the fireplace reading, and Emily was at the kitchen table mending another pair of Robert's pants. The knock on the front door that rang crisp and clear broke the silence. Pastor looked up at his daughter, "Emily, would you get the door, please. I think it's for you." She gave him a puzzled expression, but rose without comment and opened the door. As she did, a gasp of surprise escaped her lips, for standing before her was the man she loved. He nearly filled the doorway, looking very handsome with his hat in one hand and a bunch of yellow daffodils in the other.

Emily's dad laughed softly as he watched the two of them standing silently on either side of the threshold. After a minute, he suggested, "You might want to invite him in and put the flowers in some water."

She blushed and stepped aside, "Please come in."

James stepped in and held the flowers out to her. "These are for you. I remember how much you loved seeing them on our last ride together."

She took the flowers, put them and some water in an empty milk bottle, and set it in the middle of the table, saying, "Thank you. The flowers are beautiful. That ride seems like forever ago."

"It was." James offered his arm, "Come. Ride with me again. There is something I want to show you." James ignored Emily's quizzical expression and led her to the buggy. Once they were settled, he directed his horse down the scenic trail toward the south side of the ranch and continued through the heart of the ranch and around to the north side of the Hill. There on a rise stood a building Emily had never seen before. After James tethered the reins to the hitching post, he helped Emily down and reached for her hand.

"James, is this what I think it is?" Emily asked.

The man at her side smiled, but remained silent as they ascended the three steps to the front porch. James stopped and turned to face her, searching her blue eyes. "Emily, for years I have had a dream of having a home and family of my own, a place full of love and laughter . . . and you." James smoothly descended to one knee and reached for her hand. Emily's eyes glistened with tears of joy. "Please make my dream come true. Will you marry me?"

"Yes, I would love nothing more," Emily whispered.

James reached into his pocket and pulled out a tiny box. He opened it to reveal his mother's filigree ring imbedded with tiny diamonds. Emily gasped, "James, it's beautiful!"

He removed the ring from the box and slipped it on Emily's finger. James whispered, "The next time I put a ring on your finger, I'm going to kiss you afterwards."

Emily blushed and smiled. Her perfect gentleman. He slowly rose to his feet, but he didn't release her hand. She didn't mind.

James interrupted her thoughts, "So, when can we get married?"

Responding teasingly, Emily countered, "Are you in a hurry or something?"

With a twinkle in his eyes, he replied, "Yes, ma'am. I need to make you mine before your dad changes his mind."

Emily's laughter was light and musical. "Do you know who changed his mind today?" When James shook his head, she continued, "Beth. She was asking him about when he asked Grandpa if he could marry Mama. While he was telling her the story, he realized what he had done, how his decision had hurt us."

Wistfully, James spoke, "I knew I loved that little girl." He gazed into Emily's eyes and inquired once more, "When can we get married?"

Emily's smile could not be dimmed. "Persistent, aren't you?" James smiled mischievously and nodded. "Well, let's see. I wish to wear Mom's wedding dress. She and I were about the same size, so the alterations shouldn't take me long, maybe a week or two. Other than that, we just need to find out when Dad is available to perform the ceremony."

"Two weeks should be perfect." James beamed. "Welcome to our home."

She reached out with her free hand to touch the porch beam and added softly, "Our home."

James gestured to the scenery around them. "Here we are close to the river, but up on a rise to be safe from flooding. The trees behind will protect the house from the north winds. We are close to the Hill and a short ride from the barn, but out of the line of site from the ranch house, giving us both convenience and privacy." Emily's eyes had not left James' face. "May I give you a tour?"

Emily's smile had already given him the answer, but she replied, "Yes, please." James opened the latch on the door and held it for her to step through. As she entered the main living area, a soft gasp escaped her lips. "James, this is perfect!"

"And all one story," James pointed out. He escorted her from one room to the next, and Emily was awestruck. James remarked, "The construction of the house itself is complete, but we still need to finish some of the furniture. Tim and Jacob are building our dining table and chairs, and Josiah has nearly finished carving our headboard. As soon as the headboard is done, I can assemble our bed."

Emily blushed at his last comment, but inquired, "When did you find the time to do all of this?"

"I had already ordered the lumber for the house in the fall, long before the blizzard that took most of our herd. Since there was no way to return it, my brothers urged me to build. With fewer cattle to tend to, we all had some extra time to work on the house. The work gave us something constructive to do together as brothers and kept our minds off the problems here at the ranch. We all needed an outlet for the tension we were feeling. Besides, building our home let me feel close to you, even when I couldn't be." As he gazed into her eyes, he asked gently, "Why do you have tears in your eyes?"

"Tears of joy. Today has been amazing. I just hope I'm not going to wake up and find it's all a dream."

James lifted Emily's left hand and rubbed her new ring with his thumb. "This is a dream. One that is finally coming true. You are finally my fiancée, and hopefully in two weeks, you will be my wife." He chuckled and added with a twinkle in his eyes, "You know, it's too bad we're not Kiowa."

"Why do you say that?"

"The Kiowa marry the same day the proposal is given."

The color in Emily's cheeks deepened once again, but she smiled and gave him a slight nod.

James led Emily over to the mantle above the fireplace. He picked up the journal box resting there and handed it to his fiancée. "This belongs to you. Thank you for loving me even though I cannot promise you expensive satin gowns or symphonies."

"Those things are unimportant. All I want is you."

CHAPTER 23

Confrontation

Jacob worried Emma. He still worked hard, but his attitude was becoming more sour every day. One morning, Emma looked up from the washboard where she was scrubbing laundry near the water pump. Jacob had just passed her to take the pail of fresh milk into the kitchen. She dried her hands and walked over toward the kitchen door to meet Jacob when he exited.

Jacob opened the door. Spotting Emma coming his way, he tried to skirt around her, but she extended her hand and caught him gently by the arm. He turned to face her, revealing his stern features and steely gaze.

"Jacob, what is it? What is wrong?" Emma asked.

"Nothing," was his surly reply.

"You are my son. I know when something is truly wrong. Please tell me what is troubling you."

Jacob roughly pulled his arm from Emma's hand and responded through gritted teeth. "You are not my mother. I work hard and do everything you ask. What more do you want from me?"

Emma stood speechless. Jacob had not laid a hand on her,

but she felt as if she'd been struck. Tears welled up in her eyes as Jacob turned and stomped off toward the barn. She wrapped her arms around her middle and slowly descended to sit on the kitchen step.

Tim passed Jacob on his way to get a fresh bucket of water. He had not heard Jacob's words to Emma, but he did hear his biting tone. While in full stride, he dropped the empty bucket by the water pump and went straight to Emma.

He squatted down and placed his hand on her shoulder. "Did Jacob hurt you?" Tim asked protectively.

Emma's gaze was still on Jacob's retreating back. "Not physically, no, but his words left quite a wound. I feel as if I'm losing my son." Her words dissolved into tears.

Speaking with a determined tone, Tim said, "That's it. This has gone on long enough. I'm going to have a talk with that boy whether he wants it or not."

After dinner and evening chores, James went to his office in the barn while the other three headed back to the bunkhouse. Josiah climbed up in his top bunk with a book. Tim looked over at Jacob, "I challenge you to a checker rematch."

Jacob retorted, "I've won the last three times."

"I know. That's why I need a rematch."

"You're a glutton for punishment."

"Perhaps. Grab the board, and I'll pour the coffee." Tim directed.

Tim filled two coffee cups and set them on the table before maneuvering his long legs to sit on the bench. Jacob opened the board, and the two of them positioned the checkers.

The game started quietly. Tim took a sip of the warm liquid and asked his opponent, "Why are you so angry?"

"What?"

"You are spilling anger and hurting everyone around you, especially Emma." The checker moves continued, but Jacob was now distracted.

"This is a checker game, not an interrogation. Don't judge me," Jacob replied.

"There is a verse in I Samuel that says 'Man looks on the outward appearance, but the Lord looks on the heart.' That was not a condemnation, merely a statement of fact. Only God can see your heart. All the rest of us have to look at is your outward appearance. King me."

"Huh?"

Tim pointed to his checker. "King me. I'm at your end of the board. Do you remember Pastor's analogy from his sermon on Sunday? Your heart is like a cup. If you put coffee in a cup and jostle it, coffee will spill out. If you put lemonade in the cup and jostle it, you will not get coffee. Every time you are jostled, Jacob, meanness and anger come out of you. That means your heart is full of anger. Why are you so angry?"

"None of your business." Jacob jumped Tim's checker and removed it from the board.

Tim got straight to the point. "That means you haven't even taken the time to think about it. Let me ask you this, then. Do you have a personal relationship with God?"

"What kind of question is that? I prayed a prayer when I was in the orphanage, and I've never missed a Sunday service unless I was sick or on the cattle drive."

"You didn't listen to the question. I didn't ask you about praying a prayer or going to church. I asked if you have a personal relationship with God."

Jacob responded, "I don't know what you mean."

"Obviously," Tim thought to himself. To Jacob, he said, "A

relationship is a close connection you have with someone. Take me, for instance. You work with me, talk to me, live with me, hear me snore. You know my greatest ambitions and my greatest faults. You have seen me at my best and my worst, and we are still friends and brothers. We have a relationship."

Tim continued, "A relationship with God begins with confessing our sins and accepting the salvation Jesus offers, but it is far more than praying a sinner's prayer. Building a relationship requires communication: reading and meditating on God's Word and praying to Him, not because we have to do those things to obtain salvation, but because we desire to know God more."

Jacob seemed to squirm a bit, but he made his next checker move anyway. He asked rather accusingly, "What makes you think I'm not saved?"

After jumping two of Jacob's checkers, Tim replied, "God calls us to be fruit inspectors, and I don't see any fruit."

"Now you've lost me."

"Think back to that verse that says, 'Man looks on the outward appearance.' What are we supposed to look for? Fruit. Specifically, the fruit of the Spirit: love, joy, peace, patience, kindness, goodness, faithfulness, gentleness, and self-control. While none of these are necessary for salvation -- We cannot do anything to earn God's gift -- these fruits are the natural result of a changed heart, an evidence of the salvation that has already taken place."

"Jacob, in you I see a diligent worker and talented rancher, but I do not see any fruit." Tim jumped Jacob's last checker and waited until Jacob made eye contact, undaunted by the hardened gaze that met his own. "You've lost this checker game. Do not lose your soul. Find some time alone with God and search your heart."

Jacob clenched his teeth. He remained silent, but his anger was written in his body language. He pushed back the bench seat with a loud scrape and all but threw himself on his top bunk. Tim quietly gathered the checkerboard and pieces and put them away before excusing himself to the outhouse.

When the bunkhouse door shut behind Tim, Jacob nearly growled to Josiah, "Can you believe that? Who does he think he is?"

"He thinks he's your brother who cares about you."

"Oh, so you're on his side, too?" Jacob asked accusingly.

"Both of us are on your side, Jacob. He said all the things I would have said if I were better at putting my thoughts into words. Listen to him."

"Humph."

"You have been my big brother since the day I was born. You protected me and cared for me when Mom and Dad died. You even gave me your food when I was hungry and there wasn't enough to go around. You stood up for me more than once at the orphanage. I've always been proud to be your little brother, but to be honest, the changes I've seen in you lately scare me. I don't know why you're so angry all the time, but I really wish you would figure it out. I want my brother back."

Jacob laid quietly, and Josiah wondered if he had said too much or had offended Jacob in some way. Josiah took a deep breath, certain that his heart was in the right place and praying his and Tim's words would somehow get through.

A few minutes later, Jacob leaped off the bed and stomped toward the door, barging past Tim as he entered. Josiah stared after him and asked Tim, "Should I go after him?"

"No, he'll be all right."

"How do you know?" Josiah inquired.

"He had his Bible in his hand."

277

Jacob had been sitting on the bench on the Hill for nearly an hour when James joined him. James could sense the battle going on in his brother's heart.

Jacob broke the silence. "Tim asked me tonight why I was so angry. I honestly didn't know the answer. I've been sitting here asking God the same question. I've been angry for such a long time. Angry that God made us orphans. Angry that God gave us Daniel to be our dad and then took him away. Angry that Buck died. Angry that Pastor refused your request to marry Emily. Angry that God nearly destroyed our ranch." He looked over at James. "I don't want to be angry anymore, but I don't know how I can trust in a God that allows such awful things to happen."

The night was clear, and the North Star shone brightly in the sky. "Whenever Dad needed direction from the Lord, he would remember the North Star. Just as God placed the star in the sky for navigation on earth, He promises that if we truly desire His plan for our lives, He will use his Word to teach us how to navigate our hearts toward Him." James glanced over and was pleased that Jacob was paying attention. "Does the North Star disappear when the sky is cloudy?"

"No, it is still there behind the clouds."

James nodded, "In the same way, God does not disappear when tough times come. He is always with us. Always."

"What if I'm not part of His family?"

Without hesitation, James replied, "You know as well as I do that the invitation to be part of God's family is offered to everyone. Jesus died for you, Jacob. If you had been the only one on earth, He still would have died just for you because He loves you that much. He rose again and sits at God the Father's right hand. When you accept His free gift of salvation, Jesus gives you His righteousness, for the payment for your sin has already been paid in full. From the moment you ask for forgiveness, God the Father sees His Son's perfection rather than our sinfulness when He looks at us. We can come boldly to His throne in prayer because Jesus made it possible."

"I've rejected Him for so long. What if it's too late?"

"As long as you are still breathing, it's never too late. Let God adopt you into His family tonight. Then you'll be my brother in two families."

Nearly two hours later, Emma answered the knock on her door. Jacob was standing before her. Though his eyes were red, he looked as if a heavy weight had been lifted from his shoulders. "Emma, I just wanted to ask your forgiveness. I am so sorry I spoke so hatefully to you. Despite what I said before, I do think of you as my mother, and I do love you."

"I have been nearly bursting with anger, and I didn't know why. Tim challenged me to examine my heart and determine whether or not I had ever truly believed in Jesus as my Savior. God and I wrestled for a while tonight, but He won. I'm trusting in Him alone, not relying on church or baptism or reciting a prayer. I've given God my heart tonight."

Emma's eyes filled with tears. She wrapped him in a motherly bear hug. "I'm so proud of you. This moment is an answer to my prayer. There was another Jacob in the Old Testament who wrestled with God and lost, and God blessed him immeasurably. He will bless you, too."

"Thank you for not giving up on me."

"No matter what happens, you are my son, and I will always love you."

CHAPTER 24
Something New

J ames remembered something Emily had written in her journal the night of the symphony concert, and it gave him an idea. The following Friday, the boys covered for him while he made all the arrangements. That afternoon, James arrived on Emily's doorstep, just as he had done every Friday afternoon before his fateful meeting with her dad. He drove to Johnson Lake, and they found it once again surrounded by daffodils. They had a lovely walk.

"July 12th will be a wonderful day to get married," mused Emily.

"The only better day would be today, or tomorrow, or the next day . . ."

"James!" Emily scolded teasingly.

"Seriously, July 12th is still a week and a day away. I wish it would hurry up and get here."

"Me, too, but there is still much work to do," Emily replied.

Feeling contrite, James inquired, "How are the plans coming? Is there anything I can do to help?"

"The alterations on Mom's dress are almost finished. Laura has placed herself in charge of the decorating, so I know the church will be beautiful." She had a sudden thought, "We still need to ask Julie and Luke to stand with us. Don't forget. Anna's parents agreed to allow her to be a flower girl, so she and Beth can walk down the aisle together. We also need to write our vows."

"Mine are done."

"When did you find time?"

"My to-do list was shorter than yours. A wedding is more complicated that I realized," James admitted. "We could always elope."

Emily dipped her head and looked up at him as if he had lost his good sense.

He chuckled and raised his hands in surrender, "I was just kidding."

"Do you know what you need?" James asked. "A night off." Reaching into his pocket, he pulled out an envelope and handed it to her.

Scrunching her brow in curiosity, she opened the envelope and pulled out a card that read, *"Your presence is requested at seven o'clock this evening. Formal attire, please."*

"Are you serious?" Emily asked.

"Yes, I am. Shall I pick you up at seven?"

Emily smiled, "Yes, I will be ready."

At precisely seven o'clock, James knocked on the door of the parsonage. He did not have a tuxedo, but he did borrow a vest and one of Daniel's bowties from Emma. Thankfully, she was mama enough to tie it for him when he could not get it right. The bowtie and vest were a very well-dressed look with his suit coat.

When Emily opened the door, he marveled at her beauty. He bowed formally and handed her a single red rose. She read the "I love you" in the gesture and smiled. He offered his arm and asked, "Shall we?"

When James set the buggy into motion, Emily asked, "Where are we going?"

"You will see," he responded evasively.

Several minutes later, he pulled to a stop in front of the Wilsons' barn. They walked in together to soft candlelight. When they reached the middle of the floor, James bowed again and extended his hand to her, "May I have the honor of this dance?" Emily curtsied and gently placed her hand in his.

On cue, Josiah placed the needle of the Victrola on the shellac disc, and the slightly scratchy sound of the machine could not dim the music of the New York Philharmonic Orchestra that filled the room.

Emily's look of surprise melted into another smile. She placed her left hand on his shoulder and her right hand in his; he positioned his right hand on her back; and they danced. Emily asked, "How did you know I've been dreaming of a night like this, dancing with you?"

James returned, "Someone I know wrote something like this in her journal."

"I did?" Emily blushed.

"Yes, and I'm glad you did."

Josiah sat quietly in the shadows of the corner and restarted the disc every time it finished, happy that he could finally help his brother and Emily in some small way.

They danced for a couple of hours more. Neither wanted the evening to end, but propriety dictated that she be home before ten o'clock. James looked forward to a week and a day, when the clock would no longer matter, and Emily would be home with him.

The morning of July 12 was overcast, but despite the threat of rain, the sun peeked through the clouds just after noon. James and Luke arrived at the church just before two o'clock. Pastor entered a few minutes later and led them into the prayer room at the front of the church. "While the guests are coming in, let's take a few minutes to pray together."

Each of the three men prayed for James and Emily, dedicating their new family to the Lord. Twenty minutes later, Pastor excused himself to meet Emily, for he would be walking her down the aisle. At 2:25 p.m., Luke placed a hand on James' shoulder, "Are you ready?"

"Yes, I've been waiting long enough," James quipped, trying to ease his nerves.

The two brothers filed from the prayer room and stood on the right side of the church. James stood on the raised platform, and Luke stood on the floor beside him. The room was filled with family and friends, but James never noticed. His focus was on the doors at the end of the aisle. The one door opened just far enough for Anna and Beth to enter. Laura was at the back wall to direct them. The pair walked down with little baskets of flower petals, sprinkling the petals as they came, then stood next to Luke. Next, Julie entered carrying a small bouquet, walked slowly toward the front, and stood on the left side of the church, opposite Luke.

James' heart was pounding so hard, surely everyone in the church could hear it. Both doors opened, and the sunshine illuminated Emily's face and hair making her look like an angel —his angel. She was beautiful! Her gaze met his and never looked away.

Pastor Kendrick walked Emily down the aisle and placed

her hand in James' before he stepped around Luke and stood behind the couple. "We are gathered here today, in the presence of God and these witnesses, to join this man and this woman in holy matrimony."

"James and Emily have asked me to use I Corinthians 13:7 as my text today, for this verse aptly describes their journey of love. 'Love bears all things, believes all things, hopes all things, endures all things.'"

The ceremony continued, but James forgot to pay attention. He was distracted by the beautiful woman before him. Thankfully, he heard the cues for their vows and the exchange of rings. Soon, he heard the words he had wanted to hear for such a long time: "I now pronounce you husband and wife. You may kiss your bride."

James reached his arm around her and gently pulled her closer. Emily tipped up her face, and James slowly bent his head until their lips finally met. She was his.

"May I be the first to introduce to you Mr. and Mrs. James McAllister."

THE END

Almost . . . If you just don't want the story to end, I have written a bonus epilogue just for you, my readers. Find out what happens next when you download the bonus content for FREE at https://dl.bookfunnel.com/x4uv8ku2sv

Acknowledgments

Putting this long-awaited sequel into print is a milestone I could not have achieved alone. Those who helped make this book possible deserve my highest gratitude.

First, I would like to thank the wonderful man who encouraged me to pursue publication of these stories in the first place. My husband Bob has been my faithful supporter in this endeavor. His teasing persistence that my story needs a jousting scene keeps me laughing, but his serious comments have greatly shaped this story.

My friend and sister-in-law, Cindy Bower, has been my primary advisor throughout this process, and I highly value her insightful feedback and honest comments on each revision. Thank you for being on this writing journey with me.

Holly Talley performed the monumental task of the final edit. Her years of experience teaching composition enabled her to polish my manuscript into what it is now.

The lovely lady on the front cover is Bailey Goforth, our own pastor's daughter. Like Emily in the story, Bailey has a beautiful smile, a cheerful personality, and an obvious talent for music. She also has a God-given gift for teaching children, and is currently pursuing her degree in elementary education at a Christian college.

Finally, I would like to acknowledge my readers. Without your unfailing encouragement, *Emily's Hope* may have never been written. May you always trust God for your hope when the hard times come. He is faithful. Always.

About the Author

A Selah Award Bronze Medalist, Christian Author Award Winner, Will Rogers Medallion Award Winner, and Bestselling author of historical Christian fiction, Jill's writing engages the heart of her readers and leaves them empowered to fulfill God's plan for their lives. Jill's novels seamlessly weave a page-turning story with the truth of God's unconditional love. With her varied experience as an RN, a musician, and a homeschool mom, Jill creatively weaves a part of herself into each story. What sets her books apart is the way the characters point the reader to the truth of God's love.

When she can find some free time, she enjoys playing her flute, piano, and cello and thanking God for the hubby who lassoed her heart for keeps. She and her family love their church in Florida and serve in the music and children's ministries there. Jill has had a secret wish for many years to write a story that would inspire readers by reminding them of a God who loves them unconditionally and longs to have a personal relationship with them. Publishing her Rugged Cross Ranch novels has been a dream come true.

Follow Jill on Social Media:
    Facebook ~ Jill Dewhurst, Author
    Instagram ~ jilldewhurst.author
    Author Pages on Amazon, Goodreads, BookBub
    Author's Website ~ www.jilldewhurst.com

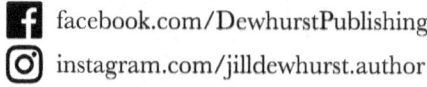

facebook.com/DewhurstPublishing

instagram.com/jilldewhurst.author

Rugged Cross Ranch

Julie's Joy

Julie Peterson had been born into a family of faith and privilege, but when her dad decides to move his family West to homestead near his sister's ranch in northeastern Oklahoma, disaster strikes, leaving Julie a nine-year-old orphan. Rescued and cared for my a migrating Kiowa village until her uncle found her years later, Julie has learned to find joy even when life turns out differently than she hoped. Meet her now as a young woman, returning home to the Rugged Cross Ranch after graduating from a college for the blind. Though she has faced many hardships in her young life, Julie spreads joy to all around her. When the biggest tragedy of all strikes, will her joy be extinguished forever?

Buck Matthews, the second oldest brother on the ranch, has given up his dreams of a family, knowing no woman would accept his heritage. When Julie arrives on the ranch, their friendship reveals they have a great deal in common. Would Julie be willing to accept his love?

Follow God's sovereign hand through this story of faith, family, and redeeming love. Be inspired to trust the One who loves us all unconditionally.

Emily's Hope

A refusal, an unexpected separation, and a catastrophic blizzard—How will shattered dreams lead to God's blessing?

Emily Kendrick, the pastor's oldest daughter, had willingly put her dreams on hold for her family, for her dad had needed her to assume the responsibility for managing the household and teaching her siblings after their mom died. Now she is ready for the next chapter of her life to begin. When God asks her to wait even longer, will she trust Him, even when hundreds of miles separate her from the man she loves?

James McAllister is the oldest of the brothers on the Rugged Cross Ranch. Though he enjoys his position as foreman, the title he truly desires is husband. He has patiently courted Emily for several years, understanding how much her family needed her. When a devastating blizzard decimates the herd at the Rugged Cross Ranch, will James carry the weight alone or will his faith allow him to trust God?

The time finally comes for him to ask Pastor Kendrick for her hand, but James does not get the answer he expects. Will they be willing to wait for Pastor's--and ultimately God's—blessing—even when their every dream has shattered?

Laura's Redemption

An abduction, a rescuer, and a picture of God's unconditional love for us—Will these be enough to convince Laura that God made her uniquely for his purpose?

Laura Kendrick stubbornly refused to follow her expected path as a pastor's daughter. She would never measure up to her sweet, servant-hearted sister Emily anyway. Nothing was wrong with marriage and motherhood, but Laura had an unwavering desire for adventure and a life of purpose beyond homemaking. Those were mutually exclusive. Weren't they?

When a case of mistaken identity leads to Laura's abduction for ransom, will the sacrifice of her rescuer be enough to save her life and convince her heart to accept his unconditional love before her final opportunity is gone?

Tim O'Brien, the third oldest brother on the Rugged Cross Ranch, has fallen in love with his best friend, the only woman he knows who has enough gumption to challenge his stubborn ways. Content with his life as a cowboy and wrangler, will he be willing to give up the life he knows and the woman he loves to follow what God has asked of him?

Heidi's Faith

A painting, a protective father, and an orphaned cowboy—Will God use these to heal Heidi's heart?

Will the brushstrokes that capture light on canvas help Heidi Müller find the light of God's promises in her soul? Will she rise above the fear that threatens to overwhelm her? When her family moves to a secret location for her protection, will she learn to trust again?

"Sometimes all you need to overcome something hard is a new perspective—and maybe a guide to help you find it." And when that new perspective is grounded in God's promises, the result is a stronger, more resilient faith in the God who loves us. The handsome stranger may have been speaking to Heidi's brother Frederick, but the message penetrated deep within Heidi's heart where she struggled with fear.

Jacob Collins desires a family of his own, but when that seems impossible, he focuses on becoming the man God wants him to be and leaves the details to Him. Will God use Jacob's desire to help his neighbor to place him where the impossible could become possible? When God uses Jacob to renew Heidi's trust in God, will a traumatic accident give Heidi the opportunity to return the favor?

Don't miss this beautiful tale of overcoming fear with unconditional love.

Coming Soon!

Clara's Courage (Book 5)

Emma's Hope (Book 6)

Subscribe to my newsletter for release updates and special offers!

www.jilldewhurst.com